The Man in Black
and Other Stories

ALSO BY ELLY GRIFFITHS

The Ruth Galloway Mysteries

The Crossing Places

The Janus Stone

The House at Sea's End

A Room Full of Bones

Dying Fall

The Outcast Dead

The Ghost Fields

The Woman in Blue

The Chalk Pit

The Dark Angel

The Stone Circle

The Lantern Men

The Night Hawks

The Locked Room

The Last Remains

The Brighton Mysteries

The Zig Zag Girl

Smoke and Mirrors

The Blood Card

The Vanishing Box

Now You See Them

The Midnight Hour

The Great Deceiver

Other Works

The Stranger Diaries

The Postscript Murders

Bleeding Heart Yard

The Last Word

Non-Fiction

*Norfolk: A photographic journey
through the land of Ruth Galloway*

The Man in Black

and Other Stories

Elly Griffiths

MARINER LARGE PRINT
Boston   New York

This is a work of fiction. Names, characters, places, and incidents are products of the author's imagination or are used fictitiously and are not to be construed as real. Any resemblance to actual events, locales, organizations, or persons, living or dead, is entirely coincidental.

THE MAN IN BLACK. Copyright © 2024 by Elly Griffiths. All rights reserved. Printed in the United States of America. No part of this book may be used or reproduced in any manner whatsoever without written permission except in the case of brief quotations embodied in critical articles and reviews. For information, address HarperCollins Publishers, 195 Broadway, New York, NY 10007.

HarperCollins books may be purchased for educational, business, or sales promotional use. For information, please email the Special Markets Department at SPsales@harpercollins.com.

The Mariner flag design is a registered trademark of HarperCollins Publishers LLC.

Originally published UK by Quercus Editions Ltd. in 2024.

FIRST HARPER LARGE PRINT EDITION

ISBN 978-0-06-341050-3

Library of Congress Cataloging-in-Publication Data is available upon request.

24 25 26 27 28 LBC 5 4 3 2 1

For Lynne Spahl

Contents

The Man in Black	1
Articulation	18
Castles in the Air	28
Max Mephisto and the Disappearing Act	43
The Only Pebble on the Beach	63
St Lucy's Day	68
The Red Handkerchief	80
Justice Jones and the Etherphone	85
The Farewell Boat	110
Harbinger: A Harbinder Kaur Story	117
One Is Silver	131
The Village Church	136
Turning Traitor	141
Ruth's First Christmas Tree	168
The Stranger by R.M. Holland	204

viii · CONTENTS

What I Saw from the Sky	221
Flint's Fireside Tale: A Christmas Story	249
The Valley of the Queens: A Ruth and Nelson Story	265
Ruth Galloway and the Ghost of Max Mephisto	312
Acknowledgements	325

The Man in Black

Ruth loves the bookshop at Jarrolds. Just a few steps down from the worldly pleasures of perfume and make-up (she admires the packaging, all sharp corners and minty colours, but never knows how to apply it) and she is among friends. She moves in an almost trance-like state around the shelves. Although this is a department in a busy department store, it has a proper bookshop feel, a sense that you could get lost behind Local History and not be found for several days.

Ruth is not looking for anything in particular. She is killing time before a meeting at Norwich museum but, somehow, she finds that she is holding two new crime novels and a book about stone circles. She'll buy the books and sit in the café reading for ten minutes. The coffee is very good, she remembers.

Ruth moves towards the till. It's nearly Hallowe'en and the children's section of the shop is decorated with giant spiders' webs and glowing arachnids. There's even a scarecrow propped up in an armchair. Should she buy a book for Kate, her daughter? Nothing supernatural. Kate's birthday is on November the first and Ruth thinks that she was lucky to avoid All Hallows' Eve and land on All Saints' Day instead. But Kate likes all sorts of books, from grim dystopian fantasies to *The Princess Diaries*. She has even shown a rather worrying interest in the lives of the saints. Besides, Kate will definitely say, 'Have you bought anything for me?' when she sees the Jarrolds bag.

Ruth pushes through the web and then stifles a small shriek. The scarecrow has risen out of its chair and is addressing her.

'Dr Galloway?'

The use of her title reassures Ruth. She sees now that the pile of clothes has transformed itself into a tall, bearded man in black.

'Yes,' she says, backing into Middle Grade Fiction.

'I'm a friend of Cathbad's,' says the apparition.

This doesn't surprise Ruth. Cathbad is a druid and one of Ruth's best friends. He also has a habit of popping up where he is least expected. Clearly this living scarecrow is one of his emissaries.

'Pleased to meet you,' says Ruth.

'Likewise.' The man grins, showing discoloured teeth. Despite this, he is younger than Ruth first thought, with dark hair only lightly streaked with grey.

'Are you looking for a children's book?' says the man.

'Yes. For my daughter. She's ten.'

'Try this.' The man is holding a book which he passes to Ruth. It's called *The Land of the Hyter Sprites* and has a rather beautiful cover, green with blue snakes meandering across it. The title sounds a bit childish but when Ruth opens the book, the type is small and she catches the words 'subterranean' and 'surreal'. This will do for Kate.

'Thank you,' she says.

'Be sure to tell Cathbad that you've seen me.'

'I didn't catch your name.'

'People call me Raven.'

Of course they do.

'Did you get anything for me?' Kate greets Ruth with a hug and a frisk, looking for hidden presents.

'A book.' Ruth proffers the purple bag.

Kate rips it open and looks at the green and blue book. 'Cool,' she says at last.

Ruth now feels that she has to hand over one of the crime novels to her babysitter, Clara.

4 · ELLY GRIFFITHS

'For you.'

'Thank you! I love this series.'

So do I, thinks Ruth. Well, she can always buy another.

'Everything OK?'

The scene is certainly very peaceful. Kate's homework books are out on the table, as is Clara's laptop. Ruth knows that Clara is studying for yet another degree, this time in psychology.

'Fine,' says Clara, although Ruth thinks that she looks strained. Maybe all this written work, on top of babysitting and bar work, is proving too much. 'I was watching the local news.'

'Another cat has gone missing,' says Kate, not looking up from her book.

There has been a rather worrying spate of cat abductions in north Norfolk recently. Ruth thanks the gods for her remote location. She doesn't know what she'd do without her cat, Flint.

'Flint's upstairs on your bed,' says Clara, reading her mind. 'I hope that's OK.'

'It's fine.' Flint lives a charmed, rule-free existence. There's more chance of Ruth sleeping on the floor than there is of Flint roughing it.

'I'd better get back before Donner and Blitzen have chewed up my flat.' Clara has recently acquired two kittens, tiny ginger lords of misrule. Ruth is willing to bet that they will have destroyed something in their owner's absence.

'Are you seeing Francis this weekend?' Through the mysterious powers of Tinder, Clara has also acquired a new boyfriend.

'Yes. We're going to see the seals at Blakeney Point. That's a wholesome-sounding date, isn't it?'

'It certainly is.' Ruth and Kate have often been to see the seals though Ruth thinks that late October might not be the best time for a boat trip. 'Hope it doesn't rain,' she says.

'Of course it will rain,' says Clara. But she doesn't seem too depressed at the prospect. She waves goodbye and runs out to her car.

Kate is still engrossed in the hyter sprites.

Kate reads until late. When Ruth goes to bed at ten thirty, she sees Kate's light still on and finds her halfway through the book, Flint watching disapprovingly from the window sill.

Kate is tired and grumpy in the morning. Ruth has to work hard to get them both ready for school and work. She drops Kate off at the cheerful gates of her primary school (mission statement: We Have Fun) and drives to the University of North Norfolk where she spends a cheery day lecturing on archaeology, bones and long-dead bodies.

She's back at the gates at three thirty. Usually the childminder collects Kate but Sandra is away and so Ruth has to take what her ex-boss Phil would definitely call a half day. Ruth has always found the other mothers rather intimidating—they all seem to know each other and stand in a circle ringed by buggies—so she's very pleased to see Cathbad sitting under a tree reading a book. Cathbad's son Michael is in Kate's year and he also has a daughter in Reception.

'Hallo,' says Ruth. 'What are you reading?'

He shows her the title. *This Hollow Land: Aspects of Norfolk Folklore* by Peter Tolhurst.

'I met a friend of yours in Jarrolds,' says Ruth. 'In the book department.'

'Oh really?' says Cathbad, marking his place with a fallen leaf. 'Who?'

'He said that people call him Raven.'

'Raven. He's hasn't been around for a few years. In fact there were rumours that he was dead. I'm glad he's resurfaced.'

Resurfaced. Ruth imagines the bearded figure rising from the earth, up through the basements and floorboard of Jarrolds, to materialise in the children's fiction section.

THE MAN IN BLACK · 7

'He recommended a book,' says Ruth. 'I have to say Kate's enjoying it.'

And, when the children come racing towards them, trailing pictures and PE bags, Kate is still holding the book. She shows it to Cathbad.

'The hyter sprites,' he says. 'They're in this book.' He taps *This Hollow Land*. 'I've heard a few local legends about them. They're usually described as malignant pixies who capture children and small animals. Children used to be told to hurry home in case the hyter sprites got them.'

'They're small with long whiskers and green eyes,' says Kate authoritatively. 'And they live in the tunnels under Blakeney.'

'*Are* there tunnels under Blakeney?' Ruth asks Cathbad.

'There are tunnels everywhere in Norfolk,' says Cathbad, 'but the tunnel in Blakeney has never been found. It's said to run from the Guildhall to the Friary. Have you heard about the violinist and the cat?'

It sounds like the start of a joke but Ruth knows that Cathbad is not much of a one for stand-up comedy. 'No,' she says.

'A violinist went into the Blakeney tunnel years ago, accompanied by his white cat. It was said that you could hear him playing underground and then, suddenly, the

8 · ELLY GRIFFITHS

music stopped. The man and his cat were never seen again. There's a carving of them on the village signpost.'

This makes Ruth think about the disappearing cats and makes her irrationally anxious to get home to Flint. She's nervous all the way home. Kate is still reading her book (one of her super-powers is being able to read in cars), and the day, which started bright, is becoming stormy. As Ruth drives across the marshes—the road the highest thing for miles around—she can see purple clouds massing over the sea. The horizon is first hazy, then disappears altogether as the rain moves inland. Ruth and Kate make it inside just in time. Flint yawns at them from the sofa.

'Sweetheart.' Ruth picks him up and cuddles him, which he endures by impersonating a ragdoll cat.

'Your phone's buzzing,' says Kate, looking up from her book.

It's Clara.

'Oh, Ruth. I don't know what to do. Donner and Blitzen have gone missing.'

'**Let me** get this straight. You want me to investigate two missing cats?'

'Six missing cats,' says Ruth. 'Six have vanished altogether.'

'It's Saturday,' says DCI Nelson. 'I'm off duty.' Actually, Nelson is on leave at the moment but he's not about to miss seeing Kate. Ruth tries not to exploit her connection with one of Norfolk's senior police officers, but this is clearly an emergency.

'Here.' Ruth pushes a piece of paper across the table. 'I've made a list.'

Nelson's lips twitch. A liking for lists is one of the few things he and Ruth have in common.

*Simon—ginger tom, 6 years old. Disappeared in
  Binham.*
*Betsy—tortoiseshell female, about 10. Disappeared
  in Stiffkey.*
*Scamander—b&w, 3 years old. Disappeared in
  Blakeney.*
*Ginger tom—name and age unknown. Disappeared
  in Morston.*
*Donner and Blitzen—10-month-old kittens.
  Disappeared in Blakeney.*

'Anything else?' says Nelson. 'Any distinguishing marks? Unusual personality quirks?'

'Simon only has one eye,' says Ruth. She suspects that Nelson is not taking this entirely seriously. 'And Betsy apparently has a skin condition.'

Nelson looks like he's about to ask another facetious

question but, at that moment, Kate rushes into the room and throws herself on him.

'Dad!'

'Hallo, Katie love.'

It's Kate, says Ruth silently. Nelson can never rid himself of the habit of adding 'ie' to their daughter's name. Ruth has almost—but not quite—given up reminding him. He does it with his three-year-old son, George, too. Ruth wonders if Nelson's wife, Michelle, protests when Nelson calls him 'Georgie'. She doubts it somehow.

'The cats all lived near Blakeney,' says Ruth. 'And almost all are ginger.'

'We should get a criminal profiler in,' says Nelson.

'We should,' says Ruth, 'but we've got to make do with you.'

'OK,' says Nelson, holding the list at arm's length. Ruth knows that he needs his glasses and is rather pleased that he's usually too vain to wear them in front of her. 'There's a clear geographical link, also, the time frame is quite tight. All the animals disappeared over a three-week period. We might be looking at a series of abductions but we might not. I mean, cats go missing all the time. They just wander off.'

Flint, who is sitting on the sofa, gives Nelson a sharp look. Unlike Ruth and Kate, he is not a fan of Norfolk's senior police officer.

THE MAN IN BLACK · 11

'Clara's cats didn't wander off,' says Ruth. 'She lives in a flat and they aren't allowed out.'

'That certainly makes it more interesting. What happened to Clara's cats?'

'She'd been out, working the lunchtime shift in the pub. When she got in, the balcony doors were open and the cats were gone. Her flat's on the first floor so I suppose someone could have climbed up.'

'A cat burglar,' says Nelson.

'It's not funny,' says Kate. 'Clara was crying.'

Ruth and Kate had driven straight over to Clara's yesterday, braving the wind and the rain. They found Clara sitting on the floor, hugging the kittens' blanket. 'Who would do this, Ruth?' she said, her face swollen with tears. 'They're still so little. How will they survive?'

Nelson becomes serious immediately. 'Sorry,' he says. 'But it's hard to know where to start looking. Legally, cats are the property of their owner so, if they were taken, it's theft. But I can't see Super Jo spending much manpower on this.'

Ruth rather admires glamorous Superintendent Jo Archer but she can't imagine her taking much interest in missing pets. It's as ridiculous as the idea that cats belong to their owners.

'We could look in Blakeney,' says Kate. 'We could see the seals too.'

Ruth thinks that this has been in Kate's mind ever since she heard of Clara's weekend plans.

'Maybe you'll find the secret tunnel,' she says.

'Oh, I know where the tunnel is,' says Kate. 'It was in that book. I finished it last night. I'll show you if you like. You'd better come too, Mum.'

As they pass the village sign, Ruth spots the violinist. He stands, bespectacled and bewigged, accompanied by his white cat, looking rather sad. Well, maybe they'll find him today. Or his remains. The thought doesn't exactly fill Ruth with excitement, although human remains are her speciality.

Kate says that the tunnel is in the church. St Nicholas' Church is famous for having two towers, one a solid edifice on top of the main building, the other a slim column at the opposite end. A light is glowing in the narrow tower, very visible in the grey, misty morning.

'It's for ships,' says Cathbad, who materialised at Ruth's cottage just in time to make one of the party. 'It's said that sailors used the two towers to guide them over the sandbanks. If you lined them up together, you were on course for the channel that led you safely to shore. This was in the days before the harbour silted up, of course.'

THE MAN IN BLACK · 13

A crossing place, thinks Ruth. That most magical of pathways.

'The tunnel's inside the church,' says Kate, who can be single-minded when she wants to be. 'By a strained glass window.'

No one corrects her. They park by the graveyard and make their way into the church. The building looks very large and impressive now that they are closer, rising out of the ground like a ghost ship in full sail. It's very dark inside, the only light filtered through the coloured glass. It smells, like all old churches, of candle wax, flower stalks and damp.

'Which stained glass window is it?' says Cathbad.

'St Nicholas.'

'What's he the saint of?' says Nelson. 'Besides being Santa, of course.'

It's Kate who answers. 'Sailors, archers and repentant thieves.'

'Jo Archer would love that,' mutters Nelson. Ruth wanders through the cool church, reading the memorials to those lost at sea. She's very conscious of Nelson walking beside her, almost close enough for her to touch his hand. Kate, meanwhile, is examining the windows in great detail and, eventually, she shouts, 'I've found him!'

St Nicholas stands by a side altar. He's dressed in red and wears what Ruth thinks is a bishop's hat. Behind him ships bob on a blue-green sea.

Kate is kneeling at his feet where there is a small cat portrayed in orange glass.

'Under the cat,' she says.

Directly under the cat is a memorial stone. 'Sacred to the memory of Felix Macavity, Musician.' Cathbad, kneeling beside Kate, pushes at the stone. It moves, very slightly.

'Jesus wept,' says Nelson.

'Very likely,' answers Cathbad. The stone moves some more and now the church is filled with horrible, unearthly wailing.

'It's the violinist,' says Ruth, before she can help herself.

'I think it's a cat,' says Cathbad.

The stone has now moved aside to reveal a black square, the entrance to a tunnel. A horrible smell is now added to the caterwauling.

'I could crawl in,' says Kate.

'No!' says Ruth and Nelson together.

'I'll have a look,' says Cathbad. He inserts his head into the hole, then moves further in. His voice echoes against centuries of stone.

'There's a hollow space here. It's full of cats.'

When he emerges, he is holding two tiny orange kittens in his arms.

Ruth rings Clara from the car park. By the time she has arrived, Cathbad has rescued all six cats. He has also found a bus pass belonging to Francis Matthews.

When Clara has finished cuddling her kittens, Ruth hands her the bus pass.

'Francis?' she says. 'He stole the cats? Why?'

'I don't know. Nelson's on his way to see him now.'

Helped by the vicar and the verger, Cathbad has got the cats into various boxes and baskets. The church is full of voices, laughter and angry meowing.

Clara looks at Ruth, wet-eyed. 'I'm done with men. From now on, it'll just be me and the cats.'

'It's a pretty good way to live,' says Ruth.

'I knew it was him,' says Kate, in bed that night. 'St Francis. Patron saint of animals.'

Ruth hadn't wanted Kate to read that book about the saints, but she supposes that it came in useful in the end. As did *The Land of the Hyter Sprites*. Nelson says that Francis Matthews was obsessed with saving animals he thought were being mistreated. He'd taken one-eyed Simon and bedraggled Betsy because he felt sorry for them. He took Donner and Blitzen because he considered it cruel that they were never allowed outside. Francis was also a 'sidesman' at the church, one of those mysterious clerical jobs which meant he knew about the secret space, which wasn't so much a tunnel as a hidden cupboard. Francis is being charged with theft, which doesn't quite seem enough.

Kate soon settles down to sleep, worn out with heroism. Ruth takes *The Land of the Hyter Sprites* from her bedside table and goes downstairs to read it.

'There is a land below this one,' she reads, 'a place of secret pathways and unspoken words . . .'

Ruth turns the book over and looks at the cover. *The Land of the Hyter Sprites* by R.B. Stone. Those blue snakes are actually tunnels, she realises. She thinks of the memorial stone below the stained-glass window. Felix Macavity, Musician. Felix the cat. Macavity the mystery cat.

She rings Cathbad. 'Can you remember Raven's real name?'

'Robert, I think. Or Richard. I remember his surname though. Stone.'

So Raven hadn't come back from the dead. He wasn't an emissary sent from heaven to point the way to the stolen cats. He was that familiar figure in bookshops the world over. An author loitering by his book, urging passers-by to read it.

Note:

Jarrolds is real.

Blakeney is real.

St Nicholas' Church is real.

The legend of the hyter sprites is as real as a legend can be.

You can see the violinist and his cat on the Blakeney sign.

This Hollow Land by Peter Tolhurst is real.

The Land of the Hyter Sprites by R.B. Stone is imaginary.

The hiding place in the church is imaginary.

R.B. Stone is imaginary, as are all the characters in this story.

Articulation

It's the worst thing, being called in to a private construction. Usually, when bones are found, it's on a building site. The foreman informs the police and then they send a forensic archaeologist. They're always expecting a man and, when they see me, five foot nothing and looking, in my high-vis jacket and wellingtons, like a sixth former on a field trip, there's a flood of witty banter, like the milky-brown water that sloshes around inside the cement mixer. 'Hallo, blondie.' 'Come over here and hold my trowel, darling.' I blush easily and know that my face is bright red as I trudge through the mud, falling over the apparently random piles of bricks that spring up all over these places, until I get to the hole where, amidst the rubble and builders' detritus, I see the tell-tale gleam of a human bone.

ARTICULATION · 19

Because that's what a forensic archaeologist does. We look at buried bodies and we can tell, by the way the soil lies on top of a corpse, whether they were deliberately laid in the earth. We look for clues, we read the landscape. Nettles, for example, prefer soil with a high nitrogen content. So, if you have nettles growing in your garden, you may have a body buried there. You think I'm joking but I'm not. Any big city is built on top of bones: graveyards, plague pits, fever hospitals, charnel houses. Richard III was found under a car park because that's what urban car parks *are*. They're places where archaeologists know something or someone is buried so they can't build a house or an office block on top. What they do is slap some tarmac over the site and park cars on it.

And what often happens is that some young couple, dreaming of private ownership after years of renting, buys a plot of land. They start building their dream house and, after a bit of digging, they find bones. A forensic archaeologist comes in and holds everyone up, digging up the bones—oh so carefully, one by one—examining them, photographing them. Then they send samples off for carbon-14 testing, which could take weeks or even months. No wonder the fresh-faced young couple soon become choleric with anger. No wonder they swear at the archaeologist, weep at them and sometimes clumsily offer a bribe. Because this isn't the way the dream of home-ownership is meant to go. It never happens on *Grand Designs* or any one of those myriad programmes where photogenic thirty-somethings build fantasies of chrome, glass and exposed brickwork. Kevin McCloud never has to stop work because some old shin bone is found in a drain. It's just not part of the plan.

And, after all that, the bones always turn out to be Vic-torian or earlier. Then, unless they are really archaeologically interesting, the building work goes on, in an atmosphere of sullen resentment, and a brand-new house is built on top of the skeleton and its fellows. Because, if you've got one body, there are probably others. Sleep well, I often think, as I drive past a year later, on top of that paupers' graveyard. The Outcast Dead, they're sometimes called. The bodies thrown into unmarked graves; the lepers, the paupers, the prostitutes. Unimportant then and now. But not forgotten by me.

But, as soon as I got to number 14 Shelley Drive, it was different. The builder, Mark Wallace, was also the home-owner. He was doing everything himself: surveying, plans, construction work, the lot. But he wasn't a typical home-improvement type. He was considerate, intelligent, even a little sad.

'It was our dream, me and my wife,' he told me, that

first day, as we drank tea in a prefabricated hut surrounded by mud and abandoned machinery. 'We had a little bungalow here but we always planned to knock it down and build our dream house. Took us ten years to raise enough money and . . . well, here I am.'

I didn't need to ask about his wife. It was obvious she wasn't around any more. Mark had the look of a man on his own. Not that he seemed lonely or pathetic in any way. He was always smartly dressed, clean and well-shaven, smelling of expensive soap. But I knew that he slept in the hut; I'd seen the folded camp bed and the suitcase. I didn't know where he had showers and used the lemon-scented soap. He talked about staying with friends but no one ever came to the site.

I started on the excavation that morning. The man driving the mechanical digger had spotted what looked like a human bone when he was churning up soil for the foundations. He had stopped work and informed the police. And the police had sent me. Climbing into the pit, I gently exposed the margins of the bone with a pointing trowel. It was a femur and I could see at once that another bone was attached.

'It's articulated,' I said.

'What does that mean?'

'Connected,' I said. 'It could mean that we've got a whole skeleton.'

I worked all day, exposing the bones but not moving them. It's important for an archaeologist to get a proper look at bones in situ. Position can be very important. A body lying from east to west could indicate a Christian burial, for example. Sometimes felons are buried face down, and there are even cases of mutilation after death to prevent evil spirits from escaping. It's a good idea, too, to let the bones dry out in the sunlight as this can harden them. And it was a sunny day. After a few hours sweat was trickling down my back and I knew that my face was fuchsia red.

Mark brought me cold lemonade (he had a mini-fridge in the hut) and we sat on planks laid over the mud and talked.

'It must be an interesting job, being a forensic archaeologist,' he said.

'It is interesting,' I said. 'I like excavating bones, I like the order of it. I could never have taught, I'm not articulate enough. I get nervous talking to people. I never fancied working in a museum. So fieldwork was all there was, really.'

'You don't seem nervous now,' he said.

'One-to-one is different,' I said.

The skeleton was lying in a shallow grave. Although the top soil had been disturbed by the digger, the layers lower down were intact. This meant that the body had, at some point, been buried deliberately. From the pelvis and the length of the bones I deduced that the deceased was female. When I saw the skull, I was sure. Male skulls have prominent brow ridges and larger nuchal crests. This skull was small and smooth across the brow, the teeth small too, with a gap between the front two. When I told Mark about the brow ridges, he said, 'Does that mean we're all Neanderthals?'

'All Europeans have between one and four per cent Neanderthal DNA,' I told him.

Mark went to the shop and bought us sandwiches for lunch. We ate them sitting on the planks, drinking water from bottles and talking about our lives. Mark was from Essex, he'd left school at sixteen and worked all round the world. He'd met his wife, Leah, while backpacking in Vietnam. 'She was into all that hippie scene,' he said with a smile, 'but it gets boring in the end and the music's terrible.' He played bass guitar, he told me, and had been in a group called Boromir's Horn. I told him about school and university, how my life had been crippled by shyness until I met Steven, who had been too self-absorbed to notice it.

In the afternoon, I excavated the bones. I lifted them out of the earth, one by one, and brushed them clean with a child's toothbrush. Then I marked each bone with a tiny number in indelible pencil and ticked them off my skeleton sheet. Mark watched me. By the time I had finished it was nearly nine but still light, the air heavy with pollen and the sounds of the city in summer: children playing in gardens, cars hooting, the far-off siren call of an ice-cream van.

'You'll be late home,' said Mark.

'It doesn't matter,' I said and felt myself blushing, because I knew I'd given something away.

But Mark didn't say anything. He helped me put the bones into evidence bags, which I then packed into a cardboard box, wedged around with newspaper. Mark laughed when he saw that it was from a butcher's.

'Very appropriate.'

'Actually I'm a vegetarian,' I said.

There was a silence. We were standing by my car, an old VW Golf. Mark's car, a new Audi, stood in the driveway. It didn't look like a car that belonged to a man who slept in a hut.

'So what happens now?' said Mark. 'Will you be able to date the bones?'

'It's difficult,' I said. 'They don't look very old but the soil is clay which can have a preservative effect. I'll send some samples away for carbon-14 testing. That'll give us a better idea.'

'What's that?'

'Carbon-14 is present in the earth's atmosphere.

Plants take it in, animals eat plants, we eat animals. So we all absorb carbon-14 until the day we die. By measuring the amount of carbon-14 left in a bone, we can estimate how old it is.'

'How accurate is it?'

'Plus or minus about a hundred years,' I said.

Mark laughed. 'I thought you'd say it would tell you exactly when a person was killed.'

'Nothing's that accurate,' I said. 'Carbon-14 testing can be skewed by lots of things—solar flares, sun spots, nuclear testing. Results can take up to six weeks.'

But somehow I knew that Mark would contact me the next day. He rang and suggested a meal in south London. It was warm enough to sit outside, one of those evenings when London feels like Paris or Rome. We ate delicious vegetarian food and drank white wine. He told me more about his wife. 'Leah was a wild child,' he said. 'Dyed hair, home-made tattoos. My parents disapproved of her but I thought she was the most exciting person I'd ever met.'

I told him about my ex-fiancé, Steven. 'He wasn't exciting and my parents approved too much. He was an accountant, very sensible, very steady. They couldn't believe it when I broke off the engagement.'

'Why did you?'

'Because he bored me senseless,' I said.

That wasn't the only reason. It was also because, although I could envisage a future of regular mortgage payments and half-board holidays in Devon, I couldn't quite face up to a lifetime of faking orgasms. But, that evening, when Mark put his hand on my arm to steer me across Wandsworth High Street, I knew that wouldn't be our problem. He took me back to the hut and we made love on an old tarpaulin, the foxes singing in the background.

The carbon-14 results took almost two months, by which time Mark was living with me in my bedsit, just until our dream home was completed. I had done many other tests on the bones found in Shelley Drive. I had found, for example, a mark on the femur that could have been a sign of a periosteal infection. There are many causes of such infections, including bone disease or a home-made tattoo that has become septic. I didn't say anything to Mark. Hadn't he said, that first day, 'I thought you'd say it would tell you exactly when a person was killed'? When they were killed, not when they died. I knew even before I saw Leah's gap-toothed grin in her wedding photos. I knew that Leah wasn't in Marrakesh with her new lover. But I didn't articulate this knowledge.

The test results, when they came, were inconclusive.

The bones were anything from ten to a hundred years old. I didn't recommend referral to the coroner. Work started on the house again. Our double bedroom with its ensuite bathroom was full of light and the dappled reflections of trees. It was spring again by the time that we moved in, the cherry blossom was in flower and Mark carried me over the threshold. It turns out that you can sleep quite happily over a burial ground. Ask anyone in London.

Castles in the Air

I got this job because I hate books. At least that's what the bookshop manager, Mr McGuire, said. I didn't think I had a chance, to be honest. There aren't many jobs in this town and I knew there'd be loads of applicants. My A levels were in DT, IT and PE. My mum said that I'd picked them because I prefer initials to real words, and she had a point. Anyway, my grades weren't that good and I thought you might need English to work in a bookshop. I also thought that it might be a bit of a girl's job. But Mr McGuire said that he was fed up with all these girls bleating on about how they absolutely *loved* books, books were their *life*, they'd just *die* if they didn't have a book by their side every second of the day. 'They might love books,' he said on my first day in the shop, 'but can they stack boxes or organise a spreadsheet? Can they make a good cappuccino? Believe me, boy, that's the future of bookshops. Cappuccinos.'

Mr McGuire is building a coffee shop on the second floor. It's going to take up the whole of the travel and biography sections. He's going to have me trained to make proper Italian coffee.

'I'm going to be a barista,' I told Mum.

'I'm so proud,' she said. 'I always wanted you to do law.' Mum likes to think she's funny. It's because she reads *Private Eye*. She's an artist and, when I was younger, I used to get embarrassed because she didn't dress like other mothers. She'd turn up to collect me from school in a smock covered with paint, or a short skirt and crazily patterned tights. I bought her a tracksuit for her fortieth and she never wore it once. Now I'm quite proud of her for being different. She's brought up my brother and me on her own (my dad left when I was ten) and she hasn't done too bad a job. My brother's dead clever, he's only fourteen but he's the school chess champion and he's grade eight on the French horn. And he reads all the time. 'It's just you, Dylan,' says Mum, 'who thinks books are the enemy.'

When people hear that my name's Dylan they think that it's after Bob Dylan or that Welsh poet. But, no, trust Mum. It's after some dozy rabbit in a children's TV programme that was on about a million years ago. It was called *The Magic Roundabout* and Mr McGuire says it was really all about drugs. That doesn't surprise me. I think Mum was pretty wild in her art school days. My brother's called Ozzie which doesn't sound so bad until you find out that it's after a poem called 'Ozymandias'. Poor kid.

I don't know quite when my battle against books started. I think I used to read when I was Ozzie's age or younger. There were these cool books about Vikings that I really liked. Then, I don't know, books started to get longer and more boring. I got a Nintendo DS and spent most of my time playing on that. The final straw was having to do *Of Mice and Men* for GCSE. I hated that book. Lennie was obviously a homicidal maniac with a rabbit fixation and George wasn't much better. It was only set for the lower stream because it was short (and they probably thought we'd identify with Lennie). When I finished it I swore I'd never read a novel again. By the time I was eighteen, I hadn't read a book for nearly two years.

Mum used to try to get me to read (exciting-looking parcels under the tree that turned out to be—gee thanks—a book) but she gave up in the end. Even so I think she was quite proud of me for getting the job in the bookshop. She was a bit worried when I didn't want to go to college. My A levels weren't up to much but I would probably have got in to read PE somewhere. But just the word 'read' put me off. More books, even when you're doing PE? No thanks. But working in a bookshop was quite a respectable job. Best of all, it was *interesting*. Mum's highest term of praise.

It was on an interesting morning in early September that I met her. I spotted her immediately because she was standing by the poetry shelves reading a book. We don't get many Readers, as Mr McGuire calls them. 'Readers aren't Buyers,' he says, 'so we don't want to encourage them. No chairs or sofas or cosy corners where they can curl up and forget the world. Overhead lighting and wipe-clean surfaces. That's what keeps the Readers away.'

But the overhead lighting didn't seem to have deterred this girl. She was leaning against the wall, apparently absorbed in her book. That was the first thing I noticed. The second thing was her hair. She had this long, reddish-brown plait that fell below her waist. I remember thinking that it was like a rope, that if you were drowning you could grab onto it and save your life. God knows why that went through my mind. I'm not the sort of person to fantasise about drowning, or about girls for that matter. Oh, I like girls, don't get me wrong. It's just that so far my relationships had been more the

32 • ELLY GRIFFITHS

'wanna go out?' 'don't mind' variety. In fact 'relation-ship' seemed too big a word for them. Those bookish girls have *relationships*; the rest of us just go out.

'Go and ask her if she's buying that book,' Mr Mc-Guire hissed. 'She can't just stand around reading all day.'

I was a bit nervous but he was the boss and I'd only been working there a few weeks. So I sidled over carrying a pile of George R.R. Martins.

'Areyougoingtobuythatbook?'

I didn't mean it to come out quite like that, but she turned and smiled.

'I don't know,' she said. 'I was just reading it. I don't know much about Gerard Manley Hopkins, do you?'

'No,' I said. It was safe to say that I'd never heard of him.

'It's extraordinary some of the things he does with words. It feels quite modern but he died in 1889.'

'Oh,' I said. Was she actually trying to have a booky conversation with me?

She must have seen my face because she laughed and said, 'Don't you like poetry?'

I was on safer ground here. 'No,' I said.

'I haven't read as much poetry as I should,' she said. 'But I'm off to uni soon and I want to get lots of reading done before I go.'

My argument against university in a nutshell. But she was smiling at me so I didn't want to be rude. She was pretty really although you didn't notice it at first. She had these wide apart eyes that were a strange colour, somewhere between grey and blue. When she was talking she looked right at you, which not many people do. It made me feel nervous.

'I need to put these on the shelves,' I said, indicating the Georges.

'I haven't even got started on *Game of Thrones* yet,' she said. She sounded genuinely worried. 'So many books, so little time.'

When I came back from the fantasy section she was at the till. Mr McGuire was wrong. She was a Buyer as well as a Reader. She bought the Gerard Manley Hopkins book and she put another in front of me.

'Try that,' she said. 'You might like it.'

After she'd gone I looked at the book. It was by T.S. Eliot and it was all about cats. I put it back on the shelf.

She was back the next day. This time she was looking at the history shelves.

'I want to find out about the Spanish Civil War,' she said.

'Are you reading History at university?' I asked. I was quite proud at the way it came out, 'reading' and everything. I sounded like one of those people from *University Challenge* (Mum and Ozzie's favourite programme).

'No,' she said. 'English. But I've just read this great book about the Spanish Civil War and I wanted to know a bit more about it.'

That was another thing I hated about English. You finish a book, hooray, let's tick that one off, and the teacher's saying that you should really read another book just to get the historical *background*, or for the *contrast* or whatever. But this girl looked absolutely thrilled at the thought of more reading.

'Modern History's over there,' I said.

Instead of moving, she held out her hand to me. 'Jo-anna,' she said.

I find hand-shaking embarrassing, but I managed it. 'Dylan,' I mumbled.

'Cool,' she said. 'Like—'

'No,' I interrupted. 'Like the rabbit in *The Magic Roundabout*.'

She laughed. 'Do you have a lunch break, Dylan? Fancy getting a sandwich in the mall? It's a lovely day.'

God knows why but I said yes. I think it was partly just to get rid of her. Sometimes now I wish I'd said no but that's not how life works, is it? It's not like a book. It only goes forwards, you don't get flashbacks.

CASTLES IN THE AIR · 35

She was right. It was a lovely day. We bought sandwiches and ate them in the little square of green opposite the 99p shop. It's funny, normally I would have felt nervous, having lunch with a girl I didn't know, but she made it seem all right. I think it was because she was so normal. She wasn't flirting or coming on to me. She was just chatting. Like we were friends.

She told me that she was eighteen and going to university in October. She was going to Cambridge, a place I'd only heard about in *University Challenge*.

'Are you really clever then?' I asked.

'No,' she said seriously. 'I just worked hard. I'm not naturally clever but I love reading and that helps with English. What about you?'

I told her about the initial A levels.

'What's your favourite sport?' she asked. I liked the way that she didn't ask about grades or any of that stuff. Even so, I felt a bit embarrassed. You see, I've never much liked football, which was a big problem at my school. You were nothing if you weren't in the football team. My sport was pretty low down in the pecking order.

'Running,' I said. 'I liked long distance running.' All the other kids used to moan about cross-country running but I loved it. Getting into the zone, running almost in a trance, the only sound your feet pounding on the grass or the tarmac or whatever. I used to train in the early mornings and even this crappy town looked good then, the mist rising from the river, the roads empty, the smell of grass and fresh, clean air.

'You used the past tense,' she said. 'Do you still run?'

'Only for the bus,' I said. 'You stop doing sport when you leave school, don't you?'

'That's like saying you stop reading when you leave school.'

'Yeah, well, I did that too,' I said.

Joanna was at St Faith's, the private girls' school out by the golf course. I knew her family must be posh, I knew it by her voice, but this just confirmed it.

'I got a scholarship,' she said, rather defensively. 'My sisters did too.'

'How many sisters have you got?'

'Three. Two.'

We said goodbye because I had to get back to work and she wanted to go to the library (natch). All afternoon I wondered about someone who didn't know how many sisters they had. Maybe she's terrible at maths (one of the annoying things about those bookish girls is how they all hate maths) but even so. About an hour before closing time she was back, holding out a book to me.

I looked at the front. It was called *The Loneliness of the Long Distance Runner.*

'I had to get it from the library,' she said. 'I didn't think you'd have it here. Don't tell your boss.'

I'd told her a bit about Mr McGuire. You won't be surprised to hear that he hates libraries.

'It's a short story,' she carried on. 'By Alan Sillitoe. I thought you might like it.'

'How long have I got to read it?'

'Three weeks.' She said it like it was an unimaginable stretch of time. It had taken me a whole term to read *Of Mice and Men* and that's only about a hundred pages long.

There was a pause and then she said, 'My sister died. That's why I said I had three sisters at first. I hate saying two. It feels like I'm disowning Elizabeth. She was ill for a long time but I wasn't prepared for her to die. It's so final, death. Not like reading a book. If someone dies in a book, they're alive again every time you read it.'

What could I say to that? 'I'm sorry,' I said at last.

'Read the book,' she said.

After that we met every day. It was a really hot September, better than August had been. We'd have lunch on the green and, after work, we'd walk down to the river. We'd sit there with our feet in the water and we'd talk. I've never talked so much in my life. My mates and I, we don't talk much. We'll meet at someone's house, play a few computer games and watch TV. We'll only talk about what's happening on screen at that particular moment. The past and the future doesn't come into it. I used to talk to Mum but, as I've got older, it's embarrassing somehow. Ozzie still chats away to her—what superpower he'd have if he could choose, what he'd like for dinner, his favourite French horn music—but mostly I just listen.

Sometimes it would get dark and we'd still be talking. Then we'd walk back into town, get some chips and maybe a couple of beers and go back to the river. The water had this strange green light sometimes, phosphorescence she called it, and we'd sit there with this glow on our faces, like aliens. Once I took a photo of her and her hair was all electric, standing up round her head like a halo. That was the only time I ever saw her hair loose.

Mum saw me with Joanna one lunchtime and was convinced that something was going on. She kept talking about my girlfriend, 'you know, the one with the lovely long hair'. 'She's not my girlfriend, Mum,' I'd tell her patiently. 'She's just a friend.' And that was true. It was the 'just' that was a lie.

We told each other everything. I told her how upset I'd been when Dad left. I even told her that I'd wet the bed for months. She told me how awful it had been when Elizabeth died. 'I thought I couldn't show any emotion because I've always been the strong one in the family.' She wasn't the oldest though. She had an elder sister who was married and a younger sister who was a bit of an airhead. 'Give me her number,' I said. 'I love airheads.' 'I'll give you her number when I go to university,' she said. 'You can take her out then. But this is our time.'

Sometimes, at night, I used to look at her Facebook profile. It was the usual thing: lots of girls fooling about in funny hats, a few pictures of her with her family and her dog (Scrabble), a few posts about books and films. It was funny though, when I looked at her Facebook page I felt that I didn't know her at all. But, when we talked by the river, I felt that I knew her better than I knew anyone. Better than Mum or Ozzie or Tom, who's been my best mate since year three. It almost felt like we were the same person.

I read the book she lent me. It was actually quite good. It's about this boy who's at Borstal. He starts running to forget about being locked up, to escape inside himself. Then he gets offered a place at a posh school. All he has to do is win a race. He's miles ahead but he stops just before the finish line. It's meant to show that he's his own person but I thought it was a bit stupid, to be honest.

'So if I'd won the county championship I could have gone to St Faith's,' I said.

'Except it's a girls' school,' said Joanna.

'All the same,' I said. 'I could have been a contender.' I meant it to be funny but it came out wrong. I sounded bitter and sarcastic.

'Dylan.' She leant forward so that her face was only a few inches from mine. Her hair was tickling my face. 'You are a contender. Not because of where you went to school but because of *you*. You're clever and funny and sweet. You've just got to believe in yourself.'

But it was enough that she believed in me.

September was endless but then it was over in a flash. One day Joanna came into the shop and started buying all these pens and notepads and things.

'Stocking up?' I said.

'Yes,' she said. 'I'm off on Saturday.'

Saturday. It was three days away. Mr McGuire came over, all happy because she was buying stationery. He thinks that's the sort of thing the shop should be selling. 'A notepad's used up in a week,' he'd say. 'And then they buy another. But a book can last for ever.' He made it sound like something disgusting. *For ever.*

'We'll miss you,' he said to Joanna. 'I've never known a Reader buy so many books.'

'We'll have to have a farewell party,' Joanna said to me later. 'Friday night, down by the river. I'll bring some wine.'

CASTLES IN THE AIR · 41

On Friday I wore my best green top and told Mum I'd be home late. 'Going somewhere nice with your girlfriend?' she said. 'Have fun.' But I didn't think I'd ever have fun again. I'd bought Joanna a present, a bicycle bell because she told me that everyone cycled in Cambridge. It had Dylan from *The Magic Roundabout* on it. I hoped it would remind her of me. I wondered how I'd cope, stuck in this stupid town with no one to talk to. Maybe I should go away, try to get into college somewhere. The night before I'd even downloaded some prospectuses.

'Excuse me,' said the girl at the counter. 'Have you got a book called "Grumpy Git in a Green Shirt"? I think it's by Charles Dickens.'

I looked up. I didn't recognise her at first, even though she was staring at me with those wide-apart grey eyes. It was Joanna but instead of her long plait, the rope that was going to save me from drowning, her hair was cut short and dyed bright red.

'You've cut your hair,' I said stupidly.

'Yes,' she said. 'Thought it was time for a new look. Do you like it?'

'Yes,' I said.

I hated it.

We went down to the river and we sat on the bank

and drank the wine. I gave her the bicycle bell and she gave me this bag that she'd made herself with big fabric stars on it. I could tell immediately that it was full of books. I have to admit that I was a bit disappointed. Joanna had done nothing else but give me books and lend me books since we'd met. I'd hoped that her leaving present would be something more personal.

She saw my face. 'It's not just a bag of books, Dylan. Each of these books is special to me. I'm in all of them. You're in all of them. That way we'll never lose each other. Just start to read and you'll see.'

She leant towards me and, just for a second, I thought about kissing her. Then a couple of drunks came staggering along the towpath and the moment was lost.

When I got home I opened the bag. Some of the books were new from the shop but some were her old books, ones she'd had as a child. She'd written her name in them. Joanna M, England, Great Britain, Europe, The World, The Universe. The first one I opened had a hideous cover showing four girls sitting in a garden.

Little Women. Well, I wouldn't find Jo in that. But it was a place to start.

Max Mephisto and
the Disappearing Act

Leeds, 1928

'How can you make a woman disappear?'

Mrs Hamm leant over the breakfast table, crumbs adhering to her purple housecoat. Max averted his eyes and refrained from making the obvious comment.

'I can't tell you all my secrets,' he said, attempting the jocu-lar tone that he'd heard other pros use with the landlady.

'What secrets could a young lad like you know?' There was a hint of challenge in her voice which could almost be interpreted as flirtatiousness. Tommy Hawkins, the juggler, said that Mrs Hamm had quite a reputation. 'There was that knife thrower a few years ago. And three of the Four Singing Trubshaws. Don't know what the fourth had done to miss out.' Max had laughed but he was uncomfortable with dressing room humour, never knowing quite how to respond. He knew that he was acquiring a reputation for being posh and standoffish but the problem was that he *was* posh. Aristocratic and poor, an uneasy combination. When Max ran away from boarding school for the third and final time, aged sixteen, his father, Lord Alastair Massingham, had made good on his threat to cut him off without a penny. Two years later, Max was becoming known as a promising young magician but he hadn't heard from his father in all that time and he wondered if he ever would again.

'Wish you could make Mr H disappear.' Mrs Hamm's laugh was too loud for the small dining room. 'But it's always women with you lot, isn't it?'

Max wondered which lot she meant. Men? Magicians? Posh people?

'Audiences want to look at pretty women,' said Eileen Dawkins, one of the chorus girls. She was rather pretty herself, Max decided, with curly blonde hair and a heart-shaped face. The hair was now covered with a green scarf but her blue eyes twinkled as she smiled at Max across the remains of the scrambled eggs. He wondered if he was blushing and hoped it didn't show on his olive skin, a legacy from his dead Italian mother.

'I'll be watching you closely tonight, young Mr Mephisto.' Again, Mrs Hamm's voice held a hint of menace and something even less welcome. Tonight was the first night and, even worse, Mondays were when the landladies got their free tickets. 'Hardest audience you'll ever face,' a previous stage manager had told Max.

'I hope you'll be satisfied,' said Max, regretting it almost immediately.

'I doubt it, lad.' Mr Hamm had entered the room. 'She almost never is.'

The lodgers broke into laughter but Max saw a glance pass between the married couple that made him glance, briefly, at the bread knife.

Max was appearing in a variety show, performed twice nightly for the good citizens of Leeds. As he approached the Dominion Theatre, two boys were pasting up the playbills.

Trixie Lee *'The Girl with the Golden Voice'*
Accompanied by **Ed Levi** *on piano*
Ronnie Arthur *'The King of the Squeezebox'*
Tommy Hawkins *'Jovial Juggler'*
Tim and Tom *'Tiny Acrobats'*
Harry the Hat *'Funniest Man in Britain'*
Syd Moose *'Cycling Supremo'*
Max Mephisto *'You'll believe a woman can disappear'*
The Babes in the Wood *Dance troupe*

Max's name was so small that it could hardly be seen without a magnifying glass. But he was confident about the premise of his act. That summer, during a season in Blackpool, he'd met a magician called Stan Parks, otherwise known as The Great Diablo. Stan had been a big star before the war but now had a reputation for drinking too much and forgetting the end of his tricks. But, for some reason, the aging pro had taken a liking to Max. They spent many hours in his dressing room, drinking whisky from a flask, and talking about magic. Stan knew the secrets of every theatre in England.

'The thing about the Dominion, dear boy, is that there's a trapdoor. You put your vanishing cabinet over it, false bottom of course. Your girl opens the trapdoor, climbs down into the space below. Hey presto—she's disappeared. Cue applause and drinking champagne out of chorus girls' shoes.'

Max couldn't afford a vanishing cabinet but thought he could perform the trick just with a table. Surely he'd be able to find a table somewhere? And he'd written to the stage manager to see if he could recommend a girl who'd be willing to disappear for an extra pound a week.

Max walked through the foyer, which had a faded crimson carpet and framed posters from the Dominion's glory days. Ellen Terry as Lady Macbeth.

MAX MEPHISTO AND THE DISAPPEARING ACT · 47

Beerbohm Tree as Hamlet. He could hear from the auditorium that the band call had already started.

Band call was when the orchestra went through the music for each act. Unlike the posters, the order was strictly democratic. Whoever got their music on stage first, secured the first slot. Max arrived to find Trixie Lee, the headline act, sitting in the third row of the stalls, wearing a fur coat and watching rather sourly as Tommy Hawkins explained the tempo for his juggling act. Trixie was billed as 'the girl with the golden voice' but the hair was covered with a scarf and 'girl' was pushing it. Max thought that the singer was probably in her forties, good-looking but rather hard-faced. She didn't glance round when Max took the seat behind her.

When it was Trixie's turn, she shrugged off the coat and climbed the steps onto the stage. A piano was wheeled on and her accompanist, a bespectacled man in braces, took his seat and plonked his way through the singer's greatest hits. 'My One and Only'. 'Girl and Boy'. 'The Last Dance.' Trixie sang in a low monotone, occasionally forgetting the lyrics and snapping her fingers with irritation. Max wondered if she was saving her voice or whether the rumours were true and she could no longer hit the high notes. The orchestra had very little to do and the first violin took out a newspaper.

48 · ELLY GRIFFITHS

Next was Harry Venables, the 'funniest man in Britain'. He became very angry when he heard that Tommy had chosen 'Swanee' by Al Jolson for his juggling act. 'It's my tune,' he shouted to Franz, the conductor, who shrugged apologetically. 'I'm known for it. I get a big laugh on those bird calls.'

'I'm sorry,' said Franz, who had a pleasant German, or possibly Austrian, accent. 'But Mr Hawkins was before you.'

Another rule of band call was that, whoever requested the song first, got to use it in their act. Harry could only mutter angrily and settle, with bad grace, on 'Charleston'.

Max was up next and he approached the stage with trepidation. He didn't have any signature music and usually performed to whatever the orchestra could busk. The results could be interesting, to say the least.

'I'm sorry,' he said to Franz. 'I don't have any band parts.'

'What is your act?'

'I'm a magician.' If he said it often enough, he might come to believe it.

'What about the "Danse Macabre"? We play it nice and slow, yes? Could become your theme tune.'

'That would be wonderful. Thank you.'

MAX MEPHISTO AND THE DISAPPEARING ACT · 49

'Not at all.' Franz smiled at him kindly. 'Always happy to help a young man on the way up.'

Was he on his way up? Max wasn't sure. His father wouldn't think so, at any rate. He'd expected his son to follow in his footsteps, running the estate in between murdering innocent wildlife and playing golf. But Massingham Hall had never felt like home in the way a theatre—any theatre—did. The Dominion had seen better days but it was still a majestic place, a Number Two venue, a step up from the fleapits where Max first started, a gawky sixteen-year-old performing card tricks by the flickering light of old gas lamps.

'Max!' Bill Waring, the stage manager, hailed him. The SM was an important personage in any theatre. He was in charge of the running order and controlled everything that went on backstage. Max stopped. 'Good morning, Mr Waring.'

'That's what I like to see. A nice polite boy.' Bill clapped him on the shoulder. 'I've found you a girl for tonight. Here she is.'

'Hi, Max,' said Eileen. 'I'm ready to disappear.'

They practised all morning. The plan was that, after Max had performed a few initial sleight-of-hand tricks, Eileen would appear from the wings and take her place on the trestle table that Max had borrowed from the stage carpenter. Max would cover her with a cloth that looked smooth but was, in fact, molded to the shape of a woman's body. Then, after some cymbal clashes and a puff of green smoke, Eileen would slide from the table and disappear through the trap door into the space beneath the stage. She would then make her way into the wings and back through the foyer to take her seat in the Royal Box, which was empty for the length of the run. The assistant stage manager, a spotty youth called Lionel, would shine a spotlight, showing Eileen waving to the crowd. The timing was all-important. Max had to keep talking long enough for Eileen to make her way through the backstage chaos and take her seat, looking calm and composed, as if she'd materialised there.

Eileen was a quick learner. With a dancer's grace she was able to slip smoothly from the table without disturbing the covering. Eileen told Max she'd had ballet lessons as a child but had to leave school when she was thirteen. She joined the Babes in the Wood troupe at sixteen. Max asked how old she was now and she said 'nineteen' but he'd noticed the pause that went before the words. You can't be a magician without reading unspoken clues.

At lunchtime Eileen suggested that they went to a

MAX MEPHISTO AND THE DISAPPEARING ACT · 51

nearby workmen's café. It was in an unprepossessing backstreet but the egg and chips were delicious. Mrs Hamm had succeeded in putting Max off his breakfast but now he ate hungrily, gulping down the sweet tea he normally hated. 'Boys always eat a lot,' said Eileen, although she'd consumed the same amount whilst managing to make it look as if the food had magically evaporated. Max wanted to protest at being called a boy but thought that, in itself, would sound childish.

After lunch, they went back to the boarding house. Eileen went upstairs to the attic bedroom she shared with Joan, another of the Babes. Max didn't want to look as if he was following her so he waited a few minutes before heading to his own room. Standing by the front door, hanging his coat on the rack, he was surprised to hear music coming from one of the back rooms. He crossed the landing, saw an open door and Mr Hamm sitting at an upright piano, hands moving as if in a dream. The tune sounded vaguely familiar. Max tried to back away soundlessly but the floorboards creaked and the landlord said, 'Is that you?'

'It's me. Max,' replied Max, wondering who 'you' was.

'Oh. The magician.' Mr Hamm turned to look at him, his expression almost embarrassed. 'I used to play the piano a bit.'

'You're very good,' said Max. 'Not that I'm an expert.'

'I wasn't good enough to be a soloist,' said Mr Hamm. 'But I once made a living as an accompanist. I used to accompany her, as a matter of fact. Trixie.'

'Trixie Lee?'

'That's right. The girl with the golden voice. She sang like an angel back then.'

And now Max recognised the song. It was 'Girl and Boy', Trixie's most famous number. It had sounded very different played in band call that morning. Mr Hamm had added trills and ornaments and a tremulous emotion that made Max feel vaguely uncomfortable.

'This was the piano I used on stage,' Mr Hamm was saying. 'It's on casters. Look.'

Max saw the wheels at the base of the piano. He'd never been in this room before and it was furnished in a different style from the rest of the house; white walls, tasteful paintings, expensive-looking furniture. French windows led into a garden where hens pecked in the freshly turned earth of Mr Hamm's vegetable patch.

'How's the act going?' said Mr Hamm.

'Quite well,' said Max. 'Eileen's going to be my assistant.'

'She's a nice girl,' said Mr Hamm. 'She's stayed here before.'

'Yes, she said so.'

MAX MEPHISTO AND THE DISAPPEARING ACT • 53

'They come and they go,' said the landlord, turning back to the keys. 'You'll be the same.'

It sounded uncomfortably like a curse.

Max felt more and more nervous as the first performance approached. 'I haven't a nerve in my body,' the older pros boasted but Max noticed that even Tommy Hawkins and Ronnie Arthur, the ancient accordionist who was second on the bill, were more silent than usual as they sat down to Mrs Hamm's famous pre-show high tea. Max couldn't eat much. The egg and chips were now churning in his stomach.

Max was the third act in the first half. He wasn't famous enough to be first or last. Harry the Hat opened the show. He was a confident figure, spotlit on the empty stage in a brightly checked suit and trademark homburg, but his slightly off-colour jokes did not seem to amuse the audience of landladies. Next was Syd Moose, whose act mostly involved circling around the stage on a penny-farthing bicycle. It was quite mesmeric, in a repetitive way, but the landladies didn't care for it and Syd's applause barely covered his exit. Then it was the Babes and then Max.

Max watched the girls doing the can-can in a line. The stage was slightly too small so there was always one dancer high-kicking on her own in the wings. Eileen was in the centre though and even Max could see that she was one of the best, her brilliant smile never faltering as her fishnetted legs flashed. Max hoped that she wouldn't be out of breath when she performed with him. The girls got unenthusiastic applause—they probably wore too few clothes for the landladies—and then they were clattering past him. 'Break a leg,' Eileen whispered. Then Max saw Franz raise his baton and the first notes of the 'Danse Macabre' drifted up from the orchestra. Max turned a circle anticlockwise (a superstition he'd recently acquired), took a deep breath and walked on stage.

'Stroll,' he told himself, 'don't be in a hurry. Make them wait for you.' Even so, it seemed to take for ever to reach his spot. He looked out over the darkened auditorium, glad that he couldn't see Mrs Hamm and Co. sitting with their handbags on their laps, daring him to entertain them.

'Good evening, ladies and gentlemen. I'm Max Mephisto. Excuse me, madam,' he addressed a woman in the front row. 'Is that something in your hair?' She put her hand up to her hat and Max shot a plume of smoke into the air, out of which flew a mechanical dove. The woman screamed, the audience laughed. He had them.

By the time Eileen appeared, Max had hit his rhythm.

MAX MEPHISTO AND THE DISAPPEARING ACT · 55

'Let me introduce you to my lovely assistant.' Eileen, still in her sparkly Babes costume, smiled and twirled. 'But don't get too fond of her, ladies and gentlemen, because I'm going to make her disappear.' He'd expected a few 'oohs' here but the landladies weren't about to commit themselves yet. Eileen climbed onto the table and arranged her hands the way they had practised. Max threw the cloth over her and opened the trapdoor with his foot.

Another puff of smoke. Eileen moved quickly, closing the trap after her. Max pulled back the cloth to show the empty table. A smattering of applause but any fool can make a girl disappear. It's bringing her back that counts.

Max started the patter that they'd timed that morning. At the word 'relief', Eileen was meant to appear in the royal box. At 'Queen' the spotlight would pick her out. But no one appeared. Thank goodness Lionel held his nerve and didn't shine the light. Max felt himself sweating. He raised his hands and did the smoke trick again. He looked under the cloth, hoping for a laugh, but the audience were silent. Just when he was wondering whether he should run away and give up magic for ever, there was a movement at the back of the box.

'And here she is,' said Max. 'Our Queen of Hearts.' The spotlight showed Eileen waving and smiling. Max bowed and exited stage left to a healthy round of applause and even a few cheers.

'I'm sorry,' said Eileen in the Green Room afterwards. 'I got lost. Nothing looked the same backstage. All the flats are on wheels so they move and change everything. I thought I was heading to the foyer and I found myself in a cupboard. I panicked.'

'So did I.'

'I'm sorry,' said Eileen again, 'but it went well in the end. The audience loved you.'

It was true that Max had been a hit. Several people had congratulated him afterwards and even Trixie patted him on the back and said that he wasn't bad for a youngster. There was only an hour before the second house. Max drank tea in the green room with Eileen and the other Babes then went back to the dressing room he shared with Tommy. He needed to change his shirt. He wished he could have a bath.

The juggler was sitting by the mirror with a greasepaint-stained towel round his neck, eating a pork pie, which made Max realise that he was hungry again.

'Good work, Maxie boy,' said Tommy, looking at his reflection. 'I think we're going to be hearing more from you in the future.'

'It was Eileen really,' said Max.

MAX MEPHISTO AND THE DISAPPEARING ACT · 57

'No, it was you,' said Tommy. 'I was watching back-stage. You've got what it takes. She was good, that little dancer, but, take my advice, don't get involved with the girls. It'll slow you down. Why do you think I never married?'

Because you look like a toad, thought Max, and an unattractive one at that. But he said nothing and absorbed this new piece of advice.

The second house went perfectly. Eileen disappeared and appeared 'as if by magic' a surprisingly enthusiastic Mrs Hamm told Max back at the house. She'd prepared a late supper and there was a comfortable, almost cosy, feeling around the table. Tommy was juggling with three boiled eggs, Joan and Eileen applauding him. Ronnie was telling Mr Hamm about Trixie forgetting her words on stage.

'It was in the middle of "Girl and Boy". She stopped and it really looked like she was going to cry. So unpro-fessional.'

'Did the audience notice?' asked Mr Hamm.

'I don't think so. Ed just kept tinkling away in the background until she caught up with him.'

'That's the secret of being a good accompanist. Keep playing until you find a bit that the singer recognises.'

'Of course, you were in the business yourself, weren't you?'

'I even accompanied Trixie. A long time ago now.'

'Do you miss it?'

Mr Hamm's face took on the dreamy expression he'd had when sitting at the piano keys. 'What's the point of talking about the past?'

'Trixie's past it, in my humble opinion,' said Ronnie, not sounding particularly humble. 'I should be top of the bill. I'm a proper musician.'

'Speaking of musicians,' said Max, talking quickly because he thought it might be an idea to change the subject, 'I thought the conductor was very good.'

'Franz?' said Mrs Hamm. 'He's German.'

'So was Beethoven,' countered her husband.

'Know all about music, do you?' said Ronnie to Max, his tone not entirely friendly.

'Not at all,' said Max. 'I had piano lessons at school, but I was terrible.'

'Did you go to public school, Max?' asked Mrs Hamm. 'Was it a famous one?'

'Oh no,' said Max. Though it was famous, if you liked that sort of thing.

'How did you end up here?' asked Joan, her gaze embracing the table with its motley collection of food and guests, the moulting stag's head over the fireplace, the faded photographs of dead Hamms.

'Just luck, I suppose,' said Max.

MAX MEPHISTO AND THE DISAPPEARING ACT · 59

Eileen winked at him as a boiled egg landed in the soup.

The pros were still sitting at the table at midnight. Max was used to this now. Variety performers were creatures of the night; they stayed up late and slept late in the mornings. Most of them didn't bother to get properly dressed for breakfast, a fact which would have made Max's father talk about shotguns and keeping the population down. But, tonight, Max decided to make his exit. He thanked Mrs Hamm for the meal and stood up, trying to catch Eileen's eye in a subtle way. At the foot of the stairs he waited. Had he been wrong? But, no, there was the creak of the floorboards. Eileen appeared, curly hair silhouetted by the porch light.

'Want a nightcap?' said Max. 'I've got a quarter of Scotch in my room.'

'I thought you'd never ask,' said Eileen.

All week, twice nightly, Max made Eileen disappear. Every night, they slept together in Max's single bed. She was his first but he hoped he'd used enough misdirection not to make this obvious. The show's producer, the much-feared Bert Billington, offered Max another run, this time at a Number One theatre in London. His wife, beautiful ex-variety star Verity Malone, smiled at Max in a way that seemed to offer even more.

'You're on your way,' Eileen said.

We could go on our way together, Max wanted to say. He needed an assistant and soon he'd be able to pay for one. But he thought of Mr Hamm saying 'they come and they go', of Tommy advising him to steer clear of girls. He still had a long way to go and there was no doubt that he'd travel faster on his own.

After the last night, there was quite a party at the boarding house. The pros clubbed together to buy wine and beer. Ronnie played the accordion and the girls danced. Max wondered if Mr Hamm would offer to play but there was no move to the piano room. The Hamms went to bed fairly early but they actually seemed on better terms than usual. Mr Hamm even had his arm round his wife's waist as they left the room. But, when Mrs Hamm didn't appear the next morning, her husband blamed the party.

'She wasn't in bed when I woke up,' said Mr Hamm, clattering saucepans. 'I expect she's gone for a walk to clear her head. The music was very loud.'

But Max remembered the landlord urging Ronnie to play 'fortissimo'. Max didn't have much appetite

MAX MEPHISTO AND THE DISAPPEARING ACT · 61

for breakfast. Eileen, her hair back in the headscarf, seemed to be avoiding his eyes. As soon as he could, Max excused himself and headed for the stairs. He had to pack his bags and embark on the long train journey from Leeds to Eastbourne, where he had his next gig. Eileen was going to Scarborough. Should they exchange addresses, arrange to meet on a station platform somewhere? As Max was pondering this, he saw that the door to the music room was slightly ajar. He pushed it open: white walls, delicate paintings, leggy furniture. Max looked again. The room was almost the same but the configuration was slightly different. The piano, which had previously been between two watercolours, was now about a foot closer to the French windows.

'Max?' Eileen had appeared behind him. 'What are you looking at?'

'Nothing.' He didn't want to explain and, besides, what was there to say?

But Eileen, it seemed, had something she wanted to say.

'This week has been wonderful,' she began.

'But . . .' prompted Max.

'But let's not pretend it meant anything more. You're on your way, you're going to be famous. We might meet again, we might not. Let's not make any promises.'

'I want to see you again,' said Max.

'Now you see me,' Eileen patted his cheek. 'Now you don't.'

Two weeks later, at the start of his London run, Max read about the mysterious disappearance of a Leeds landlady, Edna Hamm. Tommy Hawkins, when they met again on the bill in Edinburgh, said that he believed the rumour that Mrs Hamm had run away with one of the Trubshaws. A year later, preparing to headline his first show, Max read that John Hamm, forty-nine, had married singer Trixie Lee, forty-five, at a private ceremony in Torquay. He thought about John Hamm playing the piano, the convenient receptacle that had moved in the night. He thought of Eileen saying that nothing looked the same backstage because everything was on wheels, of John's face when he talked about Trixie. The girl with the golden voice.

There was no point telling anyone else any of this. And did he really think that John had killed his wife and hidden her body in a piano? Was she, even now, buried in the vegetable patch? Max didn't know but he never played the Leeds Dominion again.

And he never saw Eileen again either.

The Only Pebble
on the Beach

They were the perfect couple, that's what everybody said. Afterwards, when the police and ambulances had left and the press were sniffing around the tired little seaside town asking, 'Did you know them?' 'What were they like?'

Nobody asked me, which is just as well really. I was only a child, ten when it happened, but, as it turns out, I did know Maureen and Brian Henderson. Not well—because how well do you know any adults when you are ten?—but well enough. They were friends of my parents, which was unusual in itself because they didn't have many friends. My father was an archaeologist, my mother a painter. Brian Henderson was a writer, so I suppose that was a bond between them. He was a good writer, my mum said, though I've never read anything of his, before or since. I haven't wanted to somehow.

Maureen Henderson was an heiress. When I was a child I thought that too was a job. 'How do you get to be an heiress?' I asked my mother. I could see it was a desirable thing to be, what with Maureen's sleek red car and sleek shimmery clothes and sleek coiled hair. 'You don't have to do anything,' my mother replied, 'you just have to be born rich. There's no justice in the world.' My parents were both communists at the time.

We lived in a little town on the south coast, just a collection of houses really, perched on the edge of a cliff. Every year the sea advanced and the houses retreated. You could still see the remains of the pub, the Sailor's Rest, teetering on the edge of the precipice, the tables and beer barrels and etchings of fishing boats gradually slipping downwards onto the rocks below.

It was a lonely place to grow up but I liked it. I liked walking along the beach listening to the waves hissing against the stones. I liked the nights when the wind came roaring in from the sea, rattling our windows and howling down the chimney. I liked the rare sunny days when we would eat sandwiches on the beach.

It is one of those picnics that I remember now. The adults had been drinking wine and the women were lying back on the pebbles, dozing. My dad had taken

THE ONLY PEBBLE ON THE BEACH · 65

a large black flint from the beach and was striking it with another stone, getting the angle just right so that thin flakes fell away, creating a razor-sharp ridge.

'What are you doing?' Brian asked idly, propping himself up on one arm.

'Flint knapping,' Dad replied. 'It's how early man made his tools. It's a very ancient art. We've found flint tools in this country that are more than half a million years old.'

Brian Henderson picked up one of the discarded stone flakes and ran it across his palm. 'It's sharp,' he said.

'Incredibly sharp,' said Dad. 'Prehistoric man would have used stone tools like these to skin and butcher animals.' He carried on, striking off the blue-black flakes of rock. Brian lay watching him, shielding his eyes against the sun.

When Maureen was murdered, her throat cut as she lay sleeping in their luxury bungalow with its spectacular view of the slate-grey sea, Brian was the first suspect. The husband always is, Dad explained carefully as my mother sat sobbing on the sofa. 'He'll be released soon enough.' And he was. Although he didn't have much of an alibi, neither did he have much in the way of means. He had a motive all right, if Maureen's life insurance constituted a motive, which her family seemed to think it did. But what bothered the police, and eventually caused them to drop the case, was the complete lack of murder weapon.

Maureen's throat had been sliced with a sharp object, a knife they thought at first. But a meticulous fingertip search failed to pick up anything even slightly suspicious. I remember seeing them, swaying lines of white-suited men, moving inexorably across the beach while Brian Henderson watched from his balcony, whisky glass in hand.

It wasn't until years later that I thought about that summer's day on the beach. I'd long since left home and was visiting the area with my then boyfriend. I had some idea of showing him the place where I had grown up, but he didn't really seem interested. My parents had moved away by then and several more houses had slowly rotted into the sea. The Hendersons' luxury bungalow was boarded up. There was graffiti on its white walls and a row of beer cans on the balcony as if someone had been using them for target practice.

'What a dump,' said Tony. 'The beach isn't even sandy. What's the use of a beach without sand?'

What indeed? I stood and looked out over the expanse of grey stones, with the grey sea breaking over them and, clear as day, I heard my dad's voice: 'Prehistoric man would have used stone tools like these to

THE ONLY PEBBLE ON THE BEACH · 67

skin and butcher animals.' And I saw Brian Henderson, shielding his eyes against the summer sun, watching and listening.

And I looked back, over the hundreds and thousands of pebbles, each one worn smooth by time and tide, each one identical and yet different, each one, I saw now, capable of murder, and I wondered which stone Brian Henderson had used and if, afterwards, he had just thrown it into the sea, to be absorbed into the ever-changing, uncaring ocean. And I turned away and walked slowly back along the beach. I didn't think I'd come here again.

St Lucy's Day

'You often see the ghost lights on the marsh at this time of year. Will-o'-the-wisps. Hobby lanterns, they're called round here. Have you heard the legend?'

'No,' says Barbara, though she thinks she has. But, incredible as it may seem, standing in a graveyard talking to the verger about local folklore is probably the most satisfying human contact that she will get to-day. A social highlight, in fact.

'Well,' Henry leans comfortably against one of the taller tombstones, 'there was this blacksmith, you see, called Wicked Jack . . .'

'I'm guessing he's not a good guy?'

'You guess right, vicar. Well, he sold his soul to the devil for the price of a drink. When the devil comes for him, Jack climbs a tree and puts a cross underneath it, so the devil can't get him, you see? The Devil can't take Jack to Hell and he's too bad for Heaven, so Old Nick gives Jack a piece of hell fire.'

'Why?'

'He just does. Anyway, Jack puts the fire in a pumpkin. Like they have at Hallowe'en. They're called jack-o'-lanterns sometimes. And he's condemned to wander the earth with this light, stuck between heaven and hell.'

The Reverend Barbara Svendsen, known to friendlier parishioners as the Rev. Barbie and to the hostile majority as 'that woman vicar', looks out beyond the churchyard to the marshes stretching grey and featureless as far as the eye can see. She remembers reading once that prehistoric people saw marshland as sacred. Because it's neither land nor sea, but something in between, they saw it as a kind of bridge to the afterlife. Neither land nor sea, neither death nor life. That's why they buried bodies and treasure in marshy ground, to mark that boundary. She thinks of Tollund Man, preserved in his glass case, and of Wicked Jack, wandering the liminal zone with his flickering lantern. She thinks, too, of Jonas telling the story of Balder, god of light and joy, son of Odin. She thinks of a lake in Norway, the silver water seeping into the twilight.

'Of course,' says Henry, 'you often see them in graveyards. Corpse lights. Some say they light the way for the coffin, others say they're an omen of death.' He grins, showing four teeth like tilted gravestones.

'There are lots of legends about the dark,' says Barbara briskly. 'That's why I'm having the Night of Light on the thirteenth, to bring some light into the darkness.'

'Folk won't like it,' warns Henry. 'They'll think it's pagan stuff. You want a nice nativity for Christmas, that's what you want.'

'St Lucy's Day,' says Barbara. 'It's traditional.'

'Saints,' says Henry. 'That's Catholic. Worse than the pagans, the left-footers.'

But, Barbara muses, as she walks back to the rectory, you couldn't find anyone less Catholic than Jonas, son of a Lutheran pastor and fan of the Norse gods, but he had always celebrated St Lucy's Day. She can hear his voice now: 'The hall is dark and all the children come in with their candles and one girl, the Lucia, she has a whole crown of lights.' She wonders, almost objectively, how long it will take her to get over her husband's death. But Jonas died seven years ago, when Lucian was two, and it doesn't seem to be getting much easier. In fact, on days like today, the dark days of the soul, it seems more painful than ever.

By the telephone is the letter from the school. 'Dear Mrs Svendsen . . .' The headteacher can never bring herself to type 'Reverend'. 'We are slightly concerned about some aspects of Lucian's behaviour. Could you make an appointment to discuss this with me at the earliest opportunity? It may also be useful to have the input of the educational psychologist.'

Thinking how much she dislikes the word 'input' (is prayer a form of input?), Barbara sighs and picks up the phone.

'**So we're** concerned that he doesn't have a positive image of himself as a boy.'

'Because he wanted the part of Babushka?' Barbara is struggling to keep her temper. Everything about the interview, the headteacher's solemn yet slightly prurient manner, the box of tissues kept within reach, the inspirational texts on the wall, seems calculated to raise her blood pressure. Calm, she tells herself. All shall be well and all shall be well.

'Well, it is unusual for a nine-year-old boy to want to dress up as a woman.'

'Is it? In Victorian times he would have been dressed as a girl until he was five or six.'

The headteacher breathes through her nose. 'But we are not in Victorian times now, Mrs Svendsen. Do you know what he said to our teaching assistant, Mrs Wellbeck?'

'I'm sure you're going to tell me.'

'He said, "When I'm grown up I want to be a vicar like my mum." When Mrs Wellbeck asked him why he replied, "Because I like wearing dresses."'

'**Do you** like Mrs Wellbeck?'

'Not really.' Lucian looks out of the window, a piece of toast in his hand. He's a dreamy child, blond and blue-eyed like Jonas, but tall like her. Left to himself Lucian will often forget to eat, his lunchbox usually comes home untouched. Barbara silently adds this to her list of worries about Lucian.

'Eat your toast. Do you want Marmite on it?'

'No thanks. I don't like Marmite any more. Mum?'

'Yes?'

'Can you see the lights? Out there.'

Barbara follows her son's gaze. The rectory kitchen looks out over the churchyard. Beyond the crumbling stone wall are the marshes that lead to the estuary and, eventually, the sea. They have only been in the house a few months so they have never seen it in summer, when the grass is purple with sea lavender, or in the spring when the returning birds circle in the sky. Now, in mid-winter, the flat landscape is grey during the day and pitch-black at night. There should be no lights anywhere at all.

'Look!' Lucian points.

It must be an optical illusion but Barbara also thinks that she can see something, a faint glow, greenish-yellow in the darkness.

'They're the ghost lights, Daniel Barker says. They lure you out onto the marshes and then you drown.'

'It's phosphorescence,' says Barbara vaguely (Jonas was the scientific one in the family). 'You often find it on marshland. There are lots of legends about it. Old Henry was telling me some today.'

'Tell me.' Lucian likes Henry, who gives him peppermints and, once, let him climb the steps to the disused bell tower.

Barbara doesn't want to tell the story of Wicked Jack and the fires of hell. Not in the winter darkness with the churchyard so near. *You often see them in graveyards.*

'I can't remember,' she says. 'I wasn't really listening. Have you thought any more about your costume for the Night of Light? You could be any saint you like. St George? St Francis? St Joseph?' As she says this she wonders if she's consciously offering positive male role models. The warrior, the animal lover, the father. Is St George even a saint any more?

Lucian looks away. 'Do I have to go? No one in my class is going.'

'Lots of people will be going,' says Barbara, with more conviction than she feels. 'It'll be fun.'

74 · ELLY GRIFFITHS

But, in her heart, Barbara isn't sure if it will be fun at all. The Night of Light is her first innovation as vicar. She knows that her fascination with St Lucy goes back to Jonas but there's more to it than that. She likes the idea of light shining in the darkness. The last days of December have a rather sinister reputation in folklore. The winter solstice, the shortest days. In Scandinavia, 13 December is called Lussinatta. The Lussi is a female demon who preys on children and rides through the skies on a broomstick. In the days between Lussinatta and Christmas, trolls and evil spirits walk the earth. It was easy to dismiss these old wives' tales when she had lived with Jonas in a modern flat in Oslo, two university lecturers with their young baby. Now she is a widow—even the word has a horrid Dickensian feel— and evil sometimes seems uncomfortably near. Has she become an old wife herself?

She'd been vaguely religious since her teenage years but, after Jonas's death, had surprised herself with her desire for ordination. Three years' training and four years as a curate and now she is here, in this little church on the edge of the Suffolk marshes. She is a priest, firmly on the side of light. Why, then, does she feel so threatened by the dark? Maybe it's this church, St Thomas on the Marsh. When she first saw it, in October, she had been charmed by church and vicar-

ST LUCY'S DAY · 75

age, their nineteenth-century solidity as they hunkered down against the fields, the last buildings for miles around. The church would become a sort of spiritual lighthouse, she decided, imagining soft lights glowing as she welcomed her parishioners, a motley collection of country-folk and incomers, all stubbornly suspicious of each other. She would change things, she had thought. Of course they would have their doubts about a new vicar, especially a woman vicar, but she would dispel their fears with her kindly yet practical Christianity. And, in the process, perhaps her own heart would go some way towards being healed.

But it hasn't worked out like that. The parish remains suspicious. Even those who are fairly well disposed, like old Henry, are doubtful of her ability to keep the church going. 'People don't go to church on a Sunday now,' Henry had explained. 'They go to those DIY stores and the like.' And Barbara can't blame them really. Who wouldn't prefer a brightly lit store and an array of labour-saving goods to a dark building on the edge of no-man's land where the message is still, unmistakably, 'do it yourself' and the alternative eternal hellfire and torment?

When Lucian has gone to bed, Barbara Googles will-o'-the-wisps. Both Henry and Daniel Barker are right, she reads. The evil blacksmith story certainly exists, as do the marsh lights that lure lost travellers to their death. There's also a Welsh tradition of the pwca, an evil goblin holding fairy fire in his hands. In Cornwall the light can take the form of a pony, a colt pixie, that leads other horses astray. In Guernsey the light is said to belong to a lost soul. If encountered, the traveller must turn his coat inside out or stick a knife, blade upwards, into the ground . . .

'Mum?'

Despite herself, Barbara jumps. Lucian stands framed in the doorway. His blue pyjamas, bleached almost to white, give him the look of a choirboy or an angel. His white-blond hair stands out in a halo and his eyes are shining.

'Mum. I've decided what I want to be on the Night of Light. I found the picture in a old book of Dad's.'

On 13 December, the first snow begins to fall. That's it then, thinks Barbara, dispiritedly setting out squash and mince pies in the vestry, no one will come now. Henry, who arrives to play Christmas carols on the organ, agrees. 'Once the snow sets in, folk don't go out. In 1962, when the thaw came, we found two families frozen to death.'

'Thanks, Henry,' says Barbara. 'You're a real tonic.'

But, strangely, she doesn't feel depressed any more. Edith, who cleans the church, has brought some mulled wine and they all have a glass. Henry starts pumping out 'O Little Town of Bethlehem' and Barbara and Edith go round lighting the candles. They are everywhere, on the altar rails, around the choir stalls, arranged on the lectern below the monstrous carved eagle. Barbara has even put some lights inside pumpkins, thumbing her nose at Wicked Jack and his hellfire. Instead of goblin faces, she has carved crosses into the pumpkins and the effect, though unusual, is rather beautiful.

She looks up at the altar. The church is Victorian Gothic, heavy on stained glass and wrought iron. In the daytime it can seem rather grim but now, by candle-light, it glows and sparkles. Henry's carol is gathering for a fortissimo climax. The hopes and fears of all the years. Lighting the tall candles by the baptismal font, Barbara offers a prayer to the god she thinks of as You. 'Please give me and Lucian a good year. Please let us be happy again.'

The service is due to start at six. By five forty-five the snow is falling heavily and Henry is all for locking up. He's probably right, thinks Barbara. Who would come out in this weather just for a cup of squash and a mince pie? Lucian is meant to be coming with Dan-iel and Tom. They're getting changed at Tom's house. Barbara knows that she can rely on Tom's mother, a sensible dinner lady, to look after them. If the snow is too heavy, she supposes that they will stay where they are. She checks her phone (on silent) but there are no messages. She goes into the vestry to put away the refreshments. Then, as she passes the small mullioned window, she sees something. Lights, flickering and uncertain, moving through the graveyard towards the church. She pushes open the window. The night air is thick and cold. The lights are accompanied, not by evil pixies or possessed ponies, but by shouts of laughter and adult voices warning children to 'be careful with that shepherd's crook'. Barbara runs back through the church and flings open the main doors.

Into the church they come—St George with a stuffed dragon, several Josephs and Marys with assorted Baby Jesuses, a herd of shepherds, at least five Wise Men, a trio of giggling angels and, inexplicably, a child dressed as Scooby-Doo. They are all carrying lights: torches, candles and plastic pumpkins. Barbara moves forward, greeting the parents, shepherding children towards the altar. To her surprise, some of the parents press presents into her hands, boxes of chocolates, a bottle of wine, a mug saying 'Keep Calm and Drink Tea'.

'Thank you,' stammers Barbara. 'You shouldn't have. I didn't . . .'

'Happy Christmas, vicar,' says one of the dads, who is wearing reindeer horns. 'We're glad to have you here.'

ST LUCY'S DAY · 79

Barbara puts the presents in the vestry and ushers the children into the choir stalls. She has planned a few carols, then games and refreshments. But all the time, she is looking anxiously at the doors. Where is Lucian, her mysterious changeling son? Doesn't he realise that this is all for him, the Night of Light, the coming together against the dark, a beacon of hope for the New Year?

Then, as Henry segues into 'Hark! The Herald Angels Sing', the doors open and three boys stand silhouetted against the swirling snow. Daniel and Tom are dressed as Roman soldiers (St Paul? St Theodore?) but, between them, wearing a long white robe and a smile of ethereal beauty, is Lucian. Lucian wearing St Lucy's crown, a golden wreath supporting ten flickering candles. He processes slowly up the aisle, supported by his acolytes, a solemn yet somehow joyful figure. St Lucy bringing light into the darkness.

'Born to raise the sons of earth,' sing the children, 'born to give them second birth.'

'I hope it's OK,' whispers Tom's mother in Barbara's ear. 'I didn't light the candles until we got to the church. Lucian said it was a tradition where his dad comes from.'

'It is,' says Barbara, her eyes filling with tears.

And she rushes forward to greet her son.

The Red Handkerchief

'It must be super having a father on the stage.' That's what the girls at school said. The nicer ones, that is. The nasty ones whispered behind my back. 'Nancy hasn't got a mother. Her father's on the stage, you know. They're not quite our sort.'

Too right. I couldn't blame my father for sending me to boarding school. What else could he do when Mum died and he had his living to make? But I could, and did, blame him for sending me to St Faith's, a school whose main aim was to churn out a long line of identical paper dolls to be sent off to finishing schools in Switzerland.

I didn't want to go to finishing school. I wanted to be an actress. 'Nancy's voice is too loud,' complained Miss Phelps, the drama teacher. 'She must cultivate a

THE RED HANDKERCHIEF · 81

soft, well-modulated tone like the other gels.' When Dad heard this, he roared with laughter. 'A soft well-whatsited voice won't reach up to people in the one and nines,' he said. 'You keep on projecting, Nancy.' But it was all right for him. He only had to see the teachers once a year, when he dropped me off in September. Then they were all over him because he'd been a hero in the war. And he was handsome. The other fathers were doughy and soft with tweed suits and jobs in the city. My father was tall and dark with a pencil moustache. He didn't dress like his agent Benny Bell who wore check suits and co-respondent shoes. It was just that his shirts were whiter than anyone else's and his ties brighter. And he always wore his hat at an angle.

Matron was the worst. 'We must be nice to Nancy,' she told the other girls in my hearing. 'She's never known a mother's guiding hand.' Matron's loving guidance included telling me that my hair was too long, that I was ungainly and that I talked too much about my father. 'I know you're proud of him, dear,' she told me in her cubbyhole smelling of pear drops and stale laundry. 'It's just that the other girls probably aren't very interested in . . . well, the more *colourful* side of the theatre.' By colourful she meant music hall, shabby theatres on the ends of piers, bills that included sword swallowers and forty-year-old ingénues singing, 'My

Heart Belongs to Daddy'. Well, my heart did belong to Daddy and what was wrong with that?

Christmas was the last straw. Somehow the nastiest girls—Vicky and Leticia—had found out that Dad was in panto that year. Actually, it was a pretty good gig, a Number Two theatre and a long run. Plus Dad was the Dame, the best part. But to Vicky and Leticia the thought of Nancy Bright's father dressing up as a woman was just '*the end*'. 'Behind you,' they'd shout hilariously as I crossed the prep room. 'Is Nancy here?' the nice History teacher would enquire. 'Yes,' I'd say. 'Oh no, she isn't,' the crowd of comedians would chorus. But I wasn't going to cry in front of them. I'd hold my head up high and give them a Lady Macbeth stare number one. A proper Shakespearean actress had showed me how.

I was going to stay with Dad in Blackpool for Christmas. I was excited because we had digs with one of my favourite landladies, Mrs White. She had a poodle called Rudy (after Rudolph Valentino) and she'd promised to make us a proper Christmas dinner. I wanted to get Dad a really nice present so I asked Matron if I could take some money out of my savings account.

'I'm afraid not, dear. That money is for emergencies only.'

'But I want to get Dad a present.'

THE RED HANDKERCHIEF · 83

'Home-made presents are the best. You could knit some socks or hem a hanky.'

But I couldn't knit and she knew it. In the end I hemmed a large red handkerchief. The stitches were uneven and, to liven it up, I sewed on big white spots. Vicky and Leticia thought it was the funniest thing ever.

'Do you like it? Do you really like it?'

'Of course I do, Nance. It's really original.'

Original? Awful things were original, like Mrs White's collection of china cats with human faces. I watched Dad carefully put the handkerchief aside and carry on with his bacon and eggs. I wanted to cry but I smiled and tried to look happy. The show was starting that evening and Dad had got me a seat in a box with Benny and a couple of men from London. And he'd bought me a blue dress for Christmas. With my hair up I thought that I looked quite grown-up, almost fifteen.

It was horrible sitting there waiting for the curtain to go up. 'If tonight goes well,' Dad had said, 'this could be the start of big things for us.' The two London men were from an important theatre chain. If Dad impressed them as Widow Twankey he could get a tour of the Number Ones, maybe he'd even be on the wireless. I sat on my hands, willing him to do well. He wasn't on until the third scene but all the other characters kept talking about him. 'Wait until Widow Twankey sees that' etc. Benny was nervous too, he was sweating and looked as if his bow tie was too tight. 'Duncan Bright's a real talent,' he kept telling the London men. They sat silently, giving nothing away. But when Widow Twankey finally appeared on the stage, I knew it would be all right. The audience were laughing before he opened his mouth. Even the London men were smiling. And I was laughing too. Because Dad was in a red and white-striped dress and around his head was my red-spotted handkerchief. I thought that I might burst with pride. And, as if he knew, Dad looked up and blew me a kiss.

Justice Jones
and the Etherphone

London, November 1945

'Are *you* Justice Jones?'

Justice was used to this question. She considered a variety of answers. 'No, *you're* Justice Jones.' 'No, I'm just sitting at this desk for a bet.'

Instead she said, 'What were you expecting?'

'Someone . . .'

'Older? More male?'

'Different,' conceded the caller, rather lamely. He, on the other hand, was very much what Justice had come to expect. Most of the visitors to the Justice Jones Detective Agency were middle-aged men believing that their wives were having affairs. Many were disconcerted to be faced by a woman who looked considerably younger than her twenty-one years. 'Wear lipstick,' said Justice's stepmother, Dolores. But Justice had never really got the hang of make-up.

'I'm Justice Jones,' she said.

'Alfred Mullen,' said the man, after a pause.

'What can I do for you, Mr Mullen?' asked Justice, aiming for a brisk professional tone.

'You were recommended to me,' said Mullen, sounding as if he was already regretting the decision to climb the three flights of stairs to the attic rooms in Dyott Street where Justice lived and worked. He was a small man with a large moustache, holding a soft-brimmed hat between thin hands. His eyes were large and rather sad. Justice, who was becoming more cynical by the day, according to her friend Dorothy, thought he looked like a man with an unfaithful wife.

'Who recommended me?' she asked.

'Inspector Porlock,' was the rather surprising answer.

Inspector Porlock was a proper Scotland Yard detective. Justice had met him while she was still at school.

'It's a serious case,' said Mullen. 'A murder.'

Justice sat up straighter. 'Whose murder?'

'Mine.'

'What did he mean by that?' said Letitia. 'Sounds barmy to me.'

JUSTICE JONES AND THE ETHERPHONE · 87

Justice and her old schoolfriend Letitia were sitting in a Lyons Corner House, drinking tea the colour of rainwater. Although the war in Europe had been over since May, and Japan surrendered in September, there was still a drab, utilitarian air to London, thought Justice. Rationing was still in place ('Powdered Milk Only' read a sign over the counter) and a lot of the men were still in uniform. Justice and Letitia had been in uniform too until July, when they had both left the WAAF. Now Justice was running a detective agency and Letitia was trying to avoid being a debutante.

'It sounds barmy to everyone,' said Justice. 'Mr Mullen said that his wife and business partner thought he was going mad. But Inspector Porlock took it seriously. He told Mullen to come to me.' She tried not to sound too proud.

'But *why* does he think he's going to be murdered?' said Letitia. She sounded slightly petulant. Justice didn't know if it was because her friend had only joined Highbury House after the adventure concerning Inspector Porlock. Or maybe she was just bored with trying on hats.

'He went to a fortune teller,' said Justice, 'and she said that he would be murdered in two weeks' time. She said the killer would be someone close to him.'

'Gosh,' said Letitia. 'I thought they only said vague things like "beware dark-haired women".'

88 · ELLY GRIFFITHS

'I thought it was odd too. That's why I'm going to see Madame Adelina today.'

'Have you taken the case then?'

'Yes,' said Justice. 'I can't afford to turn down work and Inspector Porlock recommended me . . .'

She knew that this wasn't the whole truth. Her father gave her a generous allowance, as well as paying for the flat. She *could* afford to turn down the strange case of Mr Alfred Mullen. But she didn't want to.

'Where does she live?' asked Letitia, finishing her tea with a grimace.

'Dulwich.'

'Where *is* that?' Letitia tried to pretend that she didn't come from a wealthy background, that her father wasn't Lord Blackstock, but sometimes she slipped up. Justice was willing to bet that Letitia rarely stepped outside Mayfair and Chelsea. The Lyons on Tottenham Court Road was obviously a daring adventure—possibly one that Letitia was already regretting.

'South London,' said Justice. 'It's very nice apparently.' All right, Justice hadn't been there either.

And Dulwich *was* very pleasant: wide avenues full of large houses set back from the road. Here, you would hardly know that there had been a war, apart from some gardens where the iron railings had been taken

JUSTICE JONES AND THE ETHERPHONE · 89

away. Justice knew that nearby Camberwell had been badly hit, but this street seemed to have escaped almost unscathed. In Central London there were so many gaps—places where buildings had been ripped away by bombs, doors opening onto nothingness, staircases to nowhere. Now, some of these spaces were filled with wild flowers, which was lovely, but somehow sad. Justice had been stationed in Inverness during the London Blitz. Her father had initially refused to leave the capital but Dolores finally persuaded him to move to Kent with her and baby Persephone. Justice had been relieved to be free of this worry but she had been full of fear for friends and past neighbours, for unknown Londoners facing that nightly bombardment. You could hear the ack-ack guns on the south coast; Justice was sure that they would have been very loud in Dulwich.

Madame Adelina lived in a solid villa, indistinguishable from its neighbours apart from the fact that the door was painted a rather startling bright green. Justice raised her hand to knock and then paused. Music was playing in the house, silvery, uncanny notes that made Justice's nerve ends tingle. The tune was recognisable—'Jesu, Joy of Man's Desiring'—but it was as if it was being played on a celestial piano.

Justice knocked and the music stopped. A few seconds

later and the door was opened by a grey-haired woman wearing a tweed skirt and a blue jumper. There was nothing even slightly ethereal about her, although her eyes, like the knitwear, were a very pale aqua.

'Madame Adelina?' said Justice.

'Have you come for a reading then?' said the woman, in a businesslike tone.

'I'd just like to ask you a few questions,' said Justice. 'I'm a private detective.'

She was counting on this being intriguing enough to get her over the threshold. Plus, she liked saying it out loud.

'You'd better come in then,' said Madame Adelina, with a sharp blue stare.

The sitting room had a shrouded feel, partly because of the heavy net curtains but also because the sofa and chairs were swathed in cotton covers. Beside the bay window was a strange piece of furniture, like a lectern with an aerial attached and a metal ring at the side.

'What's that?' asked Justice, before realising that she should have done some social chit-chat first.

'It's an etherphone,' said Madame Adelina. 'Or theremin. Invented by some Russian before the war. You play it by waving your hands at the aerials.'

'I heard it when I was outside. It's wonderful—very atmospheric.'

JUSTICE JONES AND THE ETHERPHONE · 91

'Yes,' said the medium. 'It's useful that way. What did you want to talk to me about?'

'Alfred Mullen,' said Justice. 'I believe he came to you for a reading?'

'Yes, he did,' said Adelina. 'Forgive me, dear, but what has that got to do with you?'

'The police asked me to investigate,' said Justice, aware that she was stretching the facts and that, in her slacks and polo-neck jumper, she didn't look like someone who would assist the police in their enquiries. She obviously looked more like someone who could be called 'dear'.

'You told Mr Mullen that he would be murdered,' she added, ploughing on.

Adelina sat on one of the covered chairs. Justice followed her lead and took the sofa. Sitting was good. Sitting meant conversation.

'Alfred wanted to contact his son who died in the war,' said Adelina. 'Lots of people come for that reason. War is good for the spiritualism business. He seemed receptive enough so I said I'd try to reach the boy. David, his name was. I drew the curtains, played on the etherphone for a bit, then asked my spirit guide for help . . .'

'Your spirit guide?'

'A spirit who has gone on before,' explained Adelina

kindly. 'An entity that can move between this world and the next. They often help mediums in their work. Mine's called Effie. She used to be a scullery maid. Killed by her unkind master.'

Effie obviously had quite the backstory. Justice asked if she had managed to find David Mullen.

'Yes,' said Adelina. 'She did. He talked to his father, said that he was all right, playing cricket in heaven. Lots of them do that, apparently. Must be a regular test match up there. Anyway, after a lot more cricket talk, another voice cut in. A man's voice.'

'Did you recognise it?' asked Justice. She thought that Adelina probably had a few contacts in the spirit world.

Adelina paused. 'It was . . . the abbot.'

'The abbot?'

'A man of God who has gone to the dark side.'

'The dark side?' Despite herself, Justice shivered and looked towards the window and the outside world. The monkey-puzzle tree in the garden cast strange, misshapen shadows on the curtains.

'He's in the service of the Devil,' said Adelina flatly. 'Or one of his minions. Dark entities come through sometimes. You just have to learn to block them. Anyway, the voice said, "You will be murdered in two weeks" time. Trust no one. Not even those dear to you." It was a warning. I had to pass it on.'

'What did Mr Mullen say?'

'He was shocked, of course. Asked how he was going to be murdered. But the voice had gone silent. I couldn't tell him. I reminded him to trust no one and he said, "There's only my wife and me. David was our only child."'

Justice felt a fresh wave of sympathy for the man with the sad eyes and the fedora hat. She asked if any other spirits had come through and Adelina said, regretfully, that they hadn't. She asked if Adelina believed that Alfred Mullen would be murdered and the medium replied, 'I don't ask if the spirits are right or wrong, dear. I just pass the messages on.'

There didn't seem much else to say. When Justice got up to leave, Adelina said that she reminded her of her daughter.

'She's no longer with me.'

'Is she dead?' whispered Justice.

'No. Married a GI and emigrated to America. Might as well be dead, to my mind.'

Justice thought about it all afternoon, about the dimly lit room, the silvery notes of the etherphone and the woman saying, 'Dark entities come through sometimes. You just have to learn to block them.' That evening, she went to the pictures with Nora, another old school friend. Nora had also served in the women's forces during the war and was now reading English at London University. Nora loved a ghost story and so, on the walk from Leicester Square to Bloomsbury, Justice told her about Madame Adelina.

'It's like the three witches in *Macbeth*,' said Nora, yellow light glinting on her glasses. It was wonderful, after the darkness of the war years, to have streetlights again. 'They told him just enough to send him mad.'

'Do you remember Miss Crane putting on that funny voice?' said Justice, assuming a high-pitched quaver. '"Beware Macduff, beware the Thane of Fife"?'

They both laughed, but Justice had the feeling that she might just have missed something important. They parted at the corner of Dyott Street and Justice climbed the stairs to her flat. The lower floors were all offices so there was no one else in the building at night. Normally, this didn't bother her but, tonight, she pulled a heavy chest against the door before she went to sleep.

The next day was Saturday and Justice had promised to visit her dad and Dolores. She took the train to Headcorn and had a lovely day eating delicious food and playing with four-year-old Persephone. She was

JUSTICE JONES AND THE ETHERPHONE · 95

so full of roast beef that she slept all the way back to London. At Charing Cross, she picked up a copy of the *Evening Standard* and, as was her wont, read it from cover to cover when she got home.

At the bottom of page three, she found this:

The man killed after falling in front of a Tube train at Blackfriars has been named as Mr Alfred Mullen, 48, of Denmark Hill, London.

Justice was determined to go to the funeral. 'You can pick up clues at a funeral,' she told Letitia, making it sound intrepid in the hopes that her friend would accompany her. But the truth was that Justice felt she owed it to Alfred Mullen, the man she had only met once. On the Monday after the piece in the *Evening Standard*, Justice telephoned Inspector Porlock. She didn't have a phone in her flat so walked to the public callbox outside the Dominion Theatre. The foyer was still covered with pre-war posters advertising variety stars. *Max Mephisto: You'll Think He's Magic.* After a few minutes, the operator put her through.

'Good God,' said the inspector, when Justice told her about Mullen's death. 'Poor old Alfred.'

'Did you know him then? I know you recommended me to him.'

'I only met him that one time. I know his business partner, though, Seamus Costello. We play golf together.'

Justice couldn't imagine Inspector Porlock playing golf. It seemed too frivolous, somehow.

'Why did you send Mr Mullen on to me? Did you believe him about being murdered?'

'He seemed so agitated. It obviously wasn't a police case but I thought he'd be comforted if he felt that someone was investigating. Seamus told me that Alfred had been behaving oddly for months. Visiting the medium must have pushed him over the edge. Forgive me. That was an unfortunate thing to say.'

More than unfortunate, thought Justice. 'Do you think Alfred killed himself then?' she asked.

'I suppose it's possible. I'll look at the police reports. There will have been eyewitnesses.'

'How awful.'

'Londoners saw worse things in the war.'

Justice was sure that was true but, even so, she thought of seeing a man fall to his death before your eyes. Surely nothing could prepare you for that?

'It does seem strange that he died a day after seeing me,' said Justice.

'Strange but not necessarily suspicious,' said Inspector Porlock.

Justice wasn't so sure.

JUSTICE JONES AND THE ETHERPHONE · 97

Clothes were a problem. Justice didn't have a black dress so compromised on her WAAF uniform, now dyed forest green, under her grey coat. None of her hats were suitable either so she pulled her shoulder-length hair back in a snood. When she met Letitia at Victoria Station, she saw that her friend was wearing exactly the right coat, black with a velvet collar, and a neat beret. Oh well, detectives weren't meant to be fashionable. Although, secretly, Justice would have loved a deerstalker.

They caught the train to Denmark Hill and walked to St Saviour's. It was an odd building, more like a school than a church, with coloured brickwork and high, sash windows. Justice and Letitia sat at the back. In the front row a blonde woman sobbed quietly. That must be Alfred's widow, thought Justice. A man was comforting her. A brother?

The coffin was brought in on a kind of trolley, which surprised Justice. She had only the dimmest memories of her mother's funeral, but they involved black-coated men shouldering the casket, topped with wreaths and dreadful in its mahogany sheen. Justice shivered. She had been eleven when her mother died and, in some ways, she felt as if she'd never got any older. She was always there, in the flower-scented church, watching her mother's coffin go past.

98 · ELLY GRIFFITHS

Letitia whispered that undertakers were in short supply because of the war. That must be it then.

The service was brief. A bald man stood up to read the lesson. He had a soft Irish voice, which broke on the words 'they will find rest as they lie in death'. Then the vicar said a few words about Alfred, all of them betraying the fact that he didn't know him well: 'a family man', 'a faithful friend', 'a loving husband and father'. The service ended with 'Jesu, Joy of Man's Desiring', played on a wheezy organ. Justice thought again of Madame Adelina and the etherphone. *War is good for the spiritualism business.* Was Alfred now playing heavenly cricket with his son, David? Justice hoped so. She really did.

The congregation followed the trolley to the cemetery. Some of the graves were so old that they seemed to have sunk into the earth but, by the gates, the new war memorial was almost shocking in its whiteness. In a remote corner, under a plane tree, a new grave had been dug and, after a few prayers, lost on the cold autumn air, the coffin was lowered into it. Mrs Mullen threw in some soil and the gravediggers began their work. Rooks called from the trees.

Justice was wondering if she could possibly approach the grieving widow when, to her surprise, the blonde woman stopped in front of her.

JUSTICE JONES AND THE ETHERPHONE · 99

'Are you Justice Jones? The detective?'

Despite the circumstances, Justice couldn't help standing slightly taller.

'Yes. I'm so sorry about your husband.'

'Thank you.' The woman dabbed her eyes. 'I'm Sandra Mullen. This is Bertie, Alfie's brother.'

Bertie looked like Alfred, but without the moustache and the lugubrious look. He was taller, though, and moved slightly awkwardly.

'You must be the girl detective.'

'I'm a private detective.' Justice decided that she preferred the late Alfred to his brother. 'This is my associate, Letitia Blackstock.' She almost added the 'hon' but decided against it.

'Poor old Alf,' said Bertie. 'Going to see some supposed psychic and then a woman gumshoe. He really wasn't in his right mind.'

The eyewitness reports of the accident, relayed to Justice by Inspector Porlock, were inconclusive. Someone mentioned Alfred stumbling on the edge of the platform, another that he looked 'as if he was in a trance'. Did Alfred Mullen kill himself, whilst the 'balance of his mind was disturbed' as the inquest put it? Was he pushed? No one seemed to know.

'You can't say things like that, Bertie.' It was the man who had read the lesson in church. Then he had sounded on the verge of tears, now his voice shook with anger. 'Alfred wasn't going mad.'

'Please don't argue.' Sandra's voice was soft but it had an effect on both men. She introduced Justice and Letitia.

'Seamus Costello,' said the new man. 'Alfred's business partner.'

So this was Inspector Porlock's golfing companion. He didn't look particularly sporting, though it was hard to tell in a black overcoat.

'It's been a shock to us all.' Sandra turned to Justice and Letitia.

'Of course,' said Justice. 'Please accept our condolences.'

They watched as the three figures moved away, the blonde woman between the two men.

The vicar had mentioned a wake in a nearby pub, the Marquis of Granby. Justice persuaded Letitia to pop in. 'You can learn a lot by standing in a saloon bar,' Justice's father always said. Justice thought it was a shame that women didn't go into pubs on their own. Not that she cared about conventions, but it was the job of a private detective to look inconspicuous and a woman striding into a public house was anything but that. But here was a chance to mingle with the mourners while their tongues were loosened by drink and emotion.

The wake was in a private room upstairs. Sandra was sitting at a table surrounded by people. Seamus Costello was at the bar. Justice looked around for a possible source of family gossip and spotted an elderly woman sitting on her own with an empty sherry glass in front of her.

'Mind if we join you?' Justice had already sat down.

'Suit yourself,' said the woman draining the dregs in her glass. She was wearing a fur coat and a hat with a rather rakish feather.

'Are you David's friends?' she asked.

Justice thought about saying yes—she felt a distinct connection with the Mullens' dead son—but there was a difference between stretching the truth and outright lying.

'We're friends of the family,' she said.

'I'm one of the family' said the woman, 'and I don't know you.' Which was a good point. She then introduced herself as Sandra's Auntie Beryl.

'I'm Justice Jones,' said Justice. 'And this is Letitia Blackstock.'

'Justice,' said Beryl. 'That's a funny name.'

'My father's a barrister,' said Justice. This is part of the reason but the other was that her mother wrote

102 • ELLY GRIFFITHS

detective stories, all concerned with the quest for justice and truth. But Justice didn't want to talk about her mother, especially not after a funeral.

'Poor Alfred,' she said, trying for a sorrowful tone slightly tinged with prurience. 'Such a tragedy. It must have been a terrible shock for Sandra.'

'Terrible,' agreed Beryl, with what sounded like relish. 'On top of losing David in the war. Poor Sandra. Such a pretty little thing she was as a girl. Very clever too. Sharp as a cartload of monkeys. Seems such a shame.'

Justice murmured encouragingly.

'All the boys were mad about her. Why she chose Alfred Mullen . . .'

The thought died away. Justice said, 'Alfred seemed very nice.'

'She could have had the other brother, you know,' said Auntie Beryl. 'They were engaged but broke it off when Bertie came back from the war. The first war. He lost his leg, you know. Became a different person.'

'Sandra was engaged to Bertie?' It was important to use names, Justice knew.

'He was very dashing in the old days, Bertie. Well, weren't we all?'

She grinned at Justice, showing long yellow teeth.

'I bet you were dashing,' said Justice.

'I was the first person in my village to show my

JUSTICE JONES AND THE ETHERPHONE · 103

ankles,' said Beryl. Letitia choked and Justice patted her on the back.

'And then Sandra married Alfred?' she said, wanting to get back to the story.

'Alfred wouldn't say boo to a goose,' said Beryl. 'But he did very well for himself. The company's worth a bit of money these days.'

'What do they make?' asked Justice.

'Munitions,' said Beryl.

Munitions meant weapons and ammunition. Justice could see why Alfred had become rich. War was good for guns as well as spiritualism. She thought that the source of his wealth might also be the reason for the sadness she'd seen in Alfred Mullen's eyes.

'Of course he was going a bit doolally,' said Beryl. 'Seamus was worried about him. But now Sandra will be his business partner. Now that David's dead.'

'Was David planning to go into the business?' asked Justice.

'No,' said Beryl, with a throaty laugh. 'He wanted to be an *actor*, if you please. Well, maybe Sandra will marry Bertie now.'

Justice looked across the room. Bertie was sitting next to Sandra, their heads very close together. Suddenly Sandra laughed, flinging back her head. The sound was shocking somehow.

'Can you get me another glass of sherry?' asked Auntie Beryl.

'**Mind if** we make a detour?' said Justice.

'I don't mind,' said Letitia. 'If I go home my mother will only make me have a dress fitting.'

'It's Dulwich Village,' said Justice. 'Walking distance.'

'Isn't that where the medium lives?' said Letitia. 'Madame whatsit?'

'Yes,' said Justice. 'Well remembered.'

'I do listen, you know,' said Letitia. 'Isn't that what you used to say at school? Good detectives always listen?'

'I said a lot of things at school,' said Justice. 'I was probably an awful pain.'

'You were wonderful,' said Letitia. 'We had some fun, didn't we?'

'We did,' said Justice. Justice had hated Highbury House at first. She had been sent there when her mother died and, even now, she found it hard to forgive her father for this decision. But, almost immediately, she had found a murder to solve, which gave her a welcome extra-curricular interest. She'd found friends too: Stella, Nora and Dorothy. Letitia had arrived a year later and, with her cheerful indifference to rules, had livened up the place considerably.

JUSTICE JONES AND THE ETHERPHONE · 105

'Why do you want to see this lady again?' asked Letitia, as they walked between the respectable South London villas, scuffing their way through fallen leaves.

'It was something Nora said.'

'Nora? She only talks about books.'

Like Justice, Letitia had never really enjoyed Miss Crane's lessons, but then she had spent a lot of them pretending to be a deaf mute.

'She said something about the witches in *Macbeth*,' said Justice. 'I missed it at the time but now I think it's the key to everything. This is the house. I remember the green door.'

This time there was no ethereal music emanating from the interior. Justice and Letitia stood on the doorstep, waiting, as an errand boy shot past on his bicycle and a robin sang noisily from the monkey-puzzle tree.

'Looking for Annie?'

A woman was regarding them from the other side of the hedge. She was carrying a pair of secateurs but, as the privet was clipped to within an inch of its life, Justice judged these to be a prop.

'Yes,' said Justice, guessing that Annie must be the non-mediumistic name of Madame Adelina.

'She's gone,' said the woman, gesturing vaguely with the shears.

'Gone?'

'Gone to America to see her daughter. Don't know where she got the money.'

Justice had a pretty good idea.

'Did Annie have any visitors recently?' She thought that the woman looked the observant sort.

'Only you. I saw you here two weeks ago.'

Justice was right. 'Before me? A bald-headed man with an Irish accent?'

'Oh, him. Nice man. He complimented me on my golden-rod.'

'How did you know?' asked Letitia.

They were in Justice's flat, eating chips from newspaper. The gas fire was on, making a friendly popping sound, and the curtains were drawn. Nora had arrived a few minutes ago and, traffic noises aside, it was like being back in the common room at Highbury House. They only needed Stella, currently training to be a doctor, and Dorothy, who was at Oxford. Rose had scandalised her family by marrying an Italian prisoner-of-war whom she'd met in Scotland. Luckily for Rose, Ernesto turned out to be a rich nobleman and the couple were now living in a palazzo near Florence. Eva, the other member of Barnowls Dormitory, was living in Eastbourne, happily engaged to be married.

'It was the cricket that first made me suspicious,' said Justice. 'Madame Adelina said that David's spirit talked a lot about playing cricket. I'm pretty sure Madame Adelina didn't have that sort of knowledge. Someone gave her those details. Sandra didn't strike me as the sporty type. Bertie had lost a leg and so probably didn't like talking about sport. Beryl said that he became a different person after the war. But Seamus played golf with Inspector Porlock. I thought he'd probably enjoy other games.'

'Fancy Justice getting a PE clue,' said Letitia. 'Miss Heron would be proud.' Justice was famous at school for her lack of sporting ability.

Justice ignored this. 'Then there was the abbot. Adelina said that the warning about murder was given by a dark spirit called the abbot. I thought at the time that she made the name up on the spot. Well, she was probably thinking of Seamus Costello. Abbot and Costello.'

'Who's on first?' Letitia quoted the comic duo's catchphrase.

'So you think this Costello bribed the medium to tell Mr Mullen that he was going to die?' said Nora. 'Why?'

'It was you who gave me the idea,' said Justice, shaking more vinegar onto her chips. 'You said the witches sent Macbeth mad. Well, I think Costello wanted Alfred

108 · ELLY GRIFFITHS

to have a mental breakdown so that he would retire and Costello could take over the company. Imagine, if a businessman started saying they'd contacted a medium who foresaw their death, what would you think? You'd certainly think that they were behaving strangely.'

'But Costello got angry when Bertie said that Alfred wasn't in his right mind,' objected Letitia.

'He got angry,' said Justice, 'but he repeated it. And he made it worse. He said that Alfred was going mad, not just "not in his right mind". But I think Costello was genuinely unhappy that Alfred died. He wanted Alfred alive but in a secure institution somewhere. Now, he's got Sandra for a partner. My guess is that she'll be a match for him.'

'So Mullen's death was an accident?' said Letitia.

'Either that or suicide,' said Justice. 'Maybe Madame Adelina gave him the idea. Maybe it was the thought that David was waiting for him on the other side. I suppose we'll never know.'

There was a short silence, broken only by a boy outside yelling '*Ev'nin' Standard*! Get your *Ev'nin' Stanner.*' More news, more murders, more investigations.

'It was cruel,' said Nora suddenly. 'It was cruel to pretend to be Alfred's son and then to terrify him.'

'I think the thing about David was meant to be a kindness,' said Justice. 'I don't think Adelina was a bad

JUSTICE JONES AND THE ETHERPHONE · 109

woman, exactly. Costello probably offered her a lot of money and she wanted to see her daughter.'

'Costello didn't bargain on Mullen contacting Justice Jones,' said Letitia with a smile.

'I hate to say it,' said Justice, 'but I think he did. I think he recommended Inspector Porlock, knowing he'd recommend me. What better sign of madness than employing a girl detective?'

'More fool him,' said Letitia. Then, as if this was what they had been discussing, 'I'm not going to be a debutante. I'm going to be a horse trainer.'

'Good for you!' said Justice. She knew that horses were Letitia's real passion.

'I'm going to be a teacher,' said Nora. 'I hope I'll be more inspiring than Miss Crane. The first thing I'll tell my students is that *Macbeth* is a detective story. *Hamlet* too.'

The three friends smiled at each other.

'This is our time,' said Justice. 'It's time for the girls.'

The Farewell Boat

She first saw the boat on Christmas Eve. It was a fishing vessel with oddly coloured sails, somewhere between red and orange. She stood watching it for some time, thinking not very much and letting the words of an old song run through her head. *I saw three ships come sailing in, On Christmas Day in the morning.*

She remembered, as a child, thinking how odd it was to find a ship in a carol. Christmas seemed a landlocked thing: shops and pine forests and lighted windows in dark houses. But here, in Southwold, you could never forget the sea. It crashed against the beach all day, retreating in great sighing waves. It filled the windows of her little cottage, glittering like a mirage. On still nights the moonlight made a silver pathway across the

THE FAREWELL BOAT · 111

water, like the last shot of a romantic film. She saw the moonlight a lot.

She forced herself to be active on Christmas Eve. In the past, when she'd been looking after Jack and then Mum, she'd been genuinely busy: stuffing the turkey, wrapping last-minute presents, fixing the lights on the tree, making mince pies. Now it was a strain to write a to-do list.

Buy chicken breasts (it seemed too pathetic to write it in the singular)
Write card for next-door neighbour. Peter? Paul?
Go for a walk.

This last was hardly a task, but she needed something to fill the small page of her notebook. She added a sketch of a boat. Jack used to love her drawings. He'd demand all sorts of impossible things—'Santa Claus in a helicopter with X-ray vision and bat wings'—but always seemed pleased with the results. Now Jack was in Germany with a family of his own. He was a graphic designer so maybe his artistic childhood hadn't been wasted. She just wished he'd found things to design nearer home.

And her mother was dead. She was getting better

at saying it. People in Southwold remembered Mum—
they'd been coming there in the summer for years—and
at first she used to avoid people she knew so that she
wouldn't have to say the words. But now she managed
a brief sentence and a smile to show that it was all right
really. 'After all, she was nearly ninety and it was very
peaceful.' The trouble with sudden, peaceful deaths,
though, was that they were terribly shocking for the
person who found their loved one dead in bed, Agatha
Christie book still open on their motionless chest.

Mary and Beth, her friends who owned the cottage,
had suggested that she stay there for Christmas. 'Get
away from it all. Look after yourself for a change.' But
now that she had nothing to do all day but take baths and
light scented candles, she longed for someone to look
after, to cook for or even just to talk to. But enough of
that, she told herself, you've got chicken breasts to buy.

It was a cold, bright day. The sea was almost un-
bearably blue and there was no sign of the boat with red
sails. She walked past the Sailors' Reading Room and
the Lord Nelson pub and turned right along the High
Street. There was a festive air to the shops, the plastic fisherman on the roof of the chippie was wearing a
Santa hat and the Salvation Army were singing outside
Adnams Brewery. *Oh come, all ye faithful. Joyful and
triumphant.* She bought provisions for her Christmas

THE FAREWELL BOAT · 113

lunch and, on impulse, popped into the bookshop. She'd planned to buy a crime novel but in the end she settled for an illustrated edition of M.R. James. 'There's nothing like a ghost story at Christmas,' Mum used to say. Then she walked back by the sea, enjoying the cold air and the sight of the beach huts forming an orderly line that led to the pier. The wind whipped the sand into the air and made her eyes sting.

When she got to her cottage she remembered the card for Peter or Paul. She found a suitably neutral design, a robin in a tree, and compromised by putting 'No 3' on the envelope.

Her neighbour opened the door promptly, almost as if he was waiting for her. He was an elderly man with white hair and watery blue eyes. He seemed delighted with the card and invited her in for a glass of sherry. Her instinct was to refuse but what excuse could she offer? She could hardly say that she was going home to cook for her family. So she followed Peter/Paul into his sitting room and drank a small glass of Tio Pepe. She knew that Peter/Paul had been a fisherman so she found herself telling him about the boat.

'The sails were such an unusual colour,' she said. 'Almost terracotta.' She suddenly thought that this was the wrong word, too pretentious and middle-class, but the old man just smiled.

'You've seen the ghost ship,' he said. 'It often appears at Christmas.'

'The ghost ship?' Wasn't that the name of an Adnams beer?

'A fishing boat was wrecked off the coast about a hundred years ago,' said PP. 'It was called the Red Ship because of the sails. I remember my father talking about it. It was a terrible tragedy because the townsfolk could see it foundering but no one could save it because the waves were that high. Everyone on board died. But the boat appears at certain times. To certain people.'

'I only saw it for a moment,' she said, 'and then it vanished.'

'It didn't vanish,' said PP. 'It was sailing to another shore.'

On the doorstep she wished him Happy Christmas.

'And to you,' he answered. She asked what he was doing tomorrow (maybe she should invite him in for the other chicken breast) but he said he was going to his son and daughter-in-law in Holt. The thought made her feel lonelier than ever.

'Goodbye, Peter.' She'd decided on this name as more suitable for a fisherman. 'Thank you for the sherry.'

'You're welcome, love. And it's Patrick.'

That night the seas were high and the lighthouse

beam swept across the dark water. Then, as if caught in a spotlight, she saw the Red Ship balancing on the crest of a wave before dipping down out of sight. She stood at the window for a long time but the boat did not appear again.

Christmas morning was misty and grey, you could hardly see where the horizon ended and the sea began. She listened to carols on the radio, peeled a potato and prepared some sprouts, even though she didn't really like them. Jack Skyped at eleven and it was wonderful to see him and Petra and the children, looking so happy and wholesome in their matching jumpers. Mum would have loved it, she thought. But she didn't say this aloud because she didn't want to depress Jack. He'd been very fond of his grandmother.

Then lunch. She tried to make the chicken breast festive by wrapping it in bacon but she found she couldn't eat much of it. She'd poured herself a glass of red wine but that too was hard to finish. She washed up her plate and sat down in front of the television. A Christmas special was showing, full of people in comedy hats making jokes about mistletoe and reindeer. Despite the fake snow she thought it had probably been filmed in the summer, that halcyon time when she was still a daughter. She must have fallen asleep because, when she woke, it was dark and the moonlight was shining on the sea. Turning towards the front door she saw that there was an envelope on the mat.

It was a Christmas card showing three ships sailing on glittering blue-green waves.

'To Noelle. Wishing you a happy Christmas. Love Patrick.'

As she sat looking at the card, reflecting that her neighbour had known *her* name, a text appeared on her phone. It was from Jack.

Happy Xmas, Mum. Missing Grandma xxx

She went to the window, expecting to see the boat, but the vast sea was empty. Then she thought of Patrick's words.

It didn't vanish. It was sailing to another shore.

'Bon voyage, Mum,' she said aloud. She felt sure that she was going to sleep well that night.

Harbinger:
A Harbinder Kaur Story

'I've made you a packed lunch.'

Harbinder's heart sinks. The words bring back memories of lunchboxes opened, giggling classmates, noses held, earnest talks from teachers about cultural diversity that only made things worse. Of course, Harbinder is now above being embarrassed by the aroma of vegetable paratha. She's proud of her Punjabi Sikh heritage, she no longer feels embarrassed when seen in public with her tall father and brothers, made taller by their turbans. She's actively envious of her mother's saris and her culinary skills. But does she want to turn up for her first day at Shoreham CID with a tiffin box full of curry? She doesn't.

'There's lots of sandwich places nearby,' she says. 'It's right in the middle of town.'

'Sandwiches,' says her mother, Bibi, in tones of withering scorn. 'Your father had one at a train station once. He was ill for days.'

There are many things Harbinder could say to this. She's pretty sure that her brothers, Khushwant and Abhey, lived on sandwiches in their teenage years. She too has eaten many a Pret Christmas special without suffering dire effects. But she knows these arguments will be useless. She picks up the tin. 'Thanks, Mummyji.' She uses the Indian name to make up for her reluctance over the paratha.

'Is that what you're wearing?' says Bibi, making a quick comeback.

'Yes,' says Harbinder. 'It's plain clothes.' And she's made them as plain as possible. Black trousers, dark-grey jumper, flat black boots.

'What about a scarf?' says Bibi. 'Lots of business-women wear them.'

'I never know what to do with a scarf,' says Harbinder. She either ties them so tightly that they look like a scout's kerchief or so loosely that they fall off. They make her feel silly, like a child dressing up in adult clothes.

'You look great.' Her father, Deepak, has arrived from his early morning walk with their ancient terrier, Jack.

The dog can't manage the steps to the flat any more and is still in Deepak's arms, rolling a yellowish eye at Harbinder when she pats him. She thinks the animal's days are numbered. Her parents adopted Jack from a rescue centre so nobody knows his real age but he's been with the family for more than fifteen years. Deepak insists that he's still a good watchdog but it's hard to know what the toothless animal would do if he encountered a burglar. Fart on them? Gum them to death?

'Thanks, Dad.'

'Knock 'em dead,' says Deepak, starting to prepare Jack's special food.

'That's not really the point of being a detective,' says Harbinder.

It's a twenty-minute walk to the police station and Harbinder takes the route along the seafront. It's a beautiful April morning, the sky a clear, pale blue and the sea accessorised with tiny, white waves. From the promenade you can't feel the pebbles digging into your feet or experience the shock of the freezing water. Harbinder's not a great swimmer and she hates walking on shingle. She was an adult on holiday in Greece before she encountered a sandy beach. But, as commutes to work go, this one isn't bad. The Coffee Shack is doing a roaring trade and there are dog-walkers and cyclists galore.

Haven't they got jobs to go to? thinks Harbinder, secure in the knowledge of her recent promotion. Detective Sergeant sounds a lot better than Constable and, whilst she was sad to leave her colleagues in Chichester, she's excited to join a new team. She grew up in Shoreham and went to the local comprehensive school. She might meet some people she knows. With any luck, they'll be colleagues rather than offenders.

Harbinder crosses the bridge over the estuary and walks towards the town centre. She takes a shortcut through the churchyard and sees a homeless man sitting on a bench. She's seen him before and stops to have a chat. It's always difficult to know what to do about rough sleepers. Hostels aren't always the answer—you need ID for one thing—and most people have problems the police can't solve. Sure enough, this man, whose name is Steve, says that he avoided hostels in the past because they wouldn't take his dog. 'He's passed away now,' he says, 'I miss him. Mind you, he had a good death. I just woke up to find him lying there beside me. I knew he'd crossed the rainbow bridge. He'll be waiting for me at the other side.'

Normally Harbinder hates euphemisms like 'passed away' but she feels tears prickle behind her eyelids. It's because I'm nervous about the job, she tells herself. She gives Steve a tenner, which is against official guidance, and wishes him well.

HARBINGER: A HARBINDER KAUR STORY · 121

The police station is in a modern building behind the library. Harbinder shows her ID and is directed to the second floor. DI Donna Brice, whom she remembers from her interview, greets her at the door of the CID room. She's a tall woman in her mid-forties, with flyaway curly hair and a rather harassed expression. She's wearing jeans with Adidas trainers. Harbinder always notices shoes.

'Hallo. Welcome to Shoreham. This is DS Neil Winston. We've just had a callout. Thought you might as well go with Neil and get acquainted on the way. In at the deep end and all that.'

Harbinder welcomes the thought of starting work straight away and not going through some grim induction pack. But she's not sure about Neil Winston. He's one of those gym-honed men in their thirties who are always standing with their legs apart, as if they're too macho to fit into a normal human-sized gap. Plus, he's wearing vintage Nikes.

Neil's car, a Nissan Juke so clean it smells like new, does not predispose Harbinder in his favour. He drives like an Indian Auntie, doing the whole mirror, signal, manoeuvre thing at every junction.

'What did you say your name was?' he says, whilst proceeding cautiously onto the coast road.

'Harbinder.'

122 · ELLY GRIFFITHS

'What sort of a name's that?'

'It's Indian. What sort of name's Neil?'

'That's an ordinary name.'

'In the UK. Harbinder's ordinary in India.'

Neil seems to think about this, whilst checking his mirrors carefully. Harbinder's had this before, of course. One of her primary school teachers decided her name was too hard to pronounce and called her Mary. It took Deepak's visit to the school and a lesson in phonics before Harbinder was allowed the luxury of her own name. She bets this never happened to Neil, despite his name being less phonetically regular.

'Are you Indian then?' he says.

'I'm British,' says Harbinder. Then, relenting slightly, 'My parents emigrated here from India.' Actually, her father was born in England, his parents having left India after partition, but she doesn't think Neil will know what this means.

'What's this callout about?' she asks.

'Suspicious death,' says Neil. 'Woman found in her flat, out Worthing way. Looks like drug overdose but might be blunt force trauma. No signs of forced entry. SOCO at the scene.'

This recital seems to have given Neil confidence. 'The woman's a known sex worker,' he says. 'Not that it makes a difference to us, of course.'

HARBINGER: A HARBINDER KAUR STORY · 123

It does make a difference, thinks Harbinder, because sex work is dangerous and the women involved are vulnerable. But she appreciates the sentiment.

The terraced house has seen better days although, admittedly, the façade is not helped by police tape across the door. Neil and Harbinder pull on paper suits. As Harbinder is tucking her hair under a cap, her mobile buzzes. It's her mother.

'Just a second,' she says to Neil.

'What is it?' she hisses into the phone. 'I'm at work.'

'It's Jack. He's gone missing.'

How? thinks Harbinder. The dog is so old it can hardly walk.

'He can't have gone far,' she says.

'Your father's out looking now,' says Bibi. 'I thought the police could do something. Don't you have a dog catcher?'

'Not since the nineteen fifties,' says Harbinder. 'Try not to worry, Mum. Dad will find him. I have to go now. I'm at work.'

She turns to Neil who is looking, not exactly disapproving, but definitely quizzical. Harbinder is not about to explain though. 'Shall we go in?' she says.

The scene-of-crime officer greets them at the door, which has a canopy over it. Plastic sheeting leads through into the hall.

'Hi, Neil,' she says.

'Hallo, Meg,' says Neil. 'This is Harb . . . Harbinger.'

'Harbinder Kaur,' says Harbinder. 'I've just joined the team.'

'Welcome,' says Meg, with a half-smile. 'And sorry about Neil.'

'What do you mean?' says Neil.

'Just getting the apology in early,' says Meg. 'Victim's body is still in situ. We're waiting for the coroner's van now.'

The dead woman's name is Mary-Rose Hampton. The hyphen seems particularly poignant somehow. Her body is covered with a tarpaulin but Harbinder can still see white trainers sticking out. The small apartment is tiny and painfully bare: a sofa bed and a TV in the main room, a kitchen consisting of a rusty cooker and a fridge, a bathroom that was probably once an outside toilet. This last has a sash window which is half open.

The woman constable who was first at the scene fills in the details. 'Neighbours heard loud voices last night but didn't report it. Apparently Mary-Rose had altercations with her boyfriend before. But the next-door neighbour was worried when Mary-Rose didn't take her little dog out this morning. The neighbour, Lucy Grey, had a key and let herself in. The victim was lying on the floor of the sitting room. Mrs Grey called the emergency services immediately. Paramedics pronounced Mary-Rose dead at the scene. Could be a drug overdose—she was known to be a user—but there's bruising on her forehead. Could have been caused by the fall or could be assault.'

'Where's the dog now?' asks Harbinder.

'With the neighbour. It's a yappy little thing.'

'What do you think?' asks Neil, as they examine the window in the bathroom. There's a Body Shop shower gel on the window ledge. Harbinder wonders if it was a present. 'Someone could have got in this way.'

'Mary-Rose was wearing brand-new trainers,' says Harbinder.

'What does that prove?'

'I don't suppose she was wearing them on the street. I think she changed into them. If she was just going to watch TV, she'd wear slippers. New trainers mean she was expecting someone.'

'The boyfriend?'

'Probably.'

The black van arrives to take Mary-Rose's body away. A crowd has gathered in the street. A few people are filming on their phones but Harbinder also hears sounds of sympathy. An Irish voice says, 'God bless her.'

'Time to talk to the neighbours?' says Neil.

126 · ELLY GRIFFITHS

Lucy Grey greets them holding a dog that resembles a small pig.

'She's called Maisie,' she tells them. 'She's a chug.'

'A what?' says Neil.

'Half chihuahua, half pug. Mary-Rose adored her.'

Harbinder pats the dog and it snuffles at her. It's quite cute in its way. She thinks of her father searching for Jack and her mother waiting anxiously behind the counter of the shop.

'What can you tell us about Mary-Rose's boyfriend?' she says.

'Luke Brotherton,' says Lucy, her voice hardening. 'I never liked him. He was a layabout. Never saw him do any work but he took money off Mary-Rose all the time. She stuck up for him, said he was a different person when you got to know him. He bought Maisie a little sweater last Christmas and you would have thought he'd given Mary-Rose a diamond ring. Get him to contribute to the housekeeping, I told her. That's what counts.'

'Do you have an address for Brotherton?' asks Neil.

An hour later, an arrest warrant has been issued. The house is sealed and a PC is left guarding the door.

'Time for lunch,' says Neil. 'There's a good sandwich place near here.'

'My mother made me a packed lunch,' says Harbinder.

'Really?' Neil turns to looks at her. 'Do you still live at home then?'

'Yes,' says Harbinder. 'For now.' She tries to give the impression that the situation is temporary, that she's lodging with her parents while she house-hunts, but the truth is that, apart from a few months sharing with some fellow police cadets, Harbinder has lived in the flat above the shop all her life. She even lived at home when she was at Chichester University.

'Are you single then?' says Neil. 'Shall I set you up with one of my mates?'

'Why not?' says Harbinder. 'Do you know any single women?'

It takes Neil a few seconds to get this and, to his credit, he responds with, 'I know a few.'

'It's OK, I'm not looking at the moment,' says Harbinder. 'What about you? What's your situation?'

'Got married last year. I've been with Kelly since school. She's too good for me really.'

He shows Harbinder a photo and she has to agree. By now they are at the sandwich place and Harbinder has a cheese roll just to keep Neil company. They eat on a bench looking out to sea. Harbinder texts her mother and learns that Jack still hasn't been found. Is he on his way to the rainbow bridge? She hopes not.

Back at the station, Harbinder and Neil interview Luke Brotherton. He's a thin man in his late thirties with tattoos on his neck and covering both arms. Harbinder recognises several that usually commemorate prison sentences. Brotherton is accompanied by a solicitor who has obviously instructed him to give a 'no comment' interview. Harbinder and Neil continue regardless. They know that, if they ask the questions now, then they will be repeated in court. Harbinder is pleased to note that Neil is a patient interviewer, going over events in a reasonable voice that cries out to be answered. In fact, Harbinder could learn from him. She knows that both her tone and her body language tend towards the confrontational. She unfolds her arms and asks Brotherton, 'Was Maisie, Mary-Rose's dog, there when you visited?'

Unexpectedly, this is the question that breaks the suspect. His lips start to form 'no comment' but, suddenly, he drops his head to his hands. Harbinder and Neil are both silent, waiting.

'Do you need a break?' asks the solicitor.

Brotherton raises his head. His eyes are full of tears.

'I loved that dog,' he says. 'I loved Mary-Rose. I didn't mean to hit her. It was just once. She went down so quickly, must have hit her head on the tiles round the fireplace . . .'

HARBINGER: A HARBINDER KAUR STORY · 129

'That's why the neighbours didn't hear the dog barking,' says Harbinder afterwards. 'The neighbour said it was yappy but it didn't bark at Brotherton because it knew him and liked him.'

'Shows how stupid it is,' says Neil but he, too, is elated by the confession. When they go back into the open-plan area, they are greeted with a round of applause.

'Good work, team,' says Donna. 'And what a great first day for you, Harbinder.'

To celebrate, Harbinder opens her lunchbox and soon the whole room is munching on rajma chawal, paneer bhurji and lemon rice.

'This is the best thing I've ever eaten,' says Donna, with her mouth full. 'Tell your mother to give you a packed lunch every day.'

Bibi will be pleased at the empty tin, thinks Harbinder, but it won't compensate for the loss of Jack. She's packing her things away when there's a call from the receptionist downstairs.

'There's a man asking for you. Well, he asked for the Indian policewoman . . .'

'That'll be me,' says Harbinder. She wonders who it can be. Who knows that there's a new detective in town? And a woman of colour too.

But even her wildest imaginings don't match the

reality. It's Steve, the man from the churchyard, and in his arms, whimpering with excitement at the sight of Harbinder, is Jack.

'I found him wandering around,' says Steve. 'And I thought I'd bring him to you because we talked about dogs this morning.'

'It's my dog,' says Harbinder, dropping a kiss on the animal's bristly head. 'Well, my parents' dog. Thank you so much.'

By now, Neil and Donna have joined them.

'Community policing at its best,' says Donna. Harbinder thinks it would be even better if they could find Steve a bed for the night but, in all the excitement, he has drifted quietly away.

'How are you going to get Jack home?' says Neil. 'He doesn't look like he could walk far.'

'I'll carry him.'

'You said you live by the harbour. That's quite a way. I'll give you a lift.'

'He'll get dog hair in your car,' says Harbinder. Jack smells, too. The Nissan will never be the same again.

'It's OK,' says Neil. 'Kelly gave me a car vacuum for Christmas.'

It feels like the first gesture of friendship.

One Is Silver

It's meant to be fun. That's what I tell myself as we begin the long climb up the hill, dazzling white in the heat. A holiday in the sun. Just the two of you. A treat, a reward (for what?), a chance to recharge those batteries. Now that Laura's gone to university, it'll be an opportunity for you and Richard to spend some time together. I glance at my husband, stumping along at the side of the road, trying to keep in the meagre shade of the olive trees. He is wearing a white shirt and baggy beige shorts. His legs are thin and white. There's a plaster on his heel where his new sandals rub, and his scalp is already going pink. The thought of spending a week with him makes my heart sink.

A week in sunny Sorrento, that's what the brochure said. See the beautiful Amalfi coast, visit Pompeii and Vesuvius, sip cappuccino in charming piazzas, experience the *dolce vita*. 'You should go,' Laura kept saying, 'you've never been to Italy. You've never really been anywhere.' This from the heights of post-A-level back-packing around Europe. But it's true. When Laura was little, we spent every summer in our caravan on the Gower Peninsula. When Laura started to complain about playing endless games of Scrabble as the rain hammered on the roof, we rather gave up on holidays. Laura used to go away with her friend Megan, whose parents had a time-share in Magaluf. Richard and I stayed at home.

'Are you OK?' I ask Richard.

'Knee hurts,' he grunts.

Richard's Knee (it is always capitalised in my mind) is one of the reasons why we never go anywhere. When I met him Richard was a keen footballer. Looking at those spindly legs in front of me it's hard to believe that they were once muscular and assured, coaxing the ball past defenders and propelling it into the goal. But a lifetime of sport has left Richard with a Bad Knee. He's had two operations and endless physio but it still dominates our life, like a bad-tempered deity. Do not awake the wrath of the Great Knee.

'Nearly there,' shouts Fabio, our exhaustingly enthu-siastic guide. No one answers. We are all too hot and tired from the climb. And, at fifty-five, I'm the youngest in the group by far.

ONE IS SILVER · 133

We are on our way to visit the church of Sant'Antonino. Apparently he is the patron saint of Sorrento but, at present, I don't care who he is as long as his church is cool.

It is. Blessedly cool and smelling of flowers. As Fabio waxes lyrical about the frescos I see a small flight of stairs leading to the crypt.

'Come on,' I say to Richard. 'Let's explore.'

He mutters about the Knee but he follows me. The crypt is dark, lit only by candles burning in front of a small altar. And in front of the candles is an array of objects that makes me take a step backwards. They are all made of silver, gleaming dully in the shadows, but there is something odd about them. I move closer and see what is unmistakably a silver leg. Beside me, Richard says, 'Is that an arm?'

It is. And next to the arm are a nose and a hand. The room is full of silver body parts, some almost to scale, some in miniature, laid out before the altar.

I hadn't heard Fabio come in but, suddenly, his voice is behind us. 'This is the tradition of Sant'Antonino. You pray for healing in a part of your body. When you are cured, you make that body part in silver and you offer it to the saint, to say thank you.'

Richard and I are silent, gazing at the answered prayers.

When I wake the next morning, Richard is gone. I look around the room. It's small, just twin beds and a tiny shower cubicle. There's nowhere he could be hiding. Then, on impulse, I look out of the window. The view really is stunning; the brochure was right about that. Our window looks straight out across the Bay of Naples. But the only way to the sea is down a hundred steps cut into the rock. We've never risked it, not with the Knee. But then I look again. Is that Richard's pink head bobbing about in the impossibly blue water? It is. And, as I watch, his arms start waving. I stand there in shock. Not waving. But drowning.

Somehow I'm running down those steps in my nightdress. Richard is drowning, I keep telling myself. Hurry. Hurry. When I am about ten steps from the bottom I jump. The water is shockingly cold.

'I'm coming, Richard. I'm coming.'

'What are you doing, Hetty?'

Richard is swimming up to me with a confident front crawl.

'I thought you were . . .' I go under and swallow salt water. 'I thought you were drowning.'

Richard helps me back to the steps and we sit there in the sun. My sensible M&S nightdress is dripping, my newly streaked hair bedraggled. The first fish-

one IS SILVER · 135

ing boats of the morning are starting to chug across the bay.

'I thought you were drowning,' I say. 'Your arms were waving.'

'It was an exercise my physio taught me,' says Richard. 'For my knee.'

I want to cry but somehow, sitting there with the hot Italian sun on my face, I laugh instead. Richard looks at me in surprise and then he laughs too.

'You know something?' he says. 'My knee's feeling a lot better.'

We walk back up the steps, we shower and we lie down together on one of the single beds. The light floods through the shutters and I remember a song that Laura learnt at Brownies.

Make new friends but keep the old.

One is silver and the other gold.

And I think: new experiences are wonderful, glittering like silver in the darkness. But Richard and our twenty-eight years of marriage. That's gold.

Much later, I say, 'We should go back to Sant'Antonino. Give him a silver knee to say thank you.'

But Richard is asleep.

Note: You can visit the church of Sant'Antonino in Sorrento and see the silver body parts.

The Village Church

A walk to the graveyard was always a treat. When we were first married, Jon used to make a joke of it. 'Wow, your family really knows how to enjoy themselves. Graveyard in the morning, probably a funeral in the afternoon, then sitting down to watch *Songs of Praise* in the evening.' But, eventually, even Jon grew to enjoy the ritual. The walk over the Downs, stopping by the dew pond for sandwiches and tea from a flask, the turning into the lane where the trees met overhead and where—in spring—the banks would foam with glorious daffodils, then the silent church, the creaking gate and the walk through the graves.

It had been a proper village once, with farmworkers' cottages, even a small school. But the farm went out of business and the promised new road bypassed the vil-

THE VILLAGE CHURCH · 137

lage, leaving only a rutted track that was impassable in the winter. One by one, the residents left the cottages and there were no children for the school. Only the church remained but that was closed now too. It was a silent place, even the birds didn't seem to sing overhead and when, once, a sheep wandered into the graveyard from the fields, its bleating seemed shockingly loud, as if it could raise the villagers now sleeping beneath the turf.

We used to say that our children, Lily and Tom, learnt to read in that graveyard, spelling out the difficult Victor-ian names. Thomasina, Violet, Herbert, Archibald. It was a handy maths lesson too. 'So, if Elsie Maynard was born in 1852 and died in 1855, how old was she?' 'Three,' Lily would say, and pick daisies to put on Elsie's grave.

The most impressive grave was a stone cross near the church porch. 'Sacred to the memory of the Rev. Martin Amshore, vicar of the parish, 1870–1940. Also his beloved wife Verity 1875–1952.' Martin must have been the last vicar because the church had closed in 1932. Were there any children? The graveyard had the answer. A small white stone by the lychgate. 'Private Thomas Amshore 1897–1915. Too dearly loved to be forgotten.'

'How old was he?'

'Eighteen.'

The church was always locked but, on one visit, just before Christmas 2014, we were surprised to find the door open and an elderly couple arranging holly in the porch.

'There's going to be a carol service,' they told us, 'to commemorate the First World War. We're just cleaning the old place up a bit.'

They showed us round. The building smelt of damp but there was still that faint 'holy' aroma that I remembered from the infrequent church services of my youth: candles and incense and flower stalks. Lily and Tom were thirteen and fifteen. They hadn't wanted to come but I'd insisted. We'd had Sunday lunch at my mum's and everyone had eaten and drunk too much. 'A brisk walk over the Downs is just what we need,' I said. 'Let's go now before it gets dark.' Jon was stuck into a football match and Mum wasn't feeling too good that day. So it was just me and the kids. They'd been bored at first but I was glad to see that they were interested in the old church, asking questions and taking photographs on their phones.

'That's the leper window,' the man was telling them. 'In the Middle Ages lepers weren't allowed inside so they would queue by the window to be given Holy Communion.'

THE VILLAGE CHURCH · 139

'How old is the church?' I asked.

'Anglo Saxon originally,' said the woman, 'but it was abandoned after the Reformation. They smashed all the lovely stained glass. That window up there,' she pointed above the altar, 'it used to show the Archangel Michael with his fiery sword. The church wasn't opened again until the nineteenth century.'

'You know a lot about the history,' I said.

'Well, I used to spend a lot of time here, dear.' She turned back to her flower arranging.

On the way out I tried, rather awkwardly, to make a donation.

'No need,' said the man. He had a deep voice and it echoed against the vaulted ceiling. 'Just your presence is enough. Nice to see young people here too.'

Tom, who was standing beside me, looked embarrassed, especially when the woman put a hand on his head, 'God bless you.' She turned to me. 'Keep them close, dear. They're gone before you know it.'

'Yes,' I said brightly, 'it won't be long before they're at university.'

The woman smiled but didn't answer. As we walked away I saw her standing in the porch. I waved but she didn't respond.

When we got home, Jon said, 'Maybe they were the ghosts of Martin and Verity. Didn't the woman say she used to spend a lot of time there? Well, the place has been closed since the thirties.'

'Don't be silly,' I said. 'They were obviously just preparing the church for the carol service. It's next Saturday. I might go along.'

But I never did get to go. That night Mum had a heart attack in her sleep and died. The ramifications of selling the house went on until spring and, when we drove away for the last time, the soft green Downs disappearing in the rear-view mirror, I had no real sense that my childhood had gone for ever. I never went back to the silent village and the graveyard. But, when he was doing A-level Art, Tom printed out some of his photographs of the church. They showed the empty nave and aisle, the birds nesting in the beams, a middle-aged woman, red-faced from the walk and too much lunch, two bored-looking teenagers. They also showed an elderly couple, grey-haired and slightly sad, and, behind them, a tall youth in the uniform of the First World War, his face glowing in the light from a window which had once shown St Michael, the patron saint of soldiers.

Turning Traitor

Nothing in the world is hidden forever . . .
Sand turns traitor, and betrays the footstep that
has passed over it.

Wilkie Collins, No Name.

*A*t low tide the river is a wonderland, the mudflats are full of creatures that we can eat and the sand stretches for miles. Father says not to waste time, the tide can change very quickly and you can easily get stranded. But it's hard not to stop and look. The sand is cool under my feet and, if I rub with my big toe, it changes colour, becoming blue and grey with streaks of black. You can find shrimps there, grey-white with orange heads. If you're not quick enough, the sea birds will swoop down and take them from under your nose. Where the salt waves wash over, there are sand crabs, little creatures that burrow back down into the silt as soon as you see them. If you move fast enough, though, you can scoop them out of the sucking sand and they make good eating.

We're on the very edge here, where the river meets the big water, blue and green as far as you can see. Father says there may be more land beyond the horizon, but I don't think this can be true. We've come as far as you can, we've walked up from the great mountains, crossed the river, and are now in the most northern of lands. The Old One says the north is terrible, frozen in ice all year round, but it's beautiful here. A huge open plain with dark trees at the edge. The skies are so high and wide that, if you lie on your back, you feel as if you are swimming in the clouds. The hunting is good too: giant deer and bison, the skies full of birds that come to feed on the sandbanks. There are mammoths as well, hippos and rhinos, sabre-toothed tigers that can come in the night and drag you away from the campfire. That's why we must stick together, Father says, our family group, including the Old One.

'If this is such a rich land,' I say, 'why can't we stay here?'

'We must keep travelling,' says Father. 'If we stay too long in one place, we will use up the food. When the winter comes we will go to the south lands.'

But I want to stay here, I think. I like this place; the

plain, the river, the big water. There's plenty of food and there's shelter too, rock caves further down the river, where the water turns sweet. The river gravel is full of flints which Father and Mother work into tools, many-sided and cunning. There are birds to give feathers for arrows and, with so many deer, we'll be able to get antlers in the spring and use them for weapons. It's too cold in the winter, Father says, but we have animal hides and we make fires from driftwood and seaweed. The birds fly south, we know that, but the animals stay here all year round. In my fur over-garment I could be a mammoth, wise and considered, wading the waters in the summer and spending my winters on the low ground.

I stop and look back. It's flat here, so you can see the river twisting and turning but, eventually, it's lost in the dark. 'We don't know what lies beyond,' the Old One says. 'After summer comes winter but our lives will end one day.' I don't know what this means. I'm almost full grown, twelve summers, and I can't imagine a time when I won't be here, feeling the sun on my face and the wind in my hair. 'If we're buried in the earth,' says the Old One, 'we will bloom again one day.' That's why we put flowers around the body when we put it in the ground. If I stay here, in the same place, will I too grow roots?

I have stood here so long that my feet have sunk. I'm up to my ankles in brackish water; the tide must be turning. I can still see the others, tiny dots on the shoreline as they search for food, dutifully filling their wicker baskets. We're vulnerable because we have a young one with us, I can see her running backwards and forwards into the waves. New places are exciting at that age, you have no idea of the dangers around you. Sometimes I still feel like running in the waves but I know that it's my job to help the group, to forage for food, to collect wood for the fire, to guard against the dark.

Mother turns and waves. A 'hurry up' wave, not a friendly one. I pull my feet out of the sucking sand. They make a funny, squelching noise but it's not funny, I know. You could be trapped here when the water rises. I'm stuck deeper than I think. I struggle to free myself and hear footsteps running along the firmer sand behind me. I know that they belong to one like us but, when I look, our group is all there on the sea's edge: Father, Mother, the Young One, the Old One. I try to turn but, as I do so, the footsteps stop. I am suddenly afraid. As if the bright day has all at once become night.

We found out about the footsteps by accident. It had been raining all week so we hadn't been able to do

TURNING TRAITOR · 145

much work on the erosion project. But we turned up at Happisburgh one morning at low tide to find the beach full of people, all with machinery and ropes and measuring sticks. 'Skye and Lucy, you stay here,' said Greg, and he went hurrying down the slope, holding onto the rope handrail because the cliffs can crumble away beneath your feet. Ten minutes later he was back. Lucy and I had given up and were sitting in the back of Greg's car with the heating on.

'They're archaeologists,' he said, opening the door. 'And they've found something amazing.'

'What?' I said. I was tired and didn't fancy putting my wellies on and trudging along the beach to see an old Roman coin or something like that.

'Footprints,' said Greg. He was rummaging around in the boot to find his waterproofs. 'Fossilised footprints in the sediment. Lots of them. The tide must have washed away the sand covering them. The archaeologists are really excited.'

'What's so exciting about footprints?' I said.

'They could be really old, the archaeologists say, from the Pleistocene era.'

'What's that in English?' said Lucy.

'Old,' said Greg, sitting on the open boot to pull on his waders. 'Maybe 800,000 years old. What do they teach young people in school these days?'

146 · ELLY GRIFFITHS

This is a joke because Greg is our teacher. We're both studying Geography in sixth form. I don't really know why I chose it, perhaps because I wanted to do something sciencey and I didn't like Biology (too much medical stuff), and I thought Physics and Chemistry were too hard. Lucy did it because I did it. That's always been the way with us. We've been friends since primary school and anyone looking at us would think that Lucy is the leader and, in a way, she is. She was always the first one to do things: ride a two-wheeler, stay out late, have a boyfriend, smoke a cigarette. But, in other ways, Lucy follows me. She joined the Brownies because I did and I know she only stayed on in sixth form because I wanted to. I've always done better than Lucy in school but, in all the ways that matter, she's ahead.

Lucy's really pretty with bright-brown eyes, usually highlighted by tons of mascara. She used to have long, wavy hair but now it's short and cute. She's small and slim, great at gymnastics and dancing, the kind of girl who can sit on a boy's lap without his legs going dead. She's very popular and has sat on a lot of laps but now she has a steady boyfriend, Joe: good-looking, star striker in the football team, studies Business BTech and thinks he's Alan Sugar. I'm taller and quieter. I didn't have that many friends until I got sick in year ten and then I was madly popular because everyone thought I might die. I'm not ungrateful, I loved being voted 'Most courageous' in our year eleven yearbook, but I know it's not about me, not really. It's easy to care about the girl who's got cancer, to say she's beautiful when she loses her hair, to be her friend on Facebook and organise sponsored Zumba sessions in aid of a charity they hadn't heard of until they Googled 'teenage cancer'.

But Lucy was always my real friend. She got me through the treatment, bringing her laptop into the hospital so we could watch trashy TV while I had my chemo, shaving her own hair so we could wear matching wigs, jollying my mum along whenever she looked like crying (for some reason, my mum crying was the one thing I couldn't bear), making a friend of my little sister, even going to bingo with my gran. The best thing was that she continued to tease me—about being nerdy, about being addicted to *Friends*, about being freakishly tall—and didn't treat me like I'd suddenly become a living angel just because my lymph glands were going crazy.

I missed a lot of school in years ten and eleven but I did surprisingly well in my GCSEs. 'Don't know why you bothered coming to my lessons at all,' said Miss Rossi, my English teacher, hugging me, 'you did just fine without me.' Miss Rossi wanted me to go to university but that doesn't look like it will happen now. But I'm doing three A levels at the sixth form college and getting good grades. Lucy says that when we finish school we can get a flat together and work at one of the hotels in King's Lynn. It's good money, she says, and there's always the chance of getting off with a handsome tourist.

This project was Mr Harper's idea. He's part of a team that maps the coast to see how much damage has been done by erosion. Our part of Norfolk is slowly falling into the sea. Houses that stood a playing field's length from the cliffs are now teetering on the very edge. The pub where my dad used to drink has actually gone over, the bar stools and beer barrels ending up on the beach below, startling the sea life and turning the rock pools a nasty brown colour. Mr Harper decided that his A-level Geography class would help with the survey. 'It'll look good on your personal statements,' he told us. Except that you don't need a personal statement to work in a Travelodge. We spent most of our Easter holidays trudging up and down rainswept beaches, and along the way Mr Harper became Greg, but after a while it became boring and people stopped turning up. By May it was just me and Lucy and Charlie, a boy in year thirteen who thought that aliens had landed in Lakenheath. But then Greg met the archaeologists and everything changed.

TURNING TRAITOR · 149

We went down to the beach and there they were, a group of men and women staring intently at the ground, where the sand is dark grey and arranged in shallow steps, as tight and hard as stone. Greg bustled up to them, 'these are my students', as if they would be *thrilled* to meet Lucy and me, shivering and gormless in our fake Cath Kidston wellies.

To be fair, they were nice to us. They explained that the footprints were really significant.

'It looks like there were several people,' said the lead archaeologist. 'Maybe a family group, adults and children, walking along the shore.'

'Were they just walking along the beach?' said Lucy. I always admire the way that she isn't afraid to ask questions.

'This wasn't a beach then,' said one of the women. 'The English Channel wasn't there. It was just a river. The River Thames, in fact.'

'Isn't that in London?' I said, feeling stupid.

'It was further north in those days,' said the woman. 'And across the river was France. Well, of course, it wasn't France then, just part of the continent.'

I thought about that. Was she having us on? Was it really once possible to cross a river and walk to France? I couldn't get my head around 800,000 years ago. Were they humans like us? I had a vision of cave people with heavy brows and hanging limbs, heaving clubs and grunting.

The woman had turned away to talk to Greg.

'Happisburgh is a treasure trove for archaeologists,' she was saying. 'Because of the erosion these amazing finds keep appearing: flint tools, mammoth bones, fossilised tree stumps. But up to now we haven't found any traces of humans.'

'This is a really big project then,' said Greg.

'Yes,' she said, 'and the crazy thing is that we have to finish it in two weeks.'

'Why?' asked Lucy.

'Because, in two weeks' time, the tide will wash them away,' she said.

And that's how we got involved. Greg talked them into letting us help, saying that we were promising students, fascinated by pre-history. At the time I didn't even know what pre-history was but I knew that I wanted to be part of the project. The way Greg put it, this was a chance to find out about people, our ancestors, who had lived almost a million years ago. It was groundbreaking research, we could be in history textbooks one day. It certainly beat doing the Duke of Edinburgh award.

My parents weren't keen though. My mum was

worried that I'd exhaust myself and get ill. At first she flatly said that she didn't want me to be involved so Greg actually called round to our house. It was really embarrassing, seeing Greg sitting at our kitchen table with Evie doing her homework and Gran making one of her famous pies, pastry and flour everywhere.

'The thing is, Mr Harper,' said Mum, flustered because the proper place for a teacher was in school, not in her kitchen, 'Skye's still not right. Even after the chemo, she's just tired all the time. It's all I can do to get her up for college in the morning.'

'I do understand that, Mrs Olson,' said Greg, trying to sound like a responsible teacher and not the excitable groupie he transformed into whenever the archaeologists were around. 'But it would be a wonderful experience for her. For all of us.'

'What if she gets a cold?' said Mum. 'Her resistance is really low, the hospital said. What if she gets sick again?'

'I'll look after her,' said Greg, 'and make sure she doesn't get too cold or tired. But this project is really important. In two weeks the footprints will be gone. We've got to do it now.'

'Will there be other young people there?' said Gran, kneading away. She gave me one of her creaky winks.

152 · ELLY GRIFFITHS

I could see that, for Gran, this was just a chance for me to find a boyfriend at last. She's always wanting me to have what she calls 'a romance'. It's quite sad really.

'There's a team of the best archaeologists in the country,' said Greg, not really answering the question. 'It's the opportunity of a lifetime.'

Mum looked away then. She hates the L word.

But in the end they let me. I think it was so long since I'd actually *wanted* to do something, rather than just drearily going along with things, that I don't think they could bring themselves to refuse. 'Let the girl have some fun,' said Gran. 'Doesn't sound much fun,' said Dad, 'sounds like slave labour to me.'

And it was hard work. Cold, relentless, repetitive work. But I absolutely loved it. Lucy and I were just runners really, we fetched and carried, made tea, tried to keep the sandwiches dry, but we were part of the Footprints Project. It rained solidly all fortnight. So much for Greg saying he wouldn't let us get cold. We held umbrellas over the archaeologists as they worked but Lucy and I were always soaking wet because we didn't have expensive waterproofs, only fashion macs from Topshop. My feet would freeze in my flowery wellies and, when I got home, I'd sit with them in a bowl of hot water like a miner who had just emerged from the pit. And the funny thing was, I felt better

TURNING TRAITOR · 153

than I had for ages. I'd come home from college, have tea, do my homework and then run down to the beach in the dark to help with the arc lights. I worked at the weekends too and on my afternoons off. I didn't watch *Friends* once.

Lucy got bored quite quickly. She only kept on with the project because of me. I knew that and I was grateful. It was fun with Lucy, we used to make up mad names for the owners of the footprints—Smelly Pete, Fun Bobby, Dino Girl—we would sit in the Portakabin where the archaeologists kept their equipment, listening to the rain drumming on the roof and trying to tell our fortunes with an old pack of tarot cards we had found. But I really liked it best when I was on my own. Then, kneeling beside the one of the archaeologists, helping them brush away sand from the hollows made by those long-dead feet, I really felt that I was making a difference, that I was part of the team.

I loved watching the archaeologists at work. They were so organised, setting up screens around the footprints and marking them out with measuring rods, taking notes, drawing diagrams, plotting things on graphs. They never seemed in a rush, they would spend hours poring over one tiny square of sand, but I knew that they were really working a breakneck speed. They took photos using something called photogrammetry, hundreds of digital images that could be put together to form a 3D picture. They took samples of the sand because the little insects in it would help them date the site. I understood now how important this was. If the footprints were 800,000 years old, they would be the oldest human footprints outside Africa. Except the archaeologists didn't say human, they said 'early hominin'.

'Pioneer Man,' said Finn, one of the younger members of the team. '*Homo antecessor*, that's what they're called sometimes.'

'That's sexist,' said Lucy, trying to make him laugh. She liked Finn. She said he was sexy but it was hard to tell under all the thermal layers.

I liked the phrase, 'Pioneer Man'. I used to repeat it to myself at night when I couldn't sleep. I liked the thought of being the first to do something. Once I thought I'd be the first person in my family to go to university but sometimes I thought I was just going to be the first to die of leukaemia. 'Morbid thoughts are not uncommon in teenage cancer sufferers,' said the leaflet the hospital gave to Mum and Dad. The leaflet didn't tell you how to get rid of these thoughts, though, when you're awake at three a.m. and planning your funeral.

'In the war,' said Gran, 'my mum and I used to set the table for breakfast the night before. It was our way of saying that we didn't think that we would die in the night.'

'It would take more than an air raid to make Skye do some housework,' said Dad, trying for the light touch. But I thought I knew what Gran meant. Sometimes you have to throw down a challenge to the night, to let yourself believe that morning will come.

Down on the beach, time was running out. Every day more of the precious sediment was washed away by the tide. The site was apparently too old for radiocarbon dating so everything depended on the photogrammetry and on something they called magnetic signatures. I didn't understand it all. I just knew that, before the sand disappeared, we had to learn its secrets. One evening on the second week I was in the Portakabin making tea when Finn walked in. It was another filthy night and I was the only one there; Lucy was watching Joe play football in the rain and Greg was at a parents' evening.

'Hallo, Skye,' said Finn. He took off his coat and shook the water from it. It reminded me of a dog shaking itself dry and there was a sort of golden-retriever look to Finn, he had shaggy blond hair and the kind of mouth that smiled very easily.

'Hi,' I said. 'I'm just making tea. Do you want some?'

'That would be lovely,' he said. Lovely. I couldn't imagine any man I knew using that word but it sounded all right from Finn with his golden aura. Everything probably *was* lovely in his world.

We drank our tea and Finn broke the last biscuit in half and shared it with me. It was funny because, at that moment, the hut suddenly seemed to shrink, the prefabricated walls closing in. I was conscious of taking up too much room, as if my arms and legs were sticking out of the windows, like Alice in Wonderland when she got too big for the house.

We had been drinking in silence but then Finn said, 'Have you seen the photogrammetry results?'

'No,' I said, grateful to have something to talk about.

'We got them through today.' He went to one of the filing cabinets and got out an envelope. He laid several sheets of paper on the table. I looked over his shoulder but all I could see were shapes with little red and black numbers on them.

'Look,' said Finn, pointing. 'This shows that there were at least five different people walking along the river bed. You can see that their feet were different sizes. It looks like one of them was a young child and another was an adolescent. Look at the depth of this print here. One of the walkers, the adolescent, must have stood here for quite a time, maybe fishing or look-ing for food. They must have been standing still a long time to have made footprints that deep.'

'Maybe they were just thinking,' I said.

'Possibly,' says Finn, 'but there's another footprint here which looks as if that walker overbalanced. And a deep scrape, almost as if they were dragged along the ground.'

'What can have happened?' I say.

'We'll never know,' says Finn. 'Perhaps there was some horseplay or maybe they were even attacked.'

'I wish we knew for certain,' I say. 'I wish we knew what that person was thinking when they stood there and what happened to them afterwards.'

'I often wonder what they thought about,' said Finn, 'and whether they had hopes and fears like us. Or whether they just concentrated on where their next meal was coming from.'

This was so much what I had been thinking that I was amazed. My cave people with clubs had long since vanished and now I thought of the walkers as people I knew. Somehow Fun Bobby and Dino Girl had become my friends.

'I wonder if they knew that they were going to die one day,' I said.

Finn looked up at me. His eyes were bright blue and

158 • ELLY GRIFFITHS

his lashes were dark, unlike his hair. I thought he was going to ask where I had got this odd (morbid) notion. Instead he said, 'How old are you, Skye?'

'Seventeen,' I said.

'A levels next year?'

'Yes. English, History and Geography.'

'What next? University?'

'I don't know,' I said, 'probably not.'

I had never told any of the team that I'd been ill and I didn't want to start now. Martha, one of the anthropologists, had said that she liked my short hair and I'd just smiled and said it was easier that way. I waited for Finn to ask me why I wasn't going to university, given that I was supposedly fascinated by pre-history. Finn, I knew, had been at UCL and was now doing a PhD at Cambridge. He was twenty-three, only six years older than me.

'Do you want to go for a walk?' is what he actually said.

'It's raining,' I said.

'Have my coat,' said Finn. He picked it up from the floor and put it on me. It was a proper cold weather garment, very heavy, with double layers and flaps and zips everywhere. When I put it on I was warmer than I had ever thought possible. It smelt of Finn and of the sea.

We went down to the beach. The tide was coming

in and we could hear the waves whispering. We walked along the sand to the place where the tidal defences start. Finn had no coat but didn't seem to be cold. The rain was soft, like snow, Finn's hair was full of droplets. I put my hood (his hood) down so I could feel it on my face.

'It's sad,' said Finn, looking up at the clifftop where a long-deserted house loomed above us, like a suicide about to jump. 'Soon, this whole town will have vanished.'

'That's not sad,' I said. 'That's just life.'

I knew he was going to kiss me then and, when he did, it was like I had always imagined: hearts, flowers, an invisible orchestra playing in the dark.

The thing is, I don't want to die a virgin. It was one of the first things I thought when I knew I had cancer. Having sex, driving a car, skiing, swimming with dolphins; all the things I wouldn't ever get to do. Well I couldn't do much about the skiing and the dolphins and, though I was saving up for driving lessons, I didn't think I'd ever have enough money to take the test. But I could have sex. Lucy first had sex when she was fifteen. I could get a boyfriend and sleep with him. A tick on the bucket list. The trouble was, the chemo made me lose my hair, which wasn't a boyfriend-enticing look, and, even after the treatment, I was too tired to go out to parties and clubs. And you're unlikely to meet Prince Looks-all-right-from-a-distance when all you want to do in the evenings is watch reruns of American sitcoms. But now I felt stronger and the archaeology had given me a new interest so, when Finn asked me to meet him for a drink the next night, I did think: is this it? How quickly can you go from a drink to having sex? Was there even anywhere for us to go and do the fatal act? Finn was staying in digs with some of the other archaeologists. Surely we couldn't go there? Perhaps we'd go to the Portakabin and lie down on the photogrammetry results, with the rows of fossils and flint hand-axes looking down on us.

When I got home, only Gran was up. Dad works nights (he's a taxi driver), and Mum and Evie were in bed. Gran was dozing over Sky Sports (she loves watching the wrestling) but she woke up when I made her a cup of tea and I found myself telling her about the Footprints Project. 'It's really important,' I told her, 'they've never found human . . . early hominin . . . footprints . . . this far north. It shows that early man was more sophisticated than we thought. They had ways of keeping warm, finding shelter. Of course, they would have gone south for the winter. You could walk all the way to the south of Europe then. The English Channel wasn't there.'

'Fancy that,' said Gran, blowing on her tea. 'You know, Skye, you really should go to college.'

'I am at college. Sixth form college.' I hoped she wasn't starting to get confused.

'No, I mean university,' said Gran. 'Cambridge. You could study Archaeology.'

Gran was born on the Fens and Cambridge is probably the only university she knows. My grades weren't good enough for Cambridge but they would be good enough for somewhere. I thought of the stories I'd heard from Finn and Martha, about freshers' week and May Balls and studying all night before an exam. It was a different world and I wasn't sure that I knew the password to get in. Girls like me don't go to university. My family have always lived in East Anglia, Dad has always lived in this village. I heard one of the anthropologists say that Norfolk has a very stable population, which is another way of saying that its inhabitants never go anywhere. Gran has friends who have never been to London. It's as if people get washed up here, on the very edge of Britain, and there's nowhere else for them to go. They're not Pioneer Man, they can't just walk to Europe. They get stuck. I love my home, it's beautiful:

162 · ELLY GRIFFITHS

the sea, the wide beaches, the Broads, the quaint villages. It's just . . . it's not the only place on Earth.

But Mum would never let me apply to university. She thought I would shrivel and die if I was out of her sight for too long. And, even if I could convince Mum, the way I did with the project, there was Lucy. I knew that it was difficult for her at home. Her mum remarried a few years back and she didn't get on with her stepdad. She was living for the moment when we could leave home and share a flat together. She kept talking about what it would be like. 'We'll have candles and fairy lights all over the place. We'll give parties with food as well as drink. We'll buy a kitten and give it a name out of Harry Potter.' This was her dream. I couldn't let her down.

But what about my dreams?

Once we were talking to the archaeologists about the ages of the walkers.

'People didn't live long then, did they?' said Greg. 'I mean, you were old at thirty.' He's thirty-nine (Lucy and I sneaked a look at his driving licence) so this must have been a question close to his heart.

'You'd be surprised,' said Martha. 'Fossil records show a significant number of early modern humans lived beyond forty. Maybe even older. And the fact that the older members continued to be looked after by their tribe, even when they couldn't contribute to hunting, shows that they were valued for something else. Their wisdom, perhaps.'

Should I be valuing Gran's wisdom?

I had arranged to meet Finn in a pub. Not the Four Feathers, where the archaeologists used to drink, but a smarter place in the countryside, the kind of gastropub couples go to on their wedding anniversary. I got Dad to drop me off, saying I was meeting Lucy there.

'Splashing out a bit, isn't she, Lucy Locket?' said Dad, as he pulled up in the car park full of Range Rovers. He loves Lucy, all my family do, but he sometimes talks about her like she's a bit of a joke. I hadn't realised before how much this annoyed me.

'It's an eighteenth birthday party,' I lied.

'Whose?'

'Just one of the girls in my Geography class. Thanks for taking me. I'll get a lift back, lots of people have passed their tests.'

'Take care,' said Dad. 'Love you.'

'Love you.' We always say it now, whenever we say goodbye. It's nice, I suppose, but it has also stopped meaning anything much. It's funny how different it is when you drop off the 'I'. 'Love you' is casual, an alternative to goodbye. Bye. Take care. Love you.

164 · ELLY GRIFFITHS

Don't wait up. I don't know if I'll ever say 'I love you' to anyone.

Finn was waiting inside and, when I saw him there, too tall for the oak-beamed room, I realised that Lucy was right. He *was* sexy with his messy blond hair and rugby player's body. I was worried that we wouldn't have enough to talk about, that it would become awkward, the way it had in the Portakabin yesterday. But, actually, it was fine. We talked about all sorts of things: books, parents, favourite shows (he loved *Friends* too, said he and his flatmates watched it all the time), whether star signs mean anything and what it would have been like to have been a hunter-gatherer.

'I would be good at stalking,' I said. 'I learnt it in Brownies.'

'Why? Do they have a stalking badge?'

'No. We just spied on the Cubs a lot.'

'I think I'd be quite good at hunting animals,' said Finn. 'I was in the shooting team at school.'

'What sort of school has a shooting team?'

'A stupid private school,' said Finn and there was a slightly awkward silence. But then he bought me another drink and we started talking about the Marvel comics and everything was easy again. We ate chicken in the basket (apparently this was meant to be ironic) and stayed in the pub until almost midnight. Then

Finn asked me if I wanted to go for a drive. I wondered if he was over the limit but it was too far to walk home and so I said yes. Besides, I wanted to be alone in the car with him, music playing, a square of light on the dark roads.

We drove to Happisburgh and parked in the car park which is fenced off because half of it has fallen into the sea. The waves were crashing against the rocks below, taking chunks out of the land. In a few days the footsteps would have disappeared altogether. We kissed and Finn was breathing hard and his hair was all over his face. Was this it? I wondered. Was I about to swim with dolphins? I thought of the walkers, their long journey to reach this place, the feeling of being the first to walk along the sand. Then I sat up. 'Can I ask you something?'

'What?' said Finn.

I reached round to do up my bra strap. 'Can you help me write a personal statement?'

Lucy was furious, as I thought she would be. Worse than that, she was upset.

'You've betrayed me,' she said. 'You're a traitor. I thought we were friends.'

'We are friends,' I said. 'Best friends.'

'It's like you mugged me,' said Lucy. 'It's as if you

166 • ELLY GRIFFITHS

sneaked up behind me and hit me over the head when I wasn't looking.'

It was such an odd image that I almost laughed. But I didn't. I was almost crying and Lucy was too.

'You're my best friend,' I said again. 'That won't change.'

She laughed then, bitterly, wiping away her streaked mascara. 'Of course it will change. You'll make new friends at university. You won't bother about me any more.'

'I might not get in,' I said. 'I'm just applying. I might not get the grades.'

'You will,' said Lucy. 'You're a teacher's pet, you always were.'

This is probably true. Even before I was sick, the teachers always encouraged me, and now they were really putting themselves out to help with the UCAS forms and everything. Miss Rossi even visited my parents and tried to make them see that going to university wasn't a death wish.

'The pastoral care is very good,' she said. 'They'll look after her. And the holidays are long. Skye will be back before you know it.'

'But what if she gets sick again?' said Mum.

Miss Rossi didn't have an answer for that and Mum seemed afraid to ask the question again. She let me fill in the forms though. 'It'll be an adventure,' said Gran and I knew she was right. I knew too that I might get sick again. I'm not stupid. I know my prognosis isn't that good. I don't need the tarot cards to tell my future. But I want to be a pioneer, to make my own footsteps in the sand. And, even if they get washed away by the tide, I know that they won't be lost for ever.

Note: The Happisburgh footprints are real. They were discovered in 2013 by Nick Ashton, curator at the British Museum, and Martin Bates, from Trinity St David's University. A team of archaeologists carried out groundbreaking research on the footprints before they were erased by the tide. Pioneer Man really existed but all the characters in this story are imaginary.

Ruth's First Christmas Tree

22 December 2009

'The spirits are strong in this one,' says the man in the white robe and gumboots. 'The goddess of the forest has breathed on him.'

Ruth is not unduly disconcerted by this description. After all, it was her friend Cathbad—lab assistant and part-time druid—who recommended this Christmas tree seller to her. The empty parking lot between two warehouses has been transformed into an enchanted forest with fairy lights strung in the branches of the trees and ambient music twinkling from speakers concealed in their foliage. The seller, a young man with dreadlocks and an earnest expression, introduces himself as Leaf. His girlfriend, sitting on the steps of a caravan parked at the entrance of the site, volunteers that her name is Raindrop.

RUTH'S FIRST CHRISTMAS TREE · 169

Snowdrop would be more appropriate, thinks Ruth. It's three days before Christmas and a bitter wind is blowing across Norfolk, direct from Siberia according to the locals, bringing with it the first flakes of snow. Ruth shivers in her anorak and hopes that the snow won't settle before she has to collect her daughter, Kate, from the childminder. These days she tends to view everything through the filter of her concern for her daughter. War in Afghanistan? Hope it doesn't affect traffic on the A149. Tsunami in Japan? Hope those rising water levels don't affect King's Lynn. She doesn't like this trait in herself—she used to be interested and concerned about world events for their own sake—but she accepts it as one of the less attractive side-effects of motherhood.

'All our trees are grown in sustainable forests,' says Leaf. 'Raindrop and I talk to them every day. They're our friends.' He adds, rather more briskly, 'That one's twenty-five quid.'

Ruth looks at the tree. She can't really see anything special about it—it's green and pointy and spiky, that's about it. But she needs a tree. She has promised herself that she will make this the perfect Christmas for Kate. It's Kate's second Christmas but she didn't really register the first one, being only seven weeks old at the time. But now she can recognise Santa Claus at a hundred paces and yesterday said 'present', very loudly and clearly. So she is on her way to becoming a typical product of the consumerist society. Well done, Ruth. A triumph for modern parenting.

But this Christmas it won't just be Ruth and Kate because Ruth has also invited Max, her . . . What is Max? Her boyfriend? Surely it's ridiculous to have a boyfriend at forty-one? Her partner? Sounds too official for a relationship that has, so far, encompassed two weekends and an Aborigine repatriation ceremony. Anyway, she doesn't need a partner. She has Kate and her beloved cat, Flint. She has her job as a forensic archaeologist, her friends and a somewhat stressful relationship with Kate's father, DCI Harry Nelson. She's happy as she is. But why then is she going to so much trouble to do all the Christmassy things when usually her only concession to the festive season is watching the *Dr Who* special with a glass of white? This year she has put up her cards, bought an advent calendar and even arranged holly behind her picture frames. She has also bought a turkey (M&S, pre-stuffed), mince pies (ditto, containing brandy and grated nutmeg) and a ton of sprouts. And now she is standing in the freezing cold debating the finer points of a Christmas tree.

'I'll take it,' she says in answer to Leaf's raised eye-

RUTH'S FIRST CHRISTMAS TREE · 171

brows. 'Is it OK to collect it later? I've got some shopping to do.'

'Time has no meaning,' replies Leaf, adding that he shuts at five.

Ruth heads to the shopping centre, a place she detests. But the perfect Christmas involves ritual spending and Ruth still has to buy crackers, champagne and a present for Max. She might even find something new to wear at Shona and Phil's party tomorrow. Thinking of the party, Ruth's spirits, already lowered by the sight of a ten-foot plastic reindeer, sink below the plimsoll line.

The shopping centre is heaving. Surely real people do their shopping earlier than this? Ruth attempts to buy some wrapping paper and gives up at the sight of the queue. Kate won't care if her presents are wrapped or not and Max . . . What the hell should she get for Max? Clothes seem too personal somehow and anyway she's not sure of his size. He's tall, about as tall as Nelson, but thinner. Nelson's not overweight but somehow he seems to take up a lot of space. Mind you, having come close to death last month, he probably isn't looking his best at the moment.

Damn! She had promised herself that she wouldn't think about Nelson. Now she remembers the time when she saw him Christmas shopping, in this very mall, three years ago. She had hardly known him then but remembers watching the family—grumpy dad, glamorous wife, surly teenage daughters—and thinking what a cliché they were. But, even then, lurking behind a rack of novelty calendars, she had felt oddly drawn to Nelson, weighed down as he was by family and designer carrier bags. He had looked different, more substantial than the academic types that surrounded her, more serious, somehow more dangerous. And he had certainly proved dangerous to her peace of mind. A brief affair resulted in the birth of Kate and now Ruth is stuck with him for ever whilst Nelson—Nelson is still safe in the bosom of his nuclear family.

In desperation she buys a book about the Romans for Max aware that, as an archaeology professor, he probably possesses every known work on the subject. Still, this one has some nice pictures of Fishbourne Roman Palace where she knows Max has done some digging. She adds some Christmas socks and a novelty dog calendar. Might as well tick all the festive boxes and her only serious rival for Max's affection is his dog, Claudia. She also buys some crackers—two boxes for the price of one—and a red tablecloth decorated with snowflakes. As she heads back out into the crowd, Cliff Richard is blaring from the loud speakers. Christmas

RUTH'S FIRST CHRISTMAS TREE · 173

time. Mistletoe and wine. Ruth once found the body of an Iron Age girl with mistletoe berries in her stomach. Mistletoe was sacred to the druids who believed that the plant gave protection against illness and witchcraft. It was also linked to fertility. In fact, Cathbad once told Ruth that the juice from the berries represented the sperm of the gods. Gives a whole new perspective on kissing under the mistletoe. But mistletoe is also highly poisonous and Ruth's Iron Age girl was probably destined for a horrible death. It's a long way from Cliff's jolly Christian rhyme. Sod it, she can't be bothered to go clothes shopping. She'll just wear her black trousers and a vaguely sparkly top. Nobody will look at her anyway.

'Ruth!'

A blonde woman in a red coat is coming towards her. She is followed by a dark man, rather thinner than the vision of three years ago, but still recognisable as DCI Harry Nelson.

'Hi, Michelle,' says Ruth. 'Hi, Nelson.'

'Isn't this crazy?' says Michelle. 'I always vow I'll have all my shopping done by the end of November but there are always a few bits you forget, aren't there?'

'That's because you never stop buying things,' says Nelson. 'You've bought about a hundred presents for the girls.'

'Well, they still need their stocking presents even though they're grown-up,' says Michelle, flicking back her hair.

Ruth stares at her. Michelle knows about Kate but the knowledge is too recent for anyone to feel comfortable with it. Ruth doesn't feel that she can mention either Michelle's daughters or her own. But, standing there in the shadow of the monstrous reindeer, she suddenly feels a great affection for Michelle. In fact, she almost wishes that she could spend Christmas with her. Michelle would cook for her and buy her stocking presents. She suddenly wonders if anyone will buy her a present. Her parents, born-again Christians, sent her a card informing her that, in lieu of gifts, they have purchased a donkey for the Sudan in her name. Her brother occasionally obliges with the latest Rebus book but there's been nothing from him in the post. Will Max get her something?

Nelson looks anxious to be off but Michelle seems to feel something of the Dickensy spirit.

'Why don't we have a cup of tea?' she says. 'Or something stronger. It is Christmas, after all.'

'I'd love to,' says Ruth, 'but I've got to pick up a Christmas tree.'

'Oh we always have an artificial tree,' says Michelle, 'that way you don't get pine needles everywhere.'

RUTH'S FIRST CHRISTMAS TREE · 175

But, when Ruth returns to the parking lot, there is no sign of Leaf, the caravan or any Christmas trees. There is only a police car containing a man eating a burger. Ruth taps on the car's window.

'Clough!'

The man, DS Dave Clough, swallows the last of his bun and gets out of the car. He's dressed in jeans and a sheepskin jacket and looks rather like a successful football manager. A curly-haired dog is sitting in the passenger seat.

'Ruth. What brings you here?'

'I've come to collect my Christmas tree.'

Clough laughs. 'Been buying from Leaf, have you? Let me guess who pointed you in his direction.'

Bloody Cathbad. It's only four thirty but it's pitch black and the snow is drifting around the deserted lot. Where is Ruth going to find her perfect Christmas tree now?

'What happened to Leaf?' she asked.

'He was selling without a licence,' says Clough. 'Got a tip-off that we were on our way and did a runner. Trees, girlfriend, mood music and all.'

'What about my tree?' says Ruth. 'I'd already paid him.'

Clough smiles pityingly. 'He'll be halfway to Glastonbury by now.'

176 • ELLY GRIFFITHS

Ruth sighs. She has to pick Kate up at five. Where is she going to find a tree between here and the childminder's house? She asks Clough.

'Try the garden centre. They've got some nice ones there. Trace and I can't risk a tree this year, what with Chummy there.'

He indicates the dog, who is grinning out of the half-open car window. 'He chewed up our new leather sofa last week. Trace wasn't best pleased.'

Ruth drives home through the slanting snow feeling resentful about Cathbad, Christmas and druids everywhere. Ruth lives on a beautiful but lonely stretch of coastline known as the Saltmarsh. There are three cottages in the row but two are currently empty; one is a holiday home only occupied for a couple of weeks a year, the other belongs to an Indigenous Australian called Bob Woonunga, who is currently stretched out on a beach in North Stradbroke Island. But, as Ruth approaches, the security light flares into life, almost shockingly bright, and Ruth sees a figure silhouetted against her front gate. The figure, looming out of the swirling snow, looks sinister in the extreme, cloaked and hooded like the grim reaper, but Ruth finds herself smiling in mingled exasperation and pleasure. Cathbad.

As soon as she has parked, Cathbad appears at the

RUTH'S FIRST CHRISTMAS TREE · 177

car window, smiling at Kate who is sitting in her baby-seat next to a rather scruffy-looking Christmas tree.

'I've got a bone to pick with you,' says Ruth.

'Interesting phrase,' says Cathbad, brushing snow off his hood. 'A bit like "bone of contention". Why is it always bones, I wonder?'

At another time, Ruth, whose expertise is bones, would be happy to discuss this point, but now all she can think about is her perfect Christmas disappearing on the back of a caravan together with Leaf and Raindrop.

'Your druid friend disappeared with my tree,' she says.

'But you've got a tree,' says Cathbad, pulling faces at Kate.

'Tree! Tree!' shouts Kate.

'This is a second-best tree from the garden centre,' says Ruth. 'My first tree was special. Apparently the goddess of the forest had breathed on it.'

'That's certainly special,' agrees Cathbad. 'Do you want a hand getting this one out of the car?'

Together they haul the tree out of the car and, in a reasonably short time, it is installed in Ruth's untidy sitting room. Flint comes up and sniffs it suspiciously.

'Shall we decorate it?' says Cathbad. 'Have you got any decorations?'

'Yes,' says Ruth proudly. 'I bought them last week.'

178 · ELLY GRIFFITHS

She has even bought fairy lights—tiny lanterns in red, green and gold—tinsel and a box of baubles.

'People say the idea of putting up a Christmas tree originated in the nineteenth century,' says Cathbad, selecting a golden Santa from the box, 'but it's far older than that. It's linked to the pagan tradition of the Donar Oak.'

'What's the Donar Oak when it's at home?' asks Ruth, handing Kate a string of tinsel.

'It's a legendary oak tree sacred to the Germanic tribes,' says Cathbad. 'Also called Thor's Oak. Donar probably comes from the German word for thunder, "*donner*".'

'Isn't that one of Santa's reindeer?' says Ruth, rescuing Flint who has become entangled in the tinsel. She helps Kate twine the sparkly thread through the branches.

'Yes.' Cathbad grins. 'Dasher and Dancer, Donner and Blitzen. It's all linked. Anyway, when St Boniface came to convert the German tribes, he chopped down the Donar Oak. When he wasn't killed by a thunderbolt, they all converted to Christianity.'

'What a shame,' says Ruth, who has taken a dislike to the show-off saint. 'He sounds as if a bolt of lightning would have done him the power of good.'

'There's a Christian link too,' says Cathbad. 'The evergreen tree symbolises eternal life. In medieval times

RUTH'S FIRST CHRISTMAS TREE · 179

it was sometimes called the Paradise Tree.' He holds up a decoration in the form of an apple. 'The apples are meant to remind you of the Garden of Eden.'

'They just remind me of apples,' says Ruth. She has little patience with Christian symbolism. 'Trees are important to druids too, aren't they?' She is thinking of Leaf and Raindrop. Despite everything, she hopes the police don't catch up with them.

'Yes. The word druid comes from a Celtic word meaning "knowing the oak tree". It survives in Irish place names like Derry and Kildare. Kildare means "church of oak".'

Ruth knows that Cathbad was brought up in Ireland, otherwise his past is as mysterious as the origin of the Christmas tree. They met nearly thirteen years ago when Ruth was excavating a wooden henge found on the beach at the Saltmarsh. Cathbad and his fellow druids were protesting about the removal of the timbers. They were meant for the open air, they said, for the wind and the rain, part of the ebb and flow of the tide. But the authorities had prevailed and the remains of the henge are kept in controlled conditions inside a Norfolk museum. Looking at Cathbad now as he carefully sorts through the baubles, Ruth feels a surge of affection for him. They have been through a lot together, one way or another.

'Of course,' he is saying, 'trees are important in all

religions. Christ was killed by being hung on a tree. And Odin sacrificed himself on the world tree.'

'Yggdrasil,' says Ruth. She remembers another henge discovered nearby that had a tree buried upside down in the middle of it. Archaeologists had thought at the time that this might represent Yggdrasil, the great ash that, in Norse mythology, links heaven and hell.

'I must go to the museum,' she says. 'I haven't seen the henge for ages.'

'I was there the other day,' says Cathbad. 'Do you remember old Driffield, the curator?'

Ruth remembers a gentle old man who had made the installation of the henge timbers a more tranquil process than they had feared.

'Dear old Driff. How is he?'

'Not well.' Cathbad looks away. 'He's in hospital with pneumonia. Doesn't look good at his age. They lost some of the wood from the henge, you know. I think it's linked to his illness.'

Ruth stares at Cathbad. Just when he's being fairly normal, he comes out with something like this.

'What do you mean "linked to his illness"?'

'There are lots of stories about men's lives being linked to trees. Take the Egyptian *Tale of Two Brothers*. One brother leaves his heart in an acacia tree and, when it's cut down, he dies.'

RUTH'S FIRST CHRISTMAS TREE · 181

'He leaves his heart in an acacia tree?'

'It's just one example,' says Cathbad, rather huffily. 'There are lots of others. People hang gifts from the branches of trees as offerings to the gods. Garlands and ribbons are tied to trees to bring good luck. Think of "Tie a Yellow Ribbon Round the Old Oak Tree".'

'I try not to,' says Ruth. 'You think Driff is ill because some of the henge timber went missing? How did that happen anyway?'

'They had a big conference, lots of bigwigs there, including your boss Phil. They were looking at the timbers and, when they came to put them away, a tiny piece was missing. Driff was really upset. Thought it was all his fault. The next day, he got ill.'

Ruth is registering the fact that she didn't know about this conference whereas Phil, who was not even involved in the henge dig, was evidently a guest of honour. She is so deep in thought that she hardly notices Cathbad and Kate placing the star on top of the tree.

'Shut your eyes,' orders Cathbad.

She does so and, when she opens them, the room is in darkness apart from the little golden tree, a glittering offering to the Christian and pagan gods, spreading its laden branches in benediction.

'It's beautiful,' she says.

Ruth offers to make a cup of tea but Cathbad says that he has brought some wine.

'We could have mulled wine. It's traditional, after all.'

Ruth and Cathbad go into the kitchen. Cathbad has even brought his own spices which is a relief as Ruth's spice rack contains only some ancient curry powder and half a jar of dried basil. She feels quite triumphant, though, that she's able to brandish the luxury mince pies.

'Great,' says Cathbad. 'Let's heat them up.'

It is so cosy in the little kitchen with the wine simmering on the hob and the snow outside that Ruth forgets to check on Kate. The result of this negligence is that when Ruth and Cathbad go back into the sitting room, bearing the wine and mince pies, the Christmas tree is lying on the floor surrounded by broken baubles and Kate and Flint are sitting in the middle of the chaos wearing tinsel crowns and identical expressions of satisfaction.

23 December

In the morning the snow has gone but the wind is still howling around the house, blowing the letter box inwards and sending Flint flying through his cat flap in

RUTH'S FIRST CHRISTMAS TREE · 183

a ball of outraged fluff. In the bleak midwinter, thinks Ruth, frosty winds made moan. What a dismal carol that is. She is planning a day of domestic goddessery. She doesn't have to go into work and she wants to have the house all ready for Max's arrival tomorrow. She doesn't know exactly when he is coming, Max just said 'Christmas Eve morning', but she doesn't want to get caught unprepared. Also she doesn't think she'll feel like housework tomorrow, after a late night at Shona and Phil's party. No, Max must find a house smelling of pine needles and clean linen, with logs on the fire and gifts on the tree. Damn, now she's got that Cliff Richard song on her brain. Anyway, gifts on the tree are out of the question now. Still, some degree of Christmas spirit is still achievable. She decides to make a list.

Over breakfast, spooning porridge into Kate and trying to keep Flint off the table, she writes:

> *Make beds*
>
> *Tidy sitting room*
>
> *Wrap Christmas presents*
>
> *Make gingerbread men*
>
> *Ring Mum and Dad.*

She hasn't got any wrapping paper so the presents will have to wait. The sitting room is still covered in pine needles and broken baubles. She decides to make the beds.

It's quite a jolly morning. There is Christmas music on the radio and Ruth sings along whilst struggling with sheets and duvet covers. Kate helps delightedly, rolling on the discarded bedding. Flint waits until the pristine new sheets are in place before jumping on the bed and starting a thorough all-over clean. Ruth chases him away. Looking at the bed in all its cream and white glory reminds her that, tomorrow, she'll be sleeping there with Max. It still feels rather wicked to be having sex in a house that also contains Kate and Flint. She has now officially moved Kate's cot to the spare bedroom but she knows that it's only a matter of time before Kate joins Ruth and Max in the double. How will Ruth feel about that? Kate sleeping between her mother and her mother's boyfriend. It all feels rather decadent and uncomfortable. She wonders what Nelson would think and quickly brushes the thought aside. Nelson has no right to think anything. He is free to roll around with Michelle on their matrimonial king-size. Don't think about that.

She makes the spare room bed as well in case she ends up sleeping there with Kate.

RUTH'S FIRST CHRISTMAS TREE · 185

Downstairs she makes coffee and listens to the Christmas serial on Radio 4. It's an updating of *A Christmas Carol* about a female city banker called Mrs Scrooge. Tiny Tim is an asylum seeker called Tiny Tonderai. Ruth is ashamed to find tears in her eyes when Mrs Scrooge buys a vegetarian Christmas banquet for Tonderai's family. She must remember to get the turkey out of the freezer in time.

The postman brings more cards and an Amazon parcel from Simon, Ruth's brother. Ruth peeps inside and sees the latest Val McDermid. Three cheers for Simon. The postman hovers and shuffles on the doorstep until Ruth remembers his Christmas tip. She hastily shoves a fiver in an envelope and takes it out to him.

'Thanks very much, love,' says the postman, who dreads the daily trek out to the Saltmarsh. 'A very merry Christmas to you.'

Ruth clears away the broken decorations and puts the tree by the back door. It looks rather sad standing there, shorn of all its finery. So much for Ruth's first Christmas tree. Kate seems upset too. She keeps trying to put the star back on.

'Star! Star!'

'Maybe next year, Kate.'

Ruth gets out her recipe book and looks doubtfully at the instructions for gingerbread men. Although she loves buying cookery books she's not really much of a chef. And she's not sure if she even likes gingerbread anyway. She just likes the idea of baking something, decorating the gingerbread men with chocolate button eyes and icing sugar clothes. But where the hell is she going to find chocolate buttons or icing sugar. The nearest shop is five miles away and she doesn't feel like going out. It's bad enough that she has to go out this evening. She shuts the book. Both Kate and Flint are staring at her.

The phone rings. It's Clara, Ruth's babysitter. She's so sorry but she has flu and doesn't think she'll be able to make it tonight. Ruth sympathises but she does wonder whether Clara had just had a better offer. It's not much fun for a young woman to spend the night before Christmas Eve babysitting in the middle of nowhere. For a glorious few minutes she contemplates skipping the party altogether. After all, she has a genuine excuse now. She imagines sitting down with a mince pie and the remains of the mulled wine and watching *Miracle on 34th Street*. But Shona would never forgive her. She keeps saying that this party is her last fling before the baby is born (Shona and Phil are expecting their first child in March) and has twice rung to check that Ruth will be coming. Sighing, Ruth dials Cathbad's number.

Cathbad says that he will be delighted to babysit. He says that he can be there at six.

RUTH'S FIRST CHRISTMAS TREE · 187

'I'm going to visit Driff at the hospital but visiting ends at five and I'll be straight over.'

'How is he?'

'Not good. He's got a chest infection which is the worst thing possible. I spoke to his daughter last night and they're all really worried.'

'Any sign of the missing wood?' asks Ruth, more to distract him than anything.

'No,' says Cathbad. 'Apparently it was a small piece of oak. It's valuable because it was part of an axle; there's a square hole in it that would have been where the linchpin fitted.'

'Are they sure it's not at the museum? Those places can be very shambolic.' Ruth is thinking of the Smith Museum in King's Lynn, a place where, until recently, chaos reigned supreme.

'Not this museum. It's all very high tech. The timbers are all kept in water tanks to stop them drying out. Then they're frozen or preserved in wax. Driffield's piece of wood could be dying.'

'Dying?' This seems a melodramatic choice of word, even for Cathbad. Ruth takes an involuntary glance at the drooping tree by her back door.

'If it's left without treatment it'll disintegrate altogether.'

'But I thought you wanted the wooden posts left

188 · ELLY GRIFFITHS

where they were, they would have disintegrated eventually if they were left in the open air.'

'Yes,' says Cathbad, 'but that would have been a natural process, part of the cycle of nature. But for a piece of wood just to be lost like that. It's all wrong. These were sacred timbers. You remember what Erik used to say? "Wood represents life; stone is death."'

Ruth doesn't argue because she is grateful to Cathbad for offering to babysit. Besides, she knows what he means. She will never forget her first sight of the henge, rising up out of the flat landscape like some prehistoric monster. Erik, the archaeologist in charge of the dig, had fallen to his knees in the centre of the circle. 'Sacred ground,' he had said. She remembers, too, Erik's thoughts on wood and stone. 'Our journey is from the flesh of the body to the wood of the coffin to the stone of the tomb.' She shivers. She doesn't want to talk about Erik, whose ghost still haunts her.

'I hope Driffield feels better soon,' she says.

After that, the day goes downhill somewhat. Ruth rings her mother to be told how sad it is that she's not coming home for Christmas. 'Simon, Cathy and the boys have just arrived. They're asking for their auntie Ruth.' Ruth doubts this, her nephews have reached

RUTH'S FIRST CHRISTMAS TREE · 189

the stage when they are permanently attached to wires and communicate only in grunts.

'I'll ring on Christmas Day,' she says. 'I'm going to a party tonight.'

'Oh.' She knows this will intrigue her mother. 'Are you going with Max?'

'No, he's arriving tomorrow.'

'That's nice.' Her mother has met Max and, to Ruth's disappointment, rather approves. 'You must bring him for Sunday lunch one day.'

'I will.'

'Daddy's longing to meet him. We're both praying for you, Ruth.' Significant pause.

'I know. Thank you.'

Ruth can hear her mother's sigh all the way from Eltham. It's not easy having a daughter who's an un-married mother, an atheist unmarried mother at that. Ruth feels sorry for her parents but not sorry enough to shack up with any of the chinless Christians regularly presented for her inspection.

'Kate's really looking forward to Christmas,' she says, to placate her mother who, despite everything, adores her granddaughter.

'I'm sure she is. She'd love the crib at our church. We've got life-size cows.'

'Life-size cows. Wow. Look, Mum, I'd better go. I've got masses to do.'

'Give little Katie a kiss from her grandma.' Like Nelson, Ruth's mother can never call Kate by her plain, unadorned name. It drives Ruth mad.

'Of course I will. Bye, Mum.'

Kate is in the kitchen attempting to pick up the tree. Flint is watching from the window ledge.

'No, Kate. Leave it. We'll have a tree next year, I promise. And life-size cows if you want.'

She makes lunch, tidies the kitchen and embarks on a hunt for wrapping paper. When Cathbad arrives at six he finds Ruth wrapping presents in brown paper. 'I think it looks chic,' she says defiantly.

'And very ecologically friendly,' says Cathbad. 'I make all my own presents out of recycled driftwood.'

Ruth can believe this, having, over the years, received several dream-catchers made from shells, wood and pebbles. But, this year, though Cathbad has delivered a large present for Kate, there doesn't seem to be anything for her, recycled or not.

'When are you leaving?' asks Cathbad.

'In half an hour,' says Ruth. 'Shona said to get there for seven.' She looks doubtfully at her daughter, sitting happily on the floor surrounded by brown paper. 'I'm sure Kate will be tired soon.'

'Don't worry,' says Cathbad. 'I'm good at getting her to sleep.'

This is true. Cathbad's Celtic lullabies have an almost narcotic quality. Ruth feels pretty tired herself. How soon can she leave the party?

'I won't be late back,' she says.

'Be as late as you like,' says Cathbad. 'Enjoy yourself. It's Christmas. '

As soon as Ruth arrives at the party, she realises that enjoying herself is out of the question. For a start, Shona, who begged her to arrive early 'so I'll have someone to talk to', is already at the centre of a laughing, champagne-swilling crowd and hardly has time to acknowledge Ruth's presence. 'Get yourself a drink, Ruth. You know where it is.' Grimly, Ruth pours herself some orange juice. She can't afford even one drink if she has to negotiate the Saltmarsh road in the dark. And more snow is forecast.

Ruth wanders into the sitting room and looks round for someone to talk to. She recognises a lot of faces from the university but most people have brought their partners. She can't just insert herself into a circle and disrupt the cosy couples' chat about schools and house prices. Besides, Shona's friends from the English department are all so glamorous and

192 · ELLY GRIFFITHS

theatrical. On Ruth's left a beautiful Indian woman is holding forth on ritual and symbolism in the plays of Edward Bond. Wasn't Bond the one who wrote a play where they stone a baby to death? Hardly very Christmassy. Maybe Ruth should butt in and talk about Tiny Tonderai.

'Hi, Ruth.' Ruth turns in relief and sees Bob Bull-more, a colleague in the archaeology department, re-assuringly scruffy in jeans and an unravelling grey jumper.

'Hi, Bob. Enjoying the party?'

'I'm not really one for the beautiful people,' says Bob. 'I don't even like champagne. I brought some home-made cider but Phil looked as though I was trying to poison him.'

Ruth laughs. The pretensions of the head of the de-partment are a continual source of entertainment to his team.

'He's joined the arts crowd now,' says Ruth. 'He's even wearing a velvet jacket.'

'I know,' says Bob in awe. 'Sybil thought he was wearing lifts. I'm sure he's a good few inches taller than he used to be.'

They look across the room to where Phil is laughing heartily with two arty types dressed entirely in black. He is certainly walking tall these days. Maybe it's the

RUTH'S FIRST CHRISTMAS TREE · 193

joy of impending fatherhood, maybe it's pride at having the beautiful Shona as his partner. Or maybe it's heels after all.

'Where's Sybil?'

'She got trapped in the kitchen talking about phonics. She didn't really want to come tonight. Thought it would be disloyal to Sue.'

Sue is Phil's ex-wife, with whom he already has two children. Ruth never really liked Sue but she does feel that it's slightly sinister, the way she's been completely erased from the picture. Phil talks about the coming child as if he's never known parenthood before and the years with Sue have vanished as if they have never been. It's not a good sign when an archaeologist starts to rewrite the past.

'Does Sybil still see Sue?' she asks. She likes Sybil, a cheerful primary school teacher (hence the phonics discussion), and can't really see that she has much in common with Sue, whose main topic of conversation seemed to be aromatherapy oils.

'Sometimes,' says Bob, trying to eat a falafel and balance his glass at the same time. 'Sue's still really bitter about . . .' He inclines his head towards Phil, now throwing his head back in riotous mirth.

'I'm not surprised,' says Ruth. She thinks of Michelle and Nelson. If Nelson ever left Michelle for her, the guilt would be unbearable. But Nelson would never leave his wife and that, too, sometimes feels unbearable.

'How's Kate?' asks Bob. 'She must be growing up quickly.'

'She's just over a year old.' Ruth is grateful for the change of subject. 'How's . . .' She can't remember the names of Bob's children. Luckily, he can.

'Sam's in sixth form. Becca's at Sussex, reading Sociology. Libby's in her last year at Sheffield.'

'Do any of them want to be archaeologists?'

'God, I hope not.' Bob looks almost guiltily round the room. 'Why would anyone do a backbreaking job that pays hardly any money?'

Why indeed? thinks Ruth. She just knows that, despite the lack of money and the days spent digging in the freezing cold, she would never do anything else.

'How's your friend?' asks Bob. 'The warlock in the chemistry department.'

'Cathbad? He's babysitting.'

Bob looks suitably discomforted. Ruth takes pity on him. 'Cathbad's Kate's godfather. He's really good with her.'

Bob is obviously trying to think of something to say and is saved by the appearance of Shona, a vision in a gold smock and lots of dangly jewellery.

'Ruth! So this is where you've been hiding.'

RUTH'S FIRST CHRISTMAS TREE · 195

A remark which, like many of Shona's comments, combines to make Ruth feel both childlike and stupid. She hasn't been hiding, she is simply chatting with a workmate, and it was Shona who ignored her in the first place. Still, she knows that there's no point in saying any of this.

'Hi, Shona. You look great.'

'Thanks. I feel like a whale. A great big golden whale. Did you feel like this in the last months?'

I feel like that all the time, Ruth wants to tell her. Instead she says, brightly, 'Not long now. Are you all prepared?'

'Almost. Do you want to see the baby's room?'

Before Ruth can answer, Shona has dragged her away without a word to Bob. Ruth mouths 'bye' over her shoulder.

The hallway and stairs are now full of people. Ruth sees Liam, Shona's ex-lover, as well as Freya, a druid friend of Cathbad's, and several graduate students. For a lunatic moment, she thinks that she sees Erik, though he has been dead almost two years. But it's just another man with long grey hair and a faintly piratical expression. Shona weaves her way through the crowd, kissing cheeks and pressing hands. Ruth plods in her wake, nodding and smiling at people she knows. Surely she can go home soon.

Shona opens the door on a little room at the top of the stairs. 'We were going to use the spare room but Phil needs that for his office. Anyway, this is plenty big enough for a baby. What do you think?'

'Babies have a way of spreading,' says Ruth but she has to admit that the room is beautiful, pale yellow with a frieze of sun, moon and stars. A mobile of glittering birds hangs from the ceiling.

'It's lovely,' says Ruth. 'Perfect for a boy or a girl.'

'Oh, we don't want to know,' says Shona sinking onto a blue velvet chair. 'That would spoil the surprise.'

For Ruth there was enough surprise in getting pregnant in the first place. But thinking of her miracle daughter makes her feel warm towards Shona.

'It's so exciting,' she says. 'Are you excited?'

'Ish,' says Shona. 'I can't really imagine life with a baby. But let's talk about you. Is Max arriving tomorrow?'

'Yes.'

'That's wonderful. Your first Christmas together. Must mean that it's serious.'

'Oh, I don't know,' says Ruth. 'We don't want to rush things.'

Shona laughs. 'You're so cautious. Phil and I knew immediately that we were meant for each other.'

RUTH'S FIRST CHRISTMAS TREE · 197

Despite the fact that Phil was married to someone else, thinks Ruth. Suddenly she doesn't want to discuss Max and, more than anything, she doesn't want to go back downstairs into the glamorous, chattering throng.

'I can't stay long,' she says. 'Kate had a bit of a temperature when I left.' She crosses her fingers behind her back.

Shona immediately looks concerned. 'Oh, I'm sorry. Do you want to ring to see how she is? You can use the phone in Phil's study. It's hard to get a signal here sometimes.'

The spare room, where Ruth has spent many a night, has also been completely transformed. It is now painted dark red with bookshelves on two of the walls and a serious-looking desk in the centre of the room. Shona backs out tactfully but Ruth feels that she is still honour-bound to make the phone call. She sits in Phil's swivel chair and picks up the receiver. The desk is very tidy, a pile of letters under a paperweight, a blotter, a collection of pens in a silver tankard. No archaeology journals or exam scripts, no to-do list. Ruth suppresses the ignoble thought that Phil doesn't do any real work in here.

Cathbad answers quickly. 'Hi, Ruth. What's up?'

'Hi. Just wondered how Kate was.'

'She's fine,' says Cathbad. 'Fast asleep. Go back and enjoy the party.'

Ruth thinks that she can hear noises in the background. She wonders if Kate really is asleep. 'I won't be late back,' she says.

Putting down the phone, she thinks that she will make her excuses and leave. Pulling aside the expensive-looking brocade curtain, she sees that the snow has started again. The last thing she wants is to get snowed in with Shona and Phil for Christmas. She is just about to leave the room when something makes her look back at the desk. Blotter, pens, phone, letters, paperweight. She moves closer. She sees that what she had taken for an ornamental paperweight is, in fact, a lump of wood—oak, rounded by immersion in water, with a definite square hole where a linchpin would have fitted.

The drive home is a nightmare. The snow is falling heavily now and her windscreen wipers struggle to keep even a patch of clear window. Ruth leans forward, hands tense on the wheel, peering into the night. Her headlights seem only to reflect more snow, the flakes whirling in a funnel of watery light. It's not so bad in King's Lynn, where there are streetlights and other vehicles, buses and taxis looming up with terrifying

RUTH'S FIRST CHRISTMAS TREE · 199

suddenness, but, as soon as she hits the A149 it's a complete whiteout. Back and forth go the gallant little wipers, buckling under the weight of snow. Ruth leans even further forward, she can't see any signs or landmarks. She turns on Radio 4 to give her courage but someone is reading Jo Nesbø's *The Snowman*, which only makes her more frightened. Surely she must be near the Hunstanton turn-off by now? There is something mesmeric about the swirling snow; she imagines herself driving along this road for ever, Norfolk's answer to the *Flying Dutchman*, endlessly circling her destination, never again to reach the comfort of home. Only yesterday she bought one of those snow globes for Kate and had enjoyed seeing the child's face light up when the globe was agitated and the little plastic scene disappeared under the ensuing blizzard. Now it's as if she herself is trapped inside the glass toy, invisible behind the snowstorm. Her nose is almost touching the windscreen now. She's sure that she's missed the turning.

No. Thank God. There it is, mercifully illuminated. Ruth takes the turning wide and continues her painfully slow progress. How does that song go? Driving home for Christmas. Ruth sings a few bars and realises that she is almost crying. She so badly wants to be back in her little cottage with Kate beside her. Why did she ever go to that stupid party? But, beside her, buried in the depths of her organiser handbag, is a piece of wood which, she is almost sure, comes from a Bronze Age henge. Why had Phil taken it? To have a souvenir of the most famous find in Norfolk's history? To say that his correspondence was weighed down by a three-thousand-year-old log? Whatever the reason, Phil had no idea of the importance of the object, not only to the museum but to its elderly custodian, now lying dangerously ill in hospital. Ruth must get the wood back to Cathbad.

Then, suddenly, there's the Saltmarsh roundabout. Ruth drives round it twice before she finds her exit. Nearly there. But this is the most dangerous part of the journey. The road is raised up over the marshes, one false turn of the wheel and Ruth will be in the ditch where she could well freeze to death and be found years later, like Ötzi the iceman, the five-thousand-year-old body found on the Italian–Austrian border. Ruth the ice woman. Frosty the snowman. Nearly there. Driving home for Christmas. Ruth is singing almost manically now. I'm coming, Kate. Mummy's almost home. Christmas time. Mistletoe and wine. In the bleak midwinter. Now she can see the light from her cottage, its flickering glow like a beacon in the darkness. Flickering? Why the hell is it flickering? Ruth feels a new panic overtaking her as she parks by the gate. There is definitely something odd about the light. What's happening in her house?

She flings open the door and stands, transfixed, on the doorstep. The room is lit by dozens of candles and there, illuminated in the golden light, are Cathbad and Nelson and, hanging from a ceiling, an upside-down Christmas tree, twinkling with lights and hung with apples, oranges and stars.

'It's Yggdrasil,' says Cathbad. 'We thought, if it's up high, Kate and Flint won't be able to get at it.'

'It's amazing,' says Ruth, coming closer. 'How did you get it up there?'

'By ropes and pulleys,' says Nelson. 'Took us ages.'

'Lucky Nelson arrived when he did,' says Cathbad. 'I couldn't have managed it by myself.'

'I came to drop off some presents,' says Nelson. He gestures towards two rather clumsily wrapped parcels. One is addressed to Kate and one to Ruth.

'That's so kind of you,' says Ruth. She is afraid that she's about to cry.

'I made new decorations because yours got broken,' Cathbad explains. 'They're mainly dried fruit and paper. We wanted to make it special because it's your first Christmas tree.'

'It is special,' says Ruth. 'It's unique.'

'It has turned out rather well.' Cathbad looks modest. 'How was the party?'

'Dreadful,' says Ruth. 'Phil was wearing high heels.'

'I always knew he was weird,' says Nelson. 'Bet there wasn't even any decent beer.'

'Mainly champagne,' says Ruth. 'Bob Bullmore brought some home-made cider.' Nelson shudders. 'But I only drank orange juice.'

'Well, let's have a drink now,' says Cathbad. 'I've made some more mulled wine. Do you want some?'

'That would be lovely,' says Ruth, sinking down on the sofa, still staring up at the tree. 'I've got something for you.' And she takes the piece of wood out of her bag.

Much later, when Cathbad and Nelson have gone home, Ruth is still sitting and staring at the tree. The snow has stopped but it's still lying thick on the ground, deep and crisp and even. Nelson was confident that his heavy Mercedes could cope and he has taken Cathbad with him. Cathbad is planning to visit Driffield tomorrow, taking with him the missing piece of Bronze Age wood. 'He'll get better now. I'm sure of it.' Ruth hopes so. Even if the wood itself doesn't have special powers, she is sure that Cathbad's powerful conviction will go a long way towards healing his friend. Maybe that's what shamanism is all about. It's enough that someone, somewhere, genuinely believes that the magic will work.

Will Max be able to drive up from Brighton tomorrow? Ruth doesn't know and, at the moment, she doesn't care. All she can think of is that Nelson left his family to drive through the snow to bring her a present. She looks at the parcel, sitting under the inverted tip of the tree. It's small and irregular. It could be jewellery or an ornament of some kind. It could, knowing Nelson, be a tiny toolkit for the car. At the moment, she has no desire to open it. She too wants a surprise on Christmas morning. Still, she'd better hide the parcels before she goes to bed. Kate could never be persuaded to wait before tearing off the paper. But with age comes patience. Ruth is quite prepared to wait, looking up at her wonderful Paradise Tree, brought to her by ancient magic and the love of friends.

The Stranger
by R.M. Holland

If you'll permit me, said the Stranger, I'd like to tell you a story. After all, it's a long journey and we're not going to be leaving this carriage for some time. Actually, by the look of those skies, we might be here for a while. So, why not pass the time with some story-telling? The perfect thing for a late October evening.

Are you quite comfortable there? Don't worry about Herbert. He won't hurt you. It's just this weather that makes him nervous. Now, where was I? What about some brandy to keep the chill out? You don't mind a hip flask, do you?

Well, this is a story that actually happened. Those are the best kind, don't you think? Better still, it happened to me when I was a young man. About your age.

THE STRANGER BY R.M. HOLLAND · 205

I was a student at Cambridge. Studying Divinity, of course. There's no other subject, in my opinion, except possibly English Literature. We are such stuff as dreams are made on. I'd been there for almost a term. I was a shy boy from the country and I suppose I was lonely. I wasn't one of the swells, those young men in white bow ties who sauntered across the quad as if they had letters patent from God. I kept myself to myself, went to lectures, wrote my essays, started up a friendship with another scholarship boy in my year, a timid soul called Gudgeon, of all things. I wrote home to my mother every week. I even went to chapel. That was why I was surprised to be invited to join the Hell Club. Surprised and pleased. I'd heard about it, of course. Stories of midnight orgies, of bedders coming in to clean rooms and fainting dead away at what they discovered there, of arcane chants from the Book of the Dead, of buried bones and gaping graves. But there were other stories too. Many successful men had their start at the Hell Club, politicians—even a cabinet member or two—journalists, business tycoons. You always knew them because of the badge, a discreet skull worn on the left lapel. Yes, like this one here.

So I was happy to be invited to the initiation ceremony. It was held on October the thirty-first. Hallowe'en, of course. All Hallows' Eve. Yes, of course. It's Hallowe'en today. If one believed in the uncanny one might think that was slightly sinister.

To return to my story. The ceremony was simple and took place at midnight. Naturally. The three initiates were required to go to a ruined house in the college grounds. In turn, we would be blindfolded and given a candle. Then we had to walk to the house, climb the stairs and light our candle in the window on the first-floor landing. Then we had to shout, as loudly as we could, 'Hell is empty!' After all three had completed the task, we could take off our blindfolds and re-join our fellows. Feasting and revelry would follow. Gudgeon . . . did I tell you that poor Gudgeon was one of the three? Gudgeon was worried because, without his glasses, he was almost blind. But, as I told him, we were all blindfolded anyway. A man may see how the world goes with no eyes.

Are you cold? The wind is getting up, isn't it? See how the snow hammers a fusillade against the windows. Ah, the train has stopped again. I very much doubt if we'll get farther tonight.

Some brandy? Do share my travelling rug. I always prepare myself for the worst on these journeys. A good maxim for life, young man. Always prepare yourself for the worst.

THE STRANGER BY R.M. HOLLAND · 207

So, where was I? Ah yes. So Gudgeon and I, together with a third fellow—let's call him Wilberforce—approached the house. Three established members of the Hell Club provided us with blindfolds. They were masked, of course, but we knew some of them by their voices. There was Lord Bastian and his henchman, Clark. The third had a foreign accent, possibly Arabian.

Wilberforce was the first to don his blindfold. He set off, stumbling like a blind man, towards the ruined house. We waited and we waited. The cold November wind roared around us. Like this one, yes. We waited and, after what seemed a lifetime, we saw a candle flickering in the window embrasure. Very faintly, on the night air, we heard, 'Hell is empty!'

We cheered and our voices echoed against stone and silence. Slowly Gudgeon removed his glasses and pulled the blindfold over his eyes.

'Good luck,' I said.

He smiled. Funny, I remember it now. He smiled and made a strange gesture with his hands, splaying them out like a shopkeeper advertising his wares. I can see it as clearly as if he were standing in front of me. Lord Bastian gave him a push and Gudgeon too staggered off over the frosty grass.

We waited and we waited and we waited. A night

208 · ELLY GRIFFITHS

bird called. I heard somebody cough and someone else smother a laugh. I was breathing hard though I scarcely knew why.

We waited and, eventually, a candle shone in the window. 'Hell is empty!' Our answering cheers rang out.

Now it was my turn. I pulled on the blindfold. Immediately the night seemed not just darker, but colder, more hostile. I didn't need Bastian's push to start me on my journey. I was anxious for it to be over. Yet, how long that walk seemed when you couldn't see. I became convinced that I was heading in the wrong direction, that I had missed the ruined house altogether, but then I heard Bastian's voice behind me, 'Straight ahead, you fool!' Stretching my hands out in front of me, I stumbled forwards.

My hands hit stone. I was at the house. Feeling my way along the façade I eventually reached a void. The doorway. I tripped over the doorstep, landing heavily on flagstones, but at least I was in the building. Inside, the wind was less but the cold, if anything, more. And the silence! It echoed and re-echoed around me, seeming to weigh down on me, to press me close to the earth. I knew that I was bending almost double, like a beggar under his sack. I could hear my breathing, jagged and stertorous. It was my only companion as I inched towards the staircase.

THE STRANGER BY R.M. HOLLAND · 209

How many steps? I had been told it was twenty but lost count after fifteen. Only when I stepped on a phantom stair did I realise that I was on the landing. I had thought that Gudgeon or Wilberforce might whisper a greeting but they were silent. Waiting. I edged forwards. I had to find the window and bring this pantomime to an end. My hands swept the plaster of the wall in front of me until . . . there! . . . I found the wooden sill. My fingers shook as I lit my candle but, somehow, I managed to drip enough wax to stand it upright. I pulled off my blindfold.

'Hell is empty!'

In front of me lay two mutilated bodies.

I heard a scream echoing through the corridors of the deserted house and realised that it was mine. My friend, Gudgeon, lay dead at my feet. Wilberforce was a few yards away, his face ghastly in the flickering light of my candle. I felt for a heartbeat but I knew that there was nothing to be done. Someone, or something, had fallen on these men like a beast from hell and slaughtered them, stabbing them again and again in what could only be described as a frenzy. I was shaking, my candle making wild shapes on the wall, and, for several minutes, was frozen with fear. Because the fiend that had killed my companions was surely close at hand. Would he now descend on me, knife and hands incarnadine?

But *the ruined house was still. I could hear nothing
except the rats scuttling on the floor above. Then, from
outside, I heard a cry. 'What's happening in there?'
Then Clark, Bastian and the third man came running
up the stairs. I still held the candle and their first sight
must have been my ashen face, illuminated by the spec-
tral light, before the true horror of the scene unfolded
itself.*

*I will draw a veil—no, not a veil, a heavy curtain—
over what happened next. I wanted to inform the
college authorities but Lord Bastian pointed out that
we would get in trouble, perhaps even be sent down.
Besides, he said, the Hell Club would not be happy if
the news got out. This opinion seemed to carry great
weight with the other two, and they were all senior
men, you must remember. To cut a long story short,
I was persuaded that the best course of action would
be to leave the dread house and return to college as if
nothing had happened. The bodies would be found, of
course, and there would be an enquiry but we would
deny any knowledge of the events. We would never
speak of this night again.*

*'We must swear,' said Bastian and, to my horror, he
knelt down and pressed his hand into one of Gudgeon's
open wounds.*

'Swear,' he said. 'Swear on his blood.'

THE STRANGER BY R.M. HOLLAND · 211

Can you imagine the scene? The candlelight, the wind outside now rising to a crescendo, Bastian standing there with Gudgeon's blood dripping from his fingertips. We were all half-mad, that's the only way I can explain it. One by one we touched the pool of blood on Bastian's palm as if passing the holy water stoup in a Roman church.

'I swear,' we said, one after another. 'I swear.'

Ah, my dear young man, there's no need to look so alarmed. Time passed, as it must always do. The bodies were discovered. There was a police enquiry but no murderer was ever found. No one ever asked me about my movements that night. The junior dean made a point of consoling me over my friend's death and I said, truthfully, that I was devastated. He sympathised but quoted a chilling little epithet from Homer, doubtless intended to foster a stoical spirit. Be strong, saith my heart, I am a soldier. I have seen worse sights than this. And it was over. Consummatum est.

Or so I thought.

Listen to *the wind howling. It seems to rock the train, does it not? We're quite safe here though. After all, there's no connecting door between the carriages. No one can come in or out. More brandy?*

What happened next? Well, the prosaic truth is:

nothing much to speak of. Gudgeon's parents took his body away and he was buried at his home in Gloucestershire. I didn't attend. I don't know what happened to Wilberforce. The police never found their killer and, a year later, the ruined house was demolished. I continued my studies. I think I became quite solitary and strange. Other students would look at me oddly as I crossed the quad or sat in the dining hall. 'That's him,' I heard someone whisper once. 'The other one.' I suppose I became 'the other one' to most men in Peterhouse, possibly even to myself.

I didn't see much of Bastian or Clark. I was now officially a member of the Hell Club but I didn't attend their meetings or the infamous Blood Ball, which was held every year. I spent most of my time in my rooms or in the library. My only contact with my fellow students was with members of the shooting club. With them, at least, I managed some uncomplicated, comradely hours.

I graduated with a first, which was gratifying. I had heard that Lord Bastian had been sent down and that Clark did not complete his degree. But they were at different colleges and our paths had long since diverged. I began to read for a doctorate, continuing with the solitary, bachelor existence that I had established in my undergraduate days.

Then, in my first term as a postgraduate student, I

THE STRANGER BY R.M. HOLLAND · 213

received some rather strange correspondence. It was November, a bitterly cold day, and I remember the frost crunching under my feet as I walked to the porters' lodge to collect my post. Not that I ever received many letters. My mother wrote occasionally and I subscribed to a couple of scholarly theological journals. That was it. But on this day there was something else. A letter with a foreign postmark, inscribed in a strange, slanting hand. I opened it curiously. Inside was a cutting from a Persian newspaper. I did not, of course, understand the Cyrillic script but there was a translation, written with the same italic pen. It said that a man called Amir Ebrahimi had been killed in a freak accident involving a hot air balloon. The ascent had gone perfectly but, at some point during the flight, Ebrahimi had fallen from the basket underneath the balloon and had plummeted to his death. I turned the letter over in my hands, wondering why someone would have thought that I would be interested in this gruesome event. It was then that I saw the words written on the reverse of the paper. Hell is empty. And I remembered that Ebrahimi had been the name of the third man, the companion of Bastian and Clark.

The other one.

Of course Ebrahimi's death was a terrible shock. I remember standing there with the newspaper cutting in my hand, then going back to my rooms, lying down on my bed and shaking. Who had sent me the fateful papers? Who had written the translation with that slender, slanting pen? And who had written the words 'Hell is empty' on the reverse? Could it be Bastian? Or Clark? It seemed impossible but who else could possibly have known about the Hell Club and that terrible night?

I pondered these questions over the next few days. Indeed, I thought of little else. But in the end, I pushed my fears away and carried on with my life. After all, what else could I do? And I was young, I had my health and my strength. You understand, my dear young friend? Yes, I see that you do. Youth is arrogant, which is as it should be. I was sorry that Ebrahimi was dead—and I sincerely mourned my friend Gudgeon— but there was nothing that I could do to bring them back to life. So I continued with my studies and even began to court a young lady, the daughter of my tutor. Life was sweet that spring, perhaps all the sweeter for the thought that I had escaped from the pall of death. For, at that time, I believed that I had escaped.

How the wind howls.

'What happened next?' Ah, the perennial, unanswered question. That is the very essence of narrative,

THE STRANGER BY R.M. HOLLAND · 215

is it not? 'Please read another page,' begs the child at night-time. Anything to ward off the horrors of the dark. And you have not long left childhood behind yourself, my dear young friend. It is only natural that you should want to know what happens in the next chapter.

Another year passed. I became engaged to Ada, the daughter of my tutor. I started work on my thesis which dealt with the Albigensian heresy. I taught undergraduates too, though, in truth, I was a solid and uninspiring lecturer. I heard them whispering about me sometimes, caught the words 'Hell Club' and 'murder'. But I chose to dwell in the light that year. And I acquired a companion. Yes, the very animal that you see before you in this train carriage. My dog, Herbert. What a friend dear Herbert has been to me in my trials. Truer and more steadfast than any human acolyte.

Autumn passed and with it Hallowe'en. I confess I breathed a sigh of relief when the dread day passed without incident. But, then, several weeks later, I heard the bedders talking in the corridor and caught the name 'Clark' and the word 'killed'.

I burst out of my room and demanded, with a passion that surprised them, 'What are you talking about?'

'Mr Clark, from King's, as was, sir,' came the reply. 'We were talking about the way he died. So unnatural.'

'What happened?' I said, aware that a coldness had swept over me. Clark, the companion of Lord Bastian, had been a student at King's.

'He was killed, sir. He was driving his own carriage across the fens. He set off from Ely, as right as rain, heading for Cambridge. No one knows what happened but his horse was found a day later, running wild, still harnessed to the carriage. A search party was sent out and Mr Clark was found in a ditch. His throat had been cut, sir.'

'When was this?'

The older of the two bedders answered me. 'It was on Hallowe'en night, sir. I remember because Bert, who was one of the searchers, said it fair chilled the blood to see the horse galloping on his own as if the hounds of hell were after him.'

It was another week before the newspaper cutting reached me. 'Cambridge man found murdered on the fens.' And scrawled across the headline the handwritten words, 'Hell is empty.'

I broke off my engagement to Ada. I wasn't fit company for any decent person. I kept to my room, ostensibly working on my thesis but, in fact, writing the story

THE STRANGER BY R.M. HOLLAND · 217

with which I am now regaling you, my dear young friend. About the Hell Club and Hallowe'en at the ruined house. About the dead bodies and our vow, made in the blood of our comrades. About Ebrahimi and Clark. About the nemesis that seemed to be following me. And, again and again, I wrote the words:

Hell is empty.

When the thirty-first of October came round again, I was a mere shell. I knew people were worried about me. My tutor had tried to talk to me (though he hated me now because of the way I had treated Ada), even the junior dean had gone as far as to request an interview, during which he impressed upon me the necessity of eating well and performing regular exercises. Mens sana in corpore sano. If only he knew the true state of my mind.

All day I waited. I didn't leave my room because I knew that Nemesis would come, locked door or not. I didn't hear the news until the next day, All Saints' Day. I went for a stroll through the town, late at night. I often liked to do this, prowling the silent streets, alone with my thoughts. And, outside St John's, I saw a fellow called Egremont standing there, in the shadow of the lodge, smoking his pipe. I recognised him as a member of the Hell Club but I hurried past, not wanting to get into conversation.

218 · **ELLY GRIFFITHS**

'Hi there,' he called after me. 'You were a friend of Bastian's, weren't you?'

'I knew him,' I said cautiously, although my heart was pounding.

'Have you heard what happened to him? Awful news.'

'No,' I said. 'What has happened to him?'

'I heard it from one of the bedders just now. Bastian was in a train. One of the new sorts with connecting carriages. He was moving from one carriage to another when the train suddenly divided. He was crushed under the wheels. Poor fellow. What a terrible death.'

I looked at Egremont, saw his pale face and the skull's head badge on his lapel.

'When did this happen?' I asked.

'Only yesterday,' he replied. 'I'm sure it'll be in tomorrow's Times.'

But it was a week before the newspaper cutting reached me, with the now familiar addendum.

Hell is empty.

Well, today's the anniversary of that day and I'm the only one left. What a strange thought that is. What sprits, malign or otherwise, have brought me to this pass and this moment? And yet, despite everything, I am not unduly disturbed. After all, I am not about to go up in a hot air balloon or attempt to drive a coach and pair across the fens. I can't plummet from the air or be dragged by footpads from my carriage.

I am in a train, it's true, but I'm not about to leave this carriage.

Ah, my dear young man. How still you are. That was the brandy, of course. Atropa belladonna or Deadly Nightshade. It will give you strange visions, I fear, and your sight will be impaired. I am sure that, even now, I am metamorphosing before your eyes, becoming watery and indistinct. Perhaps I have disappeared altogether. Though who is to say what is real and what is not? As I quoted earlier, a man may see how the world goes with no eyes. How wildly you look at me, your orbs completely black now. But, of course, you cannot move. I am sorry, you know. I wish it didn't have to be this way. But whatever demonic entity it is that demands my blood—the same that has already taken the lives of Gudgeon, Wilberforce, Ebrahimi, Collins and Bastian, so many, alas, so much blood—this creature will not be satisfied until it has garnered another soul. Oh, it wants me, of course. This day, this Halloween night, was meant to be the day of my death. The day of reckoning. Hell is empty and all the devils are here. The ghoul awaits. He is hungry, I hear him in the *howling of the wind and the anger of the storm. But I think it will be satisfied with you, innocent soul that you are.*

Do not fear. The end will be painless. And who knows what will await us on the other side? Perhaps I am simply hastening your journey towards perfect felicity. I hope so. I really do.

Farewell, my dear travelling companion.

What I Saw from the Sky

'Don't ask Leanne, she'll be too scared.'

'Poor girl. She's got enough on her plate.'

That does it. If Ernestine and Bob think that the chairlift to the top of Mount Solaro will be too much for me, then I must do it. My ten-euro menu is churning in my stomach but I am determined. I tuck my hair into my baseball cap and force a cheery ready-for-anything grin.

'I'm up for it. Sounds fun.'

'Are you sure, honey?' says Ernestine. 'After . . . ?'

She obviously doesn't like to mention the moment in Ravello, when the height and dizzying beauty got too much for me and I crouched down, sobbing and hyperventilating. Ernestine helped me to a seat and, under the spotlight of her kindness and curiosity, I admitted that

222 • ELLY GRIFFITHS

I'd come on this holiday because I was recovering from a 'kind of breakdown'. 'I won't tell a soul,' breathed Ernestine, clearly thrilled by the revelation. But I was pretty sure that she'd told Bob, her husband, and Debra, her daughter, not to mention Debra's bovine husband, Ranch, and Bettina, the Swedish woman who seems to have become her best friend for the trip.

Now Debra takes my arm. 'We'll queue up together.'

Don't touch me! I want to scream. Instead I slide my arm out of hers. It's too hot for physical contact anyway. I'm only wearing shorts and a T-shirt and I'm dripping with sweat. Debra favours voluminous dresses and her face is pizza red above her frilly collar. I wonder how she'll cope with her skirt on the chairlift.

The line moves quickly and, as I get closer, I start to regret my decision. The chairlift was closed at lunchtime. 'A fault,' someone whispers and tempers are frayed amongst the passengers and the crew. The chairs really are just that, dangling seats like something from a fairground ride. You have to stand with your back to them and, when they're behind you, the attendants push you in—none too gently—click the bar down and you're off. I watch Ernestine be carried away, an increasingly tiny figure in her red Middlebury College T-shirt. Debra tries to take a photo and the attendant gestures angrily for her to put the phone away.

WHAT I SAW FROM THE SKY · 223

Now it's my turn. I back into the metal cage, the arm comes down and then the ground is falling away, terrifyingly quickly. It's too late to stop the mechanism and this realisation fills me with a panic so intense that I actually consider jumping off. This was all a mistake, I think, a terrible mistake. I'm panting, dissolving. I try to catch hold of myself, to remember the techniques that Holly, my therapist, taught me. Breath in for four, hold for four, out for four. We're climbing higher and higher, the olive trees turning into pot plants beneath my feet. I can see my shadow, very clear in the bright sunlight, growing bigger as it soars over the groves and smaller in the valleys. It's a round trip and, on my left, I can see the returning passengers, looking relaxed and happy, some of them chatting on their phones, seemingly impervious to the fact that they're one hundred metres in the air. My feet are dangling into nothingness and I begin to worry about losing my flip-flops. This anxiety gradually takes away my more pressing fears. It's very quiet up here, the sky so blue and the trees so green. I start to relax, even unclenching my toes.

The bird's-eye view is strangely serene. Below my flip-flops, the occasional advertisement appears, angled to be seen from the chairlift. Olivoncino. The Capri Bell Restaurant. Aperol like a glowing orange sun. There are houses down there too. Holiday villas. I can see a couple having lunch on their terrace, wine and salami, so clear that I can see the gleam of the man's bald patch. Then there's another villa, a terrace with arches and a swimming pool, a shimmering rectangle of blue, and a body floating, face down.

A body . . . I twist round but it's gone. I continue my stately glide towards the mountain top. Ernestine is almost at the platform. She's yanked out of her chair but, when it's my go, I'm ready and I leap out.

'Say,' says Ernestine, breathing heavily. 'That was fun.'

Debra is next, shouting '*ciao*' to the stony-faced attendants. Then Ranch, clutching his camera with both hands, then Bob. We follow the signs to the viewing platform. The sea is far below us, dotted with waves and the sails of fishing boats. Debra and Ranch take a selfie.

'Did you see it?' I say. 'The body in the swimming pool?'

'I didn't see anything but the sky,' says Ernestine.

'Didn't you look down?'

'Honey,' Ernestine squeezes my arm, 'don't look down. Always look up.'

I give up. 'I think I'll go back now.'

'Don't you want an ice cream?' says Ernestine. 'Or

one of those lemon granita things? There's a neat café over there.'

'No thank you,' I say, feeling the panic rising again. 'I just want to go back.'

This time I hold my flip-flops in one hand. In the other I've got my mobile. I'm going to try to take a picture of the swimming pool but my hand is shaking so much that I'm afraid I'll drop the phone. Is this one of the great modern fears? I'm almost more scared of losing my phone than of falling to my death. I clutch its silicone case, the hand with the shoes ready to click the camera icon. I see the house with its archways but the pool seems to have vanished. I twist round in my seat. There's the terrace, where the couple were having lunch, empty now. But no pool full of blue water. I'm too surprised to take a photo and my little chair continues its swinging descent of the mountain.

Mena, our Italian guide, is waiting in the minibus. She's chatting with the driver, Marcello, but stops when I appear in the doorway.

'Everything OK, Leanne?' Her English is excellent.

'Fine. Just a bit hot.'

'I'll switch on the air con,' says Marcello. So is his.

As I sit in the cool recycled air, I think about what I

saw. Was it real, the floating body? It's so clear in my mind. A woman in a red bikini—I can see the strings knotted in the centre of her back—with long brown hair spiralling around her. But is this what Holly meant by a 'delusional perception', something, she informs me, that is quite common in patients suffering from PTSD? But I saw her. I know I did. Below my dangling flip-flop, I can see the advertisement hoarding with the orange Aperol, then the blue rectangle with the body positioned exactly in the middle. But where did it go? How could I have missed it on the return journey?

The others are back, laughing and swinging bags of souvenirs.

'You've missed a darling church,' Ernestine tells me, 'with a floor all made of majolica.'

'I can't see the point of churches,' says Bob. Which is a surprising view for a man who wears a badge asking 'what would Jesus do?'

Mena asks about the chairlift, which she calls a '*funicolare*'. This leads to a chorus of '*funiculi, funiculà*'. Marcello starts the engine and we drive to Capri, where we pick up the rest of the party. Then it's several more hairpin bends and we're at Marina Grande, a heaving mass of sun-burned tourists and stalls selling ice cream and the little bells that are the symbol of the island. I hang back as the others surge forward to get off the bus. For some reason, they always act as if there's a reward for being first. As we leave, I thank Marcello for driving.

'It's my pleasure,' he says, with a little bow.

'Are you from Capri?' I ask.

'Born and bred.'

'I saw some villas up in the hills by Monte Solaro. Do you know anyone who lives up there?'

'Yes. Me. I live there.'

'In one of the villas?'

'No, those are for the tourists. They all want to be high up. I blame Tiberius.'

The name sounds oddly familiar, buried somewhere in my past, but I don't like to ask Marcello to explain. I say '*ciao*' and follow Stu and Donna off the coach. They are a couple from Manchester who never stop holding hands.

On the ferry back to Minori, I manage to avoid the group, who are noisily drinking Aperol spritz in the bar. I go and sit on the deck and watch the lights of Amalfi and Positano come into view. The pastel houses are golden in the twilight, the fishing boats stars in the darkening sea. Stella Maris. Star of the Sea. After Mum died I started seeing signs and portents everywhere. Robins, white feathers, two swans swimming together. But she was called Stella and I can't help thinking of her this evening. She would have loved this trip. Dad thought, and frequently said, that England was good enough for him, but Mum always wanted to travel. Unfortunately Dad's death was followed almost immediately by Covid and lockdown. I couldn't go on holiday with Mum; I couldn't even see her. We did manage a weekend in Rome in 2022 and I have wonderful memories of Mum marvelling at the Coliseum, eating ice cream on the Spanish Steps and throwing coins in the fountain. But she never did get to go back because the cancer was diagnosed only a few weeks later. Italy will always remind me of her, though, and it's partly why I chose this holiday.

Amalfi Adventures it was called, a package deal that in-cluded a three-star hotel, all meals included, and excursions including Pompeii, Herculaneum and the magical island of Capri. The hotel, the Excelsior, is on the cliffs above Minori, a charming town with beachfront cafés, myriad restaurants and a rather grand church. I've got a single room but I'm not complaining because it has a balcony facing the sea. Incidentally, not complaining makes me rather unusual in this group. The list is endless: the mountains are too high, the sea is too salty, it's scary to cross the road, the hot tap is marked C, the bread is all crust and

WHAT I SAW FROM THE SKY · 229

the menus are all in Italian. Apart from my wobble in Ravello, I must be one of the most trouble-free guests. I'm also the only person travelling on my own. 'Go on holiday,' Mum used to say, 'you might meet someone nice.' I thought of her when I paid the deposit. Maybe there would be a bookish librarian with a passion for Italian architecture. A widower with troubled eyes who was looking for someone to make his life meaningful again. I'm only thirty-two yet I was already thinking in those terms.

To take my mind off widowers, I open my laptop and look up 'Tiberius Capri'. I read that Tiberius was Rome's second emperor. Rome was a republic in Julius Caesar's time and JC was killed because it was thought he wanted to become emperor. His death led to civil war and, eventually, Augustus assumed the title. He was succeeded by his stepson, Tiberius. The names sound oddly familiar to me but I never studied Latin or Roman history. My degree is in criminology. I find a website called Veni, Vidi, Vici and it tells me that Tiberius had been a successful general but was a poor head of state. Eventually he withdrew to Capri where he 'revealed the full extent of his depravity'. I read about pornography and sexual perversion until I worry about my search engine. Then I come to the paragraph,

'Tiberius was said to throw his enemies off the cliffs at Capri. Salto di Tiberio, or Tiberius' Leap, is now a well-known beauty spot.' Is that what Marcello meant about the houses high up on the mountain? I think of the girl spread-eagled in the pool. I know that I will be going back to Capri tomorrow.

It's quite different catching the ferry on my own. The rest of the group have gone to Pompeii for the day but I told Mena that I just fancied a quiet day on the beach.

'I don't blame you,' she said. It can't be much fun shepherding fourteen grumpy tourists around Roman remains. Mena is twenty-four. We often sit together at meals—me being the awkward extra, the odd number—and so I know that she's studying law in Naples and that this is her holiday job. Her family are from Minori. She also told me the great secret that her full name is Trofimena, after the town's patron saint.

Travelling on my own makes me feel cool and independent, a rare sensation these days. But once I was what Mum would have called a 'career woman', a crime scene investigator with quite a formidable reputation. I'd been involved in several high profile cases and even had a nickname, 'Lethal Leanne', bestowed because I was adept at establishing cause of death.

WHAT I SAW FROM THE SKY · 231

'It's not right,' said Ernestine, that day in Ravello. 'A young girl like you doing work like that.'

'I loved it,' I said, which was true. Right up to the moment when, a few months after Mum's death, I broke down at a crime scene and screamed that I could see snakes in the victim's hair. A delusional perception, Holly would say, but the trouble is, even now, if I close my eyes, I can see them, dusty scales and glinting eyes.

I sit on the deck again and enjoy the salty breeze. It's another hot day and I'm back in shorts and T-shirt with my pink baseball cap. I think the hat must make me look American because that's what people always assume. When I say I'm British, they look baffled, as if I'm tricking them in some way. I don't even try to say 'Welsh', although that's what I feel.

At Marina Grande, I take a taxi to Anacapri. It's rather a lovely vehicle, open-sided with seats in film-star-blue leather. In the little piazza I see the queues for the *funicolare* and the church. I ask my driver if I can go further up into the hills. 'My friends have got a villa there.'

'What's it called? Villa Caterina?' I say yes, rather desperately, and the driver nods and backs down the hill until he takes a sharp left and we start climbing upwards, zigzagging between lemon trees and olive groves, ripe fruit falling on our roof.

232 · ELLY GRIFFITHS

'Are you American?'

I say 'yes', too terrified, by his driving and the thought of what lies ahead, to explain. He then tells me the plot of an American film he's just seen. I think it's *Oppenheimer*. But it could be *Barbie*.

Eventually he stops. 'Villa Caterina.'

It's so hard to tell but it looks like one of the villas I saw from the air. There's the Aperol advertisement, orange against the cypress trees, and the steps leading up to the terrace. I pay the driver and feel panicky when he thanks me and drives away in a cloud of dust. Then I take a deep breath and knock on the front door. I can hear music playing in the house so I know someone's in but maybe they can't hear me above the grand opera. Eventually the door is opened by a man wearing a polo shirt and chinos and carrying a copy of the *Gazzetta*, the pink Italian sports paper. This throws me. For some reason—perhaps Marcello's comment—I had been expecting a foreigner, an American or multilingual Scandinavian. I blink at him and ask if he speaks English.

'A little.' He has the impatient look of a businessman on holiday. I think his is the balding head I saw from the chairlift.

'Have you . . . have you got a swimming pool?'

WHAT I SAW FROM THE SKY • 233

'A swimming . . . ? Oh, *piscina*. No. Try next door.'

Goodness knows what he thinks I want but the door is closed. I look at the villa next door. It's bigger than the Caterina but it seems to be half-finished. There's a van outside and a pile of rubble where the front lawn should be. Nevertheless I climb the steps and approach the entrance. I can't knock on the door because there isn't one. I call 'hallo?' No answer. I step into the tiled hallway. It's blessedly cool but so dark, after the sunlight, that, for a second, I'm blind and disorientated. Then I hear noises coming from the back of the house. Voices and a radio playing one of Mum's favourite songs, 'Crocodile Rock'. I walk towards the music and soon I'm on a terrace, all dazzling white paint and blue tiles. A voice shouts, 'Can I help you, love?'

This time I'm surprised to hear an English voice. A man, shirtless and tattooed, is walking towards me.

I say, ridiculously, 'I'm looking for a house with a swimming pool.'

The man laughs and two men spreading concrete stop to laugh too.

'Want this one? All mod cons.'

The man makes an expansive gesture and I step towards him. Behind me is the terrace, which is arched like a cloister. These are definitely the arches I saw from the funicular. I look up and there it is, a ski lift in the sky, the little figures with their legs dangling, moving endlessly upwards.

'The pool?'

The man gestures again. In the middle of a tiled patio, a tarpaulin has been pulled back to show a hole, a void, a concrete box that will, at some point in time, become a swimming pool. I step forward and peer into it, as if I can somehow find the water and the floating girl. The bottom of the pool is decorated with a Romanesque mosaic. It awakens a memory that makes me, suddenly, want to cry.

'Are you OK, love?' says the man.

'Yes. I'm fine. It's just . . . I thought . . . I was on the chairlift yesterday . . .' I point upwards. 'I thought I saw a swimming pool, with water in it, and a girl, floating . . .'

'We weren't on site yesterday,' says the man, 'and this pool won't be filled with water until Franco, or whatever his name is, finishes his masterpiece.'

He must mean the mosaic. It's rather beautiful, blue and green, a mermaid surrounded by dolphins and seahorses.

'You should have some water,' says the man. 'You look faint.' I realise that I do feel wobbly. I sit on the ground while the man goes indoors and comes back

WHAT I SAW FROM THE SKY · 235

with a bottle of water. I take a gulp, feel sick and remember to sip.

'Are you all right?'

'Yes. Sorry. Just the heat.'

'It's too bloody hot. Give me Blighty any time.'

'Do you live in Italy?' I ask.

'Nah. This is a holiday job. The owners are a British
couple. From Essex. They don't trust foreign builders,
apparently. '

They sound like my dad. I sense that this man doesn't
share their xenophobia. He says, 'They're the sort that
are always changing their minds. See over there?' He
points to where the men are at work. 'Suddenly he wants
a sundial there. It was meant to be the other side, by the
roses, but all of a sudden, it's on this side.'

'That must be annoying.'

'Oh well. Can't complain. At least we're getting paid
for it. Are you feeling better?'

I stand up. 'Yes. You've been very kind.'

'No problem. Look after yourself, love.'

I'm still holding the water bottle. Outside, I sit on the
low wall and take some steadying sips. A lizard emerges
from under a stone and blinks at me with prehistoric
calm. How am I going to get back to the piazza? The
taxi took about ten minutes but that's at least a half-

hour walk, and in the blistering heat too. Well, I might as well start. I've just taken a few steps, trying to keep in the shade of the scrubby trees, when I hear a motorbike behind me. I flatten myself into the undergrowth but, to my surprise, the engine stops and a voice says, 'Amalfi Adventures?'

It's Marcello, sitting astride a red Vespa and grinning at me.

'I remember you from yesterday,' he says. 'Your pink hat.'

I'm embarrassed by the cap but I can't take it off because my hair will be so sweaty.

'I'm on my way to Marina Grande to pick up the bus,' says Marcello. 'Want a lift?'

So I climb onto the back of the bike and I want to laugh at the absurdity of it all. Me, Leanne Jones, thirty-two-year-old crime-scene investigator, flying through the olive groves with my arms around the waist of a man I hardly know. When we reach the main road, Marcello weaves in and out of the traffic in a way that would terrify me if I didn't feel so insulated from life. The sea sparkles on our left and, on our right, luxury hotels bristle with umbrellas. All too soon we are at the harbour, Marcello cutting between two buses to park his moped by the water's edge.

'How was it for you?'

WHAT I SAW FROM THE SKY · 237

Does he know the potential double meaning implied by this phrase? It makes me blush although my face is probably bright red already so, with any luck, he won't notice.

'My shift starts at midday,' says Marcello. 'Do you want to have a drink?'

He's probably just suggesting it because he's worried I'm going to die of heatstroke, I think. But I follow Marcello to a dark little bar away from the crowds. He orders us *spremuta di limone*, fresh lemon juice and water. It doesn't come in an actual hollowed-out lemon, as it does in the more touristy places, but it's delicious, icy and sharp. Marcello tells me that he's thirty and lived in America for five years (which explains the good English). He studied architecture and has come back to Capri to save the money to take his final exams. He's living with his parents which he describes as 'good but difficult sometimes'. I'm envious. I tell him that both my parents are dead and his dark eyes are instantly sad. 'Do you have brothers and sisters?' he asks. 'No,' I say lightly, 'I'm all alone in the world.' He looks as if he can't imagine this situation. His cousin owns the café, Mena is another relation. Marcello's brother, Antonio, is in the Neapolitan police force. I tell him about my job and, eventually, about the body I thought I saw from the chairlift.

238 · ELLY GRIFFITHS

'It was a woman in a red bikini floating in the water.'

'Like that?' says Marcello. We are walking towards the quay now and I look up at a huge advertisement by the bus station. It's for suncream and it shows a woman in a red bikini floating in a blue swimming pool.

Was that what I saw? I think about this all the way back on the ferry, whilst having lunch at a beach bar and during a peaceful afternoon in my air-conditioned room. Since Marcello pointed it out, I've seen the advertisement everywhere, even on the boat. Did I see the image and somehow superimpose it onto the empty pool? But the woman in the suncream picture is floating on her back, face (presumably slathered in factor 30), tilted towards the sun. My woman was face down, her hair, which has become impossibly long in my memory, floating on the water. I can see it so clearly, the flash of white from the terrace, the blue water below my black flip-flops. But I saw the snakes too, back in Cardiff, at the house where the stabbing happened. The victim, her long red hair turning into writhing snakes, striped orange and white. I think of the mosaic, the mermaid and the seahorses, and that memory slithers over my brain again. It's disconcerting but, somehow, it's also almost comforting.

That night there's a 'Roman Feast' at the hotel, in

honour of the trip to Pompeii. I see Ernestine looking anxiously at the menu: mussels, scallops, pear and gorgonzola, pork belly, fruit salad. I know from experience that Ernestine and Bob suffer from an impressive list of what they call allergies but what really seems to be a preference for a very bland, mostly beige, diet.

'Bob can't eat mussels,' she says to Mena. 'Or blue cheese. Or pork.'

'I'm sure the chef can make you something else,' says Mena.

'Pasta,' says Ernestine. 'We both like pasta.' It is beige, after all.

'Of course,' Mena says to me as Ernestine glides away, 'the Romans didn't have pasta. Marco Polo is said to have brought it back from China.'

'How was Pompeii?'

'It's amazing. They've excavated so much since lockdown but some of the group . . .' she lowers her voice, 'thought it was too hot and they were upset by the pornography.'

'Pornography?'

'The frescos in the suburban baths. Bob said he didn't come to Italy to look at people having sex. Stu and Donna seemed to like it though.'

'Did they hold hands all the time?'

'Every second.'

240 · ELLY GRIFFITHS

Mena seems to think she's gone too far in gossiping about the other members of the party. She switches back into guide mode. 'It's a pity you missed Pompeii,' she says, 'but, if you're interested, did you know there's a Roman villa here in Minori?'

'No I didn't.'

'There's only the lower floor left but there are some interesting . . .' she pauses, thinking of the word, 'relics. It must have belonged to a wealthy family. In the Claudian era.'

'Claudian?'

'In the reign of the Emperor Claudius.'

All through the five delicious courses, I think about her words and, when I'm having a digestion-soothing stroll before bedtime, it comes back to me. *I, Claudius.* A TV programme that Mum used to have on DVD. We'd watch it together. Dad, of course, had no patience with foreign people, especially those that spent their time having orgies and poisoning each other. The names of the emperors come back to me: Augustus, Tiberius, Caligula, Claudius. I remember the title sequence, the Roman letters with Vs instead of Us so that I always called the show I, Clavdivs. A mosaic head with a snake trailing over it. That must be why the mosaic today made me feel both sad and comforted. It reminded me of Mum.

WHAT I SAW FROM THE SKY · 241

Snakes. A woman's hair turning into snakes. The woman in the bikini, face down with her hair spiralling around her. I think of the mosaic mermaid, her hair in wild strands, picked out in tiny tiles, brown against blue. Was it possible that what I saw was a woman face down on the floor of the empty pool? The green and blue tiles had been designed to look like water and could have been covered by the tarpaulin on my return journey. What I had taken for floating hair could have been the mermaid's stone tresses. I have to investigate.

Marcello gave me his phone number. His *cellulare*. I'm nervous about ringing him but, after pacing my room several times, I make myself click on his name. He answers immediately.

'Leanne?'

He must have my name stored too.

'I'm sorry to call so late.' It's only ten o'clock—we eat early in the hotel—but probably too late for a social call. 'You must think I'm mad but I keep thinking about the woman I saw. The woman I thought I saw. Now I'm wondering if it really was a body lying in the empty pool. There was a mosaic . . .' My voice trails away.

Is Marcello going to ring off? Block my number? Implore me to get help? Instead, after a pause, he says,

'I'll go to the house with you but it must be early. I start at nine tomorrow.'

'I'll catch the early ferry.'

'I have a better idea. My friend Davide is a fisherman. He can bring you in his boat. Meet him on the pier at six.'

It feels very daring, sneaking out of the hotel so early. The streets are deserted but, as I near the beach, I see that the sea is already busy. Fishermen are pulling their nets up onto the shore, two women are loading mussels into containers full of ice, a lifeguard is painstakingly sweeping the black sand.

Davide's boat is called *Lady Gaga*. I long to ask him about this but, unlike Marcello, he speaks no English. It's very different being in a speedboat and not the cumbersome ferry. We rise up over the waves and fall into the space created by them. In a few seconds I'm drenched with spray. I wonder why I, who felt scared of a chairlift, should be so exhilarated by this roller-coaster ride. It's like being on the moped with Marcello.

Marcello is waiting at the dock. He and Davide exchange a few sentences in Italian, so fast that the vowels merge into one, and then Marcello is reaching down a hand to help me out of the boat. The marina looks very different without the tourists. The streets have been washed clean and there's a briny smell in the air. Buckets of fish are being unloaded from boats and waiters are putting out tables. Marcello asks if I've had breakfast and, when I say no, he takes me to his cousin's café where we eat delicious croissants, called *cornetti*, and drink tiny cups of coffee. We sit outside although Marcello says that only tourists do this. I can feel the salt drying on my skin. I took my cap off on the boat, to stop it being blown away, and my hair is still wet. I run my hands through it.

'I like your hair,' says Marcello.

It's the first personal thing he's ever said to me and I know I'm blushing again. My hair is very ordinary, shoulder-length and brown, but for a moment I feel like Rapunzel. Next to us, a stallholder is arranging strings of Capri bells and shell necklaces.

'You know the story about the bell?' says Marcello. 'A poor shepherd boy lost his sheep. He was terrified because the sheep was all he and his mother had. He searched everywhere and then he heard a bell ringing. It led him to the top of the mountain where there was an angel, all in gold. It was St Michael. He had the sheep in his arms and he gave the boy a bell. Ring it, he said, and help will always come.'

'I want to buy one,' I say.

'Let me bargain for you,' says Marcello. 'Otherwise the price will go up.'

He talks to the stallholder and comes back with a tiny blue-and-white bell.

'How much do I owe you?'

'It's a present.' He grins. 'Don't worry, I got a good deal.'

I put the bell carefully in my backpack and Marcello says, 'Shall we go and see about this body?'

We ride the moped again and the air is cool and fresh. I know that my hair will be hopelessly tangled but I don't care. Then there are the villas, white against the mountain, the Aperol sign glowing behind them. The shutters are closed in Villa Caterina but the unfinished house is open to the elements. The builders haven't started work yet but, as there's no front door, it's easy to walk straight through. It's very quiet on the terrace. The *funicolare* isn't moving and the neighbours aren't playing their music. The only sound is the cicadas. Bougainvillea hangs down between the arches and the air smells of lemon and lavender. I think how lovely it will be when it's finished. There's an outside kitchen and a shower, even a pizza oven. I imagine sitting here at a long table, eating mussels and fruit, like a Roman Emperor.

WHAT I SAW FROM THE SKY · 245

The pool is covered by the sand-coloured tarpaulin and I can easily see how, from the air, this would have made it disappear altogether. We pull back the cloth and the tiled floor is exposed. The mermaid looks up at me, her hair dark against the blue.

'That's beautiful,' says Marcello. 'I know the artist, Fausto de Angelis. He's quite famous on the island.'

Something about the way he says it makes me think that he doesn't like Fausto much.

There are steps leading into the pool and I climb down, careful not to touch the sides. I'm looking for something, anything, that will prove that a body was once here. Every contact leaves a trace, that's what my forensics tutor used to say. There's a strong smell of bleach in the air and it strikes me as suspicious that this half-finished artwork should have been cleaned so thoroughly. But, if the body had fallen face down onto a hard surface, there would have been blood, and lots of it. I climb back up the ladder and start examining the tiles around the pool.

'What are you looking for?' asks Marcello.

'Blood travels a surprising distance,' I say, 'and bigger drops go furthest.'

I'm aware that I'm talking in a different way and that my movements are swift and decisive. Lethal Leanne is back. At the edge of the patio there's a brown spot that could be significant. Dried blood is surprisingly hard to identify. Under a microscope it's easy because the droplets have a distinctive doughnut-like shape. But I don't have a microscope and I doubt that the police will be interested in one brownish stain. Frustrated, I look back at the terrace. Marcello is sitting by the concrete plinth the men were building yesterday.

'What's the time?' I say. 'Will you have to be at work soon?'

Marcello gets out his phone. 'I can't look at the sundial,' he says, 'because it's in shadow. In fact, it won't ever get sunlight, where it is. The mountain is in the way.'

I stare at him. Who would build a sundial in a place that is always in shadow? I think of the men smoothing the concrete yesterday, the builder saying, 'It was meant to be the other side, by the roses, but all of a sudden, it's on this side.' I say, 'Who asked them to move the sundial?'

It turns out the answer is the mosaicist, Fausto. He told the builders that it was the owners' idea. When the police break up the concrete base, they find the body of twenty-three-year-old Carla Fabri, Fausto's girlfriend. 'She was sunbathing on the terrace while I worked,' he said. 'I went to join her and we started

WHAT I SAW FROM THE SKY · 247

play fighting. She fell in the pool. It was an accident. I panicked.' Fausto may have panicked but his actions tell a different story. He didn't call an ambulance or the police. He pulled the tarpaulin over the pool and, later, buried his girlfriend in the garden, telling the builders to place the sundial over the spot where her body lay. Did anyone see or hear the fight and the fall? The neighbours at Villa Caterina wouldn't have heard anything over *Il Trovatore* and it was Fausto's good luck that the incident happened during the half hour when the chairlift was shut at lunchtime. It was his bad luck, of course, that I was one of the first passengers when it started moving again.

Marcello tells me all this. His brother got the information from the Capri police. It's the first murder on the island since Tiberius, the papers are saying. Marcello thinks that Fausto will plead guilty to manslaughter but that doesn't account for the fact that he left Carla there to die, unseen except for the silent witness up above. 'Silent witness', by the way, is a phrase from a book by the famous American forensic scientist, Dr Paul L. Kirk, describing the traces left by a criminal. 'Wherever he steps, whatever he touches, whatever he leaves, will serve as a silent witness against him.'

On my last night, Marcello and I eat at a restaurant by the beach in Minori. Then we go out on Davide's

248 · ELLY GRIFFITHS

boat. I'll always remember the sea in the moonlight, the waves rocking us gently. It's all I have, except for the little bell hanging on my balcony. I can see it as I look through the files from my latest case. I'm rejuvenated by my holiday, everyone agrees. 'What did you do in Italy?' my boss asks. 'Nothing much. Went on a day trip to Capri.'

As the song goes, I'll never know a better time. Until I visit Marcello in the new year, that is.

Flint's Fireside Tale: A Christmas Story

I expect you've been wondering when you would hear from me. After all, I've been here for everything. I was here when She found the hidden path across the marshes. I was here when my best friend was murdered. I was here when She ran out into the night and didn't come back until the next morning, babbling about underground prisons. I was here when she came home with a child of her own, *The* Child. I was here when the house was being watched by one of the creepiest humans I've ever seen. I was here when The American started visiting with his clothes that smelt of lavender and horses. I liked The American. He was respectful of my space and he made her keep the heating on all night. But I knew that She didn't like him as much as The

Policeman because She didn't give off the same vibrations. The Policeman's all right but recently he's started smelling of dog. I'm not scared of dogs, don't get me wrong, it's just that I find them rather unoriginal.

I've kept my silence through all of these events. Cats are good at that. If, sometimes, the solution was so obvious that I was reduced to clawing the sofa with irritation (this intellectual frustration is often misinterpreted by her), I didn't attempt to point them in the right direction. They wouldn't listen anyhow. The Druid often says that I'm clever but I notice that he rarely asks my advice. This despite being able to speak my language, in a basic kind of way.

The reason I'm speaking to you now is to tell you something that happened last Christmas. It was a mystery and, as usual, I solved it, but something still bothers me about the solution. So I thought I'd share it with you because you know her pretty well by now. And I know how much humans like a ghost story at Christmas.

It was after the time when her friend came to stay, a woman who wore something inexplicably called a dog collar. She had been emotional for some time. You wouldn't know it because She usually looks calm and collected, especially when She is talking about her Work. But, in the evenings, when She sits with me on

FLINT'S FIRESIDE TALE: A CHRISTMAS STORY · 251

the sofa drinking her dark red drink, She is tense and often unhappy. I comfort her as best I can—that's my job after all—but I can't tell her what must be obvious to everyone. The Policeman is never going to live here. His huge Policeman's shoes would hardly fit through the door for one thing. For another, he is too tightly bound to his other life. The one with the dog in it.

These feelings always become stronger when the nights get darker and Christmas approaches. She wants so much for it to be perfect and the rational and irrational thoughts battle in her head until She feels exhausted, irritable and unhappy. At around this time The Mother contacts her a lot. Her voice on the answering machine fills the room when I'm here on my own. I let the words flow over me, 'duty . . . Christian . . . family . . . disappointed', but I wish I could make them disappear so She won't hear them when She comes home and She's at her lowest. The Mother lives far away in a place called El Tham, and the further the better I sometimes think. She loves her mother, though, in that useless way that humans often yearn after the maternal relationship long after it has ceased to be any use to them. Anyway, the plan was that She and The Child would go to El Tham for Christmas and I would be looked after by The Rainbow Man, the rather interesting human who sometimes lives in the house next door and plays music on a strange pipe with deep, dark notes. I don't mind being on my own—I can sleep on all the beds and indulge in my passion for rug-shredding—but I know She doesn't like leaving me, especially at this special, magical, mysterious time of the year.

But, at the last minute, She changed her mind. It was something to do with the words on the machine ('marriage . . . God . . . children need fathers') but She suddenly decided to stay at home. 'It'll be just the three of us,' She told me, 'you, me and Kate.' I was glad that She put me first, something She has often neglected to do since The Child was born. 'We can have a tree,' She said, 'eat turkey, watch terrible films on the television.' I purred encouragingly. I like the tree. It's quite difficult to prise off the baubles and I like to give myself the occasional physical challenge.

The preparations seemed to go well. She got a bit tearful, especially when The Policeman came round with his presents and talked about 'going to the pantomime with Michelle and the girls'. Idiot. Doesn't he realise by now that the name Michelle raises her blood pressure? Apparently not. He also talked about Bruno, whom I take to be his resident canine. He's one of those panting, eager-to-please sheepdog types. I can tell by his smell.

FLINT'S FIRESIDE TALE: A CHRISTMAS STORY · 253

Anyway, it was Christmas Eve. The tree was up, doing its twinkling, symbolic thing. We'd all watched one of those brightly coloured films that The Child likes and she cooked sausages and gave me half of one of my Special Christmas Tins. Earlier that day, The Druid had also come round with presents. Luckily he didn't have *his* canine with him, for a stupider animal I have seldom encountered. He didn't have The Police-woman or The Little Boy with him either and I was sorry about that. I like The Little Boy. He shows definite promise in the art of cat communication.

When She was out of the room making one of her endless hot drinks, The Druid bent down and said to me, 'Look after her. Christmas can be a difficult time.' He said it without words. He's the only human I have ever met who has learnt the rudiments of animal language. It makes me distrust him slightly. I like humans who realise that we are different species. She is perfect in this regard. She loves me and respects me but She doesn't expect to understand me. The Druid always wants to understand everything. It makes him rather tiring company. But I do acknowledge that he's a rather unusual human. Anyway, I assured The Druid (silently) that I would look after her and he put his hand on my head and said, 'May the Goddess bless you, Flint.' Slightly pretentious but there you are.

The Druid had lit the fire for us. It's one of his talents, I must admit. She seems to lack the fire-starting gene and he has it in abundance. So we were all comfortable in the warmth of the flames and I was doing my best to exude protective vibrations while gently kneading the sofa cushions. She'd turned the television off and was trying to say it was bedtime. The Child started saying that she wanted to stay up to see Father Christmas (a mythical figure humans have cobbled together out of a mishmash of Christian and pagan legends). She said that the sooner The Child went to bed the sooner Christmas would come. They were still arguing gently when there was a knock on the door.

The thing is, people don't knock on the door at eight o'clock on Christmas Eve night. She knew that. She stiffened and the hand that had been stroking me tensed and was still. The Child didn't seem to pick up on the atmosphere (though she's normally quite good about that sort of thing). She said, 'Who's that? Is it Daddy?' Daddy is another word that raises her blood pressure.

But maybe She thought it was The Policeman because She got up and went to the door. 'Who is it?' She called, but whoever was outside couldn't hear because it was one of the nights when the wind howls over the Saltmarsh like the wolves from the sea. I went and

FLINT'S FIRESIDE TALE: A CHRISTMAS STORY · 255

stood beside her. If necessary I would throw myself at the intruder. A large cat armed with teeth, claws and intent can do a surprising amount of damage to a hostile human.

She opened the door and there, on the doorstep, was a young woman. I'm not good on human ages so I will just say that she was fully grown but only just, definitely younger than her but older than the boy who delivers our post. She had brown eyes and long brown hair and was shivering, despite being warmly dressed in a coat lined with fake animal fur.

'Sorry to bother you,' she said, 'but my car's broken down. Could I come in and wait for the AA?'

She must have weighed up the dangers and decided that She could overpower The Stranger in a fight. She stepped back and let her in.

'Hallo,' said The Stranger, bending down to stroke me. Now I'm a brave cat but I couldn't help myself. I ran away and hid behind the sofa.

'Flint!' She laughed. 'What are you doing?'

I was embarrassed but I still kept flat to the floor, claws out, eyes as wide as they would go. Why was I so terrified by this apparently innocuous human?

Because she smelt a thousand years old.

She didn't seem to notice. She ushered The Stranger

to the sofa and offered her a cup of hot chocolate. This being accepted, She actually went out of the room and left The Child with The Stranger. Despite my fears I knew what I had to do. I came out of my hiding place and placed myself on the sofa between the two humans. The vibrations between them were so strong that I'm surprised the Christmas tree lights didn't start to flicker.

'What's your name?' asked The Stranger.

'Kate,' said The Child. 'What's yours?'

'Perdita,' said The Stranger after a tiny, infinitesimal pause. Lies, I thought, all lies.

'Like in *The Hundred and One Dalmatians*,' said The Child. She loves to read to The Child at bedtime and I have to say I enjoy it too. She sits on the end of The Child's bed and I lie in the nice warm space between them. So many books about adventurous children, talking animals, magic, wizardry, boarding school, neglectful parents, flying horses, imaginary worlds. The Child has a good memory but I have a better one. The Child had remembered the name of the liver-spotted Dalmatian but I remembered its meaning.

The lost one.

'Have you rung the AA?' She said, coming back into the room with a tray. She'd even included some of those strange Christmas cakes that taste of fermented dates.

FLINT'S FIRESIDE TALE: A CHRISTMAS STORY • 257

'Yes,' said The Stranger. 'They said they were very busy tonight.'

'They don't like coming out this far,' She said. She's quite proud of how isolated our house is. She gets angry when The Policeman says we should move.

'It's a lonely place,' said The Stranger. 'I bet you know lots of stories about it.'

'A few,' She said and She couldn't stop herself looking towards the curtained window and the darkness that was out there.

'Let's tell stories,' said The Stranger. 'It's the perfect thing to do on Christmas Eve. Let's tell stories while I wait to be rescued.'

I didn't like how she put that and even She seemed to feel that there was something odd about the request but She was still feeling friendly and even protective towards The Stranger. I could feel it. Even though I knew it was a mistake.

'Stories!' said The Child excitedly. 'Let's tell stories.' She was only doing it because she didn't want to go to bed but it was Christmas Eve and children must be obeyed on Christmas Eve.

'I'll start,' said The Stranger. 'It's about a girl. A girl that goes missing.'

Of course it is, I thought.

'Once upon a time there was an old couple. They

were sad because they didn't have any children. They longed for a baby with brown hair and brown eyes and a heart full of love. Then, one year, on St Lucy's Day, the woman was walking across the marshes. It was a cold, dark night and fog came down so the woman couldn't see her way. She walked in the darkness for a while and then she found her way back onto the path. At least she thought it was the path but really it was the other way. The way into the world that lies below our own. A way into the underworld.'

'I don't like this,' said The Child. You're not the only one, I thought.

'Don't worry, Kate,' said The Stranger. 'The story has a happy ending.

'The old woman followed the path,' she continued, 'and she started to feel that soon she must see the lights from her cottage but instead there was only darkness going on and on. No beginning, no end. Only darkness.'

'I wonder,' She nodded towards The Child who was on her lap now, 'if this is quite . . .'

The Stranger did not seem to have heard her. She carried on, smiling into the firelight. 'Then, just when the woman thought she must wander in the darkness for ever, a shape appeared in front of her. A black shape with wings. It was a cormorant.'

'What's a cormorant?' asked The Child.

FLINT'S FIRESIDE TALE: A CHRISTMAS STORY · 259

'It's a bird,' said The Stranger. 'It's also one of the disguises of the Devil.'

She let this sink in and continued. '"What are you doing, human woman,"' said the bird, "walking the path between life and death?" "I'm lost," said the woman, "and I can't find my way home." "I'll make a bargain with you," said the cormorant. "I'll show you the way home if you give me your child." "Alas, I don't have a child," said the woman. "You will," said the bird. "You will have a baby with brown hair and brown eyes and a heart full of love. Then, when the child is five years old I will come for her and I'll fly away with her and keep her in my nest." Well, the woman didn't think she'd ever have a child so she agreed.'

'Big mistake,' She said. I could hear that She was trying to keep her voice all light and it'll-soon-be-Christmas-ish.

'Yes,' said The Stranger. 'Big mistake. The bird flapped its wings and the darkness vanished and the woman was on the path again. She could see her cottage ahead of her. Well, much to her surprise the woman found that she was with child and, in nine months' time, she gave birth to a baby girl.'

'With brown hair and brown eyes?' said The Child.

'Exactly, Kate. Well, the woman almost forgot the cormorant's bargain but she always made sure that the doors of her cottage were securely locked at night. But then, one night when she was five years old, the child was in her bed when she saw a beautiful bird outside her window. The bird's wings were golden and its eyes were jewels. The little girl clapped her hands and opened the window so that she could see the bird better but, as soon as she did so, the creature grasped her in its claws and flew away with her. They flew miles over the marshes towards the sea. There, in a ruined tower, the bird had its nest. He put the girl in the tower and told her never to answer if anyone called her by her real name. She must only answer to the name Will-o'-the-wisp. Every day the bird would come and call 'Will-o'-the-wisp' and he would drop food into her mouth from his beak. The girl lived in the tower and the years passed and she grew older. She would look out over the marshes at night and see the little lights glowing that were the spirits of drowned children. In the daytime she would hear the birds calling but she didn't know what they were saying. She dreamed of escape but there was no door to the tower and, besides, she had started to think that the other world no longer existed. There was only this: the endless marshes, the whispering grasses and the lost spirits calling from the sea.'

FLINT'S FIRESIDE TALE: A CHRISTMAS STORY · 261

The Stranger paused and, outside, the wind seemed to howl with new vigour. The wolves were coming closer. She still had The Child on her lap and I moved closer to them while, all the time, keeping my all-seeing cats' eyes on The Stranger.

The Stranger smiled at us. 'I'm getting to the happy bit,' she said. 'One day, when the girl was fifteen, there was a terrible storm, a wild wind like tonight but with thunder and lightning. The girl was frightened and she almost wished the bird would come but then there was a sudden lull in the storm and she heard a woman's voice calling her real name.'

'Did she answer?' asked The Child.

'She almost didn't. She'd obeyed the cormorant so long that she almost didn't dare think for herself. But something in the woman's voice made the girl trust her. So she called out and she told the woman that she was a prisoner. The woman told her to be brave. She told her that it was darkest before dawn and that she was going to help the girl get back to her parents. "How can I do that?" asked the girl. "Has the bird left any feathers about the place?" said the woman. "Yes," said the girl. "Well, make the feathers into wings," said the woman. "Glue them together with candlewax and fly away." The girl was scared but she did as the wise woman told her.

262 • ELLY GRIFFITHS

She made herself wings and she flew out of the tower. The cormorant came after her but then the sun came up and he couldn't bear the brightness so he went back into the underworld. The girl flew home to her parents and they all lived happily ever after. The end.'

There was a silence. We listened to the voice of the wind calling outside. I tried not to hear the words 'will-o'-the-wisp'.

'Did they say thank you?' said The Child. 'Did the parents say thank you to the woman? The woman who helped the girl escape?'

'I'm sure they were very grateful,' said The Stranger. 'But they moved away and didn't see her again.'

Another silence and then a bleep. One of those electronic bleeps that I hate because I know that it means her attention will be taken up by the little book of light that She keeps in her pocket.

The Stranger looked at her own light book. 'It's the AA,' she said, 'but the signal's bad.'

'It's usually better in the kitchen,' She said. Her voice was odd, as if She'd been crying, but I didn't feel that She was unhappy.

The Stranger went into the kitchen and I stayed on the sofa, guarding my humans. After a few minutes the Stranger came back.

FLINT'S FIRESIDE TALE: A CHRISTMAS STORY · 263

'The AA van is outside,' The Stranger said. 'Thank you for the hot chocolate and the mince pie.'

'Shall I come with you?' She said. 'It's dark out there.'

'No, you stay inside in the warm. Goodbye. Happy Christmas.'

'Happy Christmas,' She said. 'Hope you get home safely.'

'Happy Christmas,' said The Child.

Much later that night, when The Child was asleep and we'd filled her stocking and put it on the end of her bed, we sat on the sofa together. She was drinking her dark-red drink and I'd had the second half of my Special Tin.

'That was strange, wasn't it?' she said to me. She often asks me questions but fails to wait for my answers. 'Do you know who I thought of? Lucy. Lucy Downey. The girl that I rescued that time. The one who was imprisoned on the Saltmarsh for ten years.'

I purred reassuringly. Of course, I'd thought of Lucy too. It was all too obvious: the lost child, St Lucy's Day and all that. But what bothered me was the smell. The old, old smell that recalled, not a modern young human with a car and a light machine, but firelight and thatched roofs and little round houses sheltering against the wind. I saw a bronze torque around her neck and leaves plaited in her hair. I heard chanting and saw the fire flickering, fear reflected in her eyes. And I thought of that other girl that She had found, all those years ago. The Iron Age Girl who had been left on the marshes to die. The Lost Girl of the Marshes. Perdita.

Was it Perdita who had sat by our fire and told stories?

How do I know? I'm only a cat.

The Valley of the Queens:
A Ruth and Nelson Story

Old Hunstanton, Norfolk. November 2022

'Ruth,' says Nelson, 'we've won the lottery.'

Ruth eyes him warily. 'We don't do the lottery. You always say it's a tax on gullibility.'

'Not that one,' says Nelson. 'The real one. The Police Benevolent Society.'

Ruth takes the proffered envelope. Living with Nelson for a year has taught her many things about him. He whistles in the bathroom. He makes tea for them both every morning and always has his in a special Blackpool mug. He is allergic to Radio 4, although he leaves the *Today* programme on if Mishal Husain is presenting. And he is capable of telling jokes with a very straight face. Is this one of them?

She smooths out the letter.

266 · ELLY GRIFFITHS

Dear Harry Nelson,

Congratulations! You have won the first prize in this year's Mega Draw—two tickets for a Luxury Nile Cruise! See the temples of Luxor and Karnak! Explore the Valley of the Kings! Sail down the Nile on board the Queen Nefertari! *Live out your Agatha Christie fantasies!*

Ruth blinks. The exclamation marks are giving her a headache.

'Is this real?' she says.

'Seems real,' says Nelson, putting on his glasses to read the letterheading. 'There's a number to ring. Egypt though. Pyramids and all that. I would have thought it's your dream holiday.'

And, in a way, it is. Twenty years ago (was it really that long?) Ruth and Shona went to Cairo and saw the Pyramids and the Sphinx. She remembers both the timeless view across the sands and the effect of Shona's beauty on the local population.

'It's Luxor and the Nile, not the Pyramids,' she says. 'But it does sound wonderful.'

She reads the letter again. There's nothing on the back of the paper and only those few sentences on the front.

'Agatha Christie,' she says. '*Death on the Nile.*

That's not a great advertisement. At least three people died on that cruise, as I remember.'

'Mia Farrow was in the film,' says Nelson. 'She used to be married to Frank.'

Frank Sinatra is Nelson's musical icon. They are on first name terms, much as Ruth is with Bruce.

'Why are you talking about Frank?' says a voice from the door. Kate, their daughter, is standing in the doorway. She has just turned fourteen and is as tall as Ruth now and, to her mother's not entirely unbiased eye, extremely beautiful. She has Nelson's dark hair, worn long with a fringe, and his brown eyes. Wearing pyjama trousers and a vest top, she has a rangy elegance that doesn't seem to come from either parent but Nelson's older daughters, Laura and Rebecca, have it too so Ruth has to concede it to his gene pool. Maybe it comes from Nelson's mother, Maureen, though this is hard to imagine.

Ruth knows that Kate thinks they are talking about Ruth's ex-boyfriend, Frank. Although Kate had got on well with Frank, she doesn't want him to come back into their lives. Not when she has finally got both parents living under the same roof.

'Frank Sinatra,' says Ruth, with a slight eye roll.

'"My Way",' says Kate. 'I know. Dad and I listen to it in the car.'

'Indoctrination,' says Ruth.

'Says the woman who taught her daughter the words to "Thunder Road" before she could speak.'

'That doesn't make any sense, Dad,' says Kate, getting out the cereal.

Saturday mornings are one of Ruth's favourite times. There's none of the hassle of getting Kate to school and her parents to work. Even Flint, Ruth's cat, seems more relaxed. At least he does when Nelson's dog, Bruno, isn't making one of his custody visits. And Ruth never tires of the view from their kitchen table; the wide blue sea and the multicoloured cliffs, the seagulls swooping low over the beach. Shona says that Ruth should put in a new kitchen, knock down walls and make the ground floor open-plan. But Ruth likes the house as it is.

'We've won a competition.' Nelson pushes the letter across the table to Kate.

'Cool,' says Kate. 'Can I come?'

'It says "for two" . . .' begins Ruth. She's already worrying about Nelson's son, George. If Kate comes, will he feel left out? He's only six, but these things fester. Ruth worries a lot about being fair to George, which sometimes gets in the way of her relationship with him.

'Oh, it's next week,' says Kate. 'I can't go. It's the ski trip. Remember?'

THE VALLEY OF THE QUEENS · 269

As the ski trip has loomed large in their lives all year, this is surely a rhetorical question. But Ruth hardly notices this. She's thinking: *next week?*

Luxor

'**Mr and** Mrs Nelson?'

Ruth is too numb from the three a.m. flight to correct this. Nelson says, 'Dr Ruth Galloway and Harry Nelson,' but the guide, who introduces himself as Hammid, doesn't seem to register this. Ruth knows that she will be Mrs Nelson for the rest of the trip.

The whole week has passed in a blur: organising for Laura to catsit Flint, rearranging Ruth's teaching and Nelson's casework, seeing Kate off on the ski trip and waiting for the school to tell them that she has arrived. Then there was the five-hour flight to Cairo, the drive through traffic that seemed to have transformed itself into a single terrifying entity, the night at a hotel that they never saw in daylight, the second taxi ride and the dawn flight to Luxor. Now they are being shepherded through customs by Hammid, a slim, elegant man in a red shirt. There's no time to take in the rest of their group, who all seem to be dressed in white linen and wearing straw hats. Ruth is wearing linen too—

dark-blue trousers and pale-blue shirt—but her clothes seem mysteriously more creased and travel-worn than those of her fellow adventurers. Nelson views men who wear hats with extreme suspicion and Ruth can see his lips moving in a heartfelt 'Jesus wept' as he follows two panamas onto the coach.

Hammid explains that they will go straight to the Temple of Luxor, then the boat, where they'll have lunch. In the afternoon they'll visit the Valley of the Queens.

'Don't you mean the Valley of the Kings?' says a female American voice.

Hammid smiles as if he has heard this before. 'We will visit the Valley of the Queens *and* the Valley of the Kings. The Valley of the Queens actually contains my favourite tomb, that of Queen Nefertari.'

'That's the name of our boat,' says the same voice, as if this contradicts the guide's statement.

'Exactly,' says Hammid.

Hammid tells them that he's Nubian Egyptian and that he'll be their guide for the next three days. He asks their names and gives them each the identity of a God. Ruth is Nut, the goddess of the Sky, and Nelson is Geb, whose domain is the Earth. 'How do the sky and the earth conceive?' asks Hammid. 'By using an obelisk.'

'Good to know,' says Nelson.

The Temple of Luxor is vast, awe-inspiring and, to

THE VALLEY OF THE QUEENS · 271

a jet-lagged Ruth, almost impossible to process. They walk between pillars, white against the bright-blue sky, and past huge statues of Rameses II, the megalomaniac king.

'He wanted images of himself everywhere,' says Hammid.

'I know footballers like that,' says Nelson.

Standing by the obelisk—originally one of two, the other now in France—Hammid gives them a quick summary of the Egyptian gods. Sett, the evil god, killed Osiris and cut him into fourteen pieces. Isis, his wife—also, worryingly, his sister—found thirteen of them but the fourteenth, his penis, remained lost, supposedly eaten by a catfish. The male members of the party wince.

'But still Isis conceived a child,' says Hammid. 'The god Horus.'

'How?' asks the American woman, whose name is Tia.

'She laid an egg,' says Hammid. 'She could take the form of a bird.'

'Cheaper than IVF,' says someone.

By the time they have arrived at the mooring, Ruth has her fellow guests arranged by their own name and that of their god. She employs the technique she sometimes uses with her students, remembering one physical attribute to go with each name.

Tia—Isis, American, 50s. Red hair.
Dirk—Osiris, her husband, 50s. White beard.
Vanessa—Hathor. British, 40s. Long dark hair.
Miles—Hapi. Her husband. 40s. Bald, glasses.
Simon—Sett. British. 30s. Blond hair.
Fergus—Horus. Irish. His husband. 30s. Bushy beard.
Raymond—Ra. British. 30s? Travelling on his own.
Wears headphones and wraparound sunglasses.
Muriel—Tefnut. French. 50s. Short dark hair.
Camille—Bastet. 20s. Her daughter. Cleopatra fringe.

Bastet is a warrior goddess who takes the form of a cat. Tefnut is apparently the goddess of humidity. 'Couldn't I have a more glamorous deity?' says Muriel, in mock outrage. And she is rather elegant, neat and petite in an orange linen dress that looks as if it has been freshly ironed.

'She's also the goddess of rainfall,' says Hammid. 'Vitally important in Egypt.'

'I'm happy with mine,' says Camille. 'I miss my cat.'

Camille becomes Ruth's favourite.

The *Queen* *Nefertari* is bigger than Ruth imagined. It's three storeys high with a sun deck on top. Inside, the style is opulent art deco, lots of chrome and dark wood. The ship's manager assigns their cabins. 'Mr and Mrs Nelson. You're in the presidential suite.' Nelson

THE VALLEY OF THE QUEENS · 273

and Ruth exchange glances which turn out to be justi-
fied. Hammid told them earlier that the word 'luxury'
comes from the city of Luxor and their suite lives up to
its place of origin. Situated at the prow, it has windows
that run the length of the cabin, which has a huge double bed and a seating area with sofas and chairs. There's
a bottle of champagne in an ice bucket on the coffee
table.

'Blimey,' says Ruth. 'How much money does the
Police Benevolent Society have?'

There's a letter propped up against the ice bucket.
It's addressed to DCI Nelson.

Nelson opens it and Ruth watches his expression
change from mild interest to incredulity to exasperation.
Then he says the last thing that she expects, 'Bloody
Cathbad!'

'What?'

In answer, Nelson hands her the letter.

Dear Harry,

I hope you will forgive the presumption but my
old friend Cathbad has spoken of you so often that
I feel as if we, too, are old friends. Please forgive
also the harmless deception involving the Police
Benevolent Society. I have made a donation to that
esteemed body as a token of my respect. But, to

get down to brass tacks (as you say in your part of the world), I have an assignment for you.

Harry, like you, I have a daughter and that daughter is the most precious thing in the world to me. My dear child is, at present, on the very boat where you are an honoured guest. I have reason to believe that she is in danger. Cathbad says that you have strong protective powers. Please protect Tia, DCI Nelson. That is all I ask of you.

In friendship and gratitude,
Ashraf Khalid

Ruth looks at Nelson. He is breathing heavily. 'Even here,' he says, 'even here Cathbad sends his lunatic friends to torture me.'

Ruth knows that Nelson is, in fact, very fond of their mutual friend Cathbad, a druid whose life has been intertwined with theirs for many years. He is now married to DCI Judy Johnson, a protégée of Nelson's who now has his old job heading the serious crimes squad. Nelson is leading the newly formed cold cases team.

'It sounds as if we wouldn't be here without this particular lunatic friend,' says Ruth. 'This Ashraf Khalid. He must have paid for the whole thing.'

THE VALLEY OF THE QUEENS · 275

'But how?' says Nelson. 'I talked to the woman from the Benevolent Society. She said how lucky we were and that it was her dream to go to Egypt.'

'I suppose she was working for Ashraf,' says Ruth. 'We never checked where the tickets were sent from.'

Nelson gets out his phone. 'I'm ringing Cathbad right now . . . Bugger, no signal.'

'It says here,' Ruth is reading the welcome pack, 'that Wi-Fi is intermittent onboard.'

'I'll ring as soon as we're back on dry land,' says Nelson.

'Is there a phone number for Ashraf Khalid?' says Ruth. She picks up the letter which is written with blue ink on thick cream-coloured paper. There are no contact details. She starts to Google the name and realises that this, too, is impossible.

'I wonder which is his daughter?' says Nelson. 'Must be the French girl.'

'Tia is the American woman,' says Ruth. 'The one with red hair.'

'Her?' says Nelson. 'She's about fifty. And she's a pain.'

It's true that Tia has been the most vocal member of the party. Luxor was too big; Hammid's talk about the gods was too confusing; the sun is too hot, and she didn't like putting her Gucci handbag through the

276 · ELLY GRIFFITHS

scanner on entry to the temple complex. It's hard to think of her being anyone's dear child and means that Ashraf must be at least seventy. But then, Ruth realises suddenly, Cathbad himself must be nearly sixty. Ruth will reach the dreaded milestone in six years' time.

'What does this man want me to do?' says Nelson, looking at the letter again. 'He doesn't even say where this supposed danger is coming from.'

'But you have strong protective powers,' Ruth reminds him.

'Jesus wept,' says Nelson.

Lunch takes the form of a lavish buffet. Nelson eyes it with disfavour. To Ruth's amazement, he hands her his plate. 'Can you just choose me some things I like?'

'Of course not,' says Ruth. 'It's a buffet. The idea is you help yourself.'

Did Michelle really do this for him? Ruth wonders, as she browses the delicious-looking salads. This isn't the first time she's come across something that Nelson seems inclined to outsource to his partner. See also: clothes shopping, present buying and sending Christmas cards. She can sympathise with some of these—she hates shopping too—but putting food on his plate is a step too far. She's glad to see Nelson get up and approach the buffet. He rolls his eyes at her in a quizzical way but

THE VALLEY OF THE QUEENS · 277

seems resigned to his fate. That's another good thing about Nelson; he's not a sulker.

After lunch, the manager introduces his team: the chef, Mohammad; the ship's doctor, Ismael; the housekeeper, Fatima . . . One by one they troop into the dining room for a round of applause. Ruth can see Nelson looking impatient, even as he does his peculiarly loud clapping. Ruth knows that he's keen to get off the boat, contact Cathbad and inform Ashraf Khalid that he won't be his personal watchdog. Some of the other diners look bored too, which makes Ruth feel sorry for the staff, who will no doubt work hard all week while the guests lounge around eating buffet lunches. Tia doesn't even bother to stay for the whole retinue, she storms out after the doctor.

Eventually, they are rounded up onto the deck, given a boarding pass and shepherded onto the coach by Hammid. Tia asks Simon and Fergus to change places with her and Dirk because she gets travel sick. Nelson gives Ruth a meaningful glance, as if to say that Ashraf's dear child is going to need protection from her fellow travellers before too long. Hammid tells them about the Valley of the Queens and the newly restored tomb of Queen Nefertari. 'The colours will blow your mind.' His English is excellent. Nelson is busy trying to buy data roaming for his phone. From his frequent

278 · ELLY GRIFFITHS

sighs it seems that he is unsuccessful. Ruth tries too but she doesn't have a strong enough signal to connect with her service provider. It's quite a scary feeling. What if something happens on the ski trip? She has given Cathbad's name as a secondary contact but Cathbad, too, seems lost in the ether.

The Valley of the Queens is a disappointment at first. There seems to be nothing there but sand and rock, wrought into fantastic shapes by the wind, and a row of depressed-looking stalls selling souvenirs. Hammid ushers them through the gates, complete with the scanner so disliked by Tia, and they are walking up a track leading to the tombs. The sand is white—bone-coloured, thinks Ruth—and there's a strange expect-ant feeling in the air.

'Is it far?' asks Tia, though she must see that it isn't. 'I think I'm suffering from heat exhaustion.'

'Wear my hat,' says Dirk, her husband, handing over his panama.

'It'll make my hair go flat,' says Tia.

Ruth is hot too. It's strange to go from chilly Norfolk winter to Egyptian winter where the temperature is a mean thirty degrees. But Ruth's archaeologist's senses are beginning to take over. She wonders when the site was excavated and by whom. She gets her answer when the plaque at the entrance to Nefertari's tomb is in

THE VALLEY OF THE QUEENS · 279

Italian. SCOPERTA DALLA MISSIONE ARCH ITALIANA NELL'ANNO 1904.

From the start of the trip, Ruth has been slightly dreading going underground. She is rather claustrophobic and, on her earlier visit to Egypt, turned down the chance to explore inside one of the pyramids. Shona crawled all the way into the main chamber and emerged triumphant, to applause from her admirers. But this is far less frightening, a well-lit staircase and plenty of room to stand upright. Inside, the frescos are dizzyingly brilliant, a vibrant comic strip of shapes that are both familiar and wonderfully strange: the red disc of the sun, gods with the heads of falcons, ibises and beetles, a vulture spreading its wings over a door, Anubis like an elegant watchdog, the flail of power crooked into his back leg, Nefertari herself, in all her long-eyed beauty. Nelson looks at Ruth and smiles. She knows that, unusually for him, he too is under the spell of the past.

They emerge, blinking, into the daylight. Hammid has embarked on one of his long stories but most of the group are drinking from their water bottles and fanning themselves in the shade. Ruth only starts listening at the words, 'the first murder trial . . .'

'The Queen plotted with her son to kill the Pharoah Rameses the Third. She was found guilty and burned to death. Her son was buried in the sand and left to die. They found his mummy at Deir el-Bahari, not far from here. It's called the screaming mummy because of the expression of agony on his face.'

'How horrible,' says Ruth.

'Archaeologists knew that the mummy had been buried in disgrace,' says Hammid, 'because the body was wrapped in goatskin not in linen. But they've only just identified him as Prince Pentewere.'

Ruth wants to ask whether DNA analysis was involved but she's not ready to come out as an archaeologist quite yet. Tia walks over and announces that she's had enough of the tombs.

'Onwards to the Valley of the Kings,' says Hammid, with unflagging enthusiasm.

They return to the boat at sunset. Ruth's head is full of funerary architecture, animal-headed gods and bone-coloured hills. She can't wait to tell Kate that she actually went into Tutankhamen's tomb, though, in fact, this had been one of the least exciting. Only one chamber was decorated and all that remained was the rather badly embalmed body of the boy Pharoah. A sad place but not one that seemed particularly doom-laden. Ruth noticed Nelson crossing himself before entering, though.

THE VALLEY OF THE QUEENS · 281

The group have bonded slightly and Ruth has a good chat with Simon and Fergus on the way back. They are web designers from Brighton and this is both a honeymoon trip and the ten-year anniversary of their civil partnership.

'How long have you two been married?' asks Simon, who is the chattier of the two.

'We're not married,' says Ruth, who feels unable to ex-plain the complexity of her relationship with Nelson. 'But we have a fourteen-year-old daughter.' Nelson, who is still trying to get a signal on his phone, certainly looks detached enough to be a long-term partner.

Refreshments are served on the deck of the *Queen Nefertari*. Ruth drinks lemon juice and mint, a newly discovered favourite, and Nelson has a Sakara beer. Simon and Fergus join them, as do the other English couple, Vanessa and Miles. They have 'done' Egypt before and are going to do the Maldives next. They thought they'd treat themselves to a Nile cruise and seem a bit put out that the best suite has been taken. 'I wonder who has it?' says Vanessa. 'Probably the Americans.' Ruth and Nelson keep quiet.

At this point Dirk strolls over. 'Where's your lovely wife?' says Vanessa, who obviously doesn't have a system with names.

282 · ELLY GRIFFITHS

'Gone to see the ship's doctor for her heat exhaustion,' says Dirk. 'I'll have a beer, thanks,' he says to a passing waiter, obviously disinclined to make the short trip to the bar.

Most of the group, including Hammid and the silent Raymond, are now sitting at the same two tables, watching the sun set over the Nile. Only Muriel and Camille are slightly apart, side by side on a sunbed, drinking cocktails and laughing at something on Camille's phone. Ruth likes to watch mother and daughter together, imagining that this will be her and Kate in a few years' time. The two French women certainly seem close and even look alike, both petite with dark hair. Tefnut and Bastet, the goddess of humidity and the cat deity. Ruth really must contact Laura and ask about Flint.

Vanessa seems determined to place people according to her own social register. She expresses interest in Simon and Fergus's jobs and tells them that she has lots of gay friends. 'How very liberal of you,' says Simon. Dirk describes himself as a 'venture capitalist', which seems a sketchy description to Ruth. She sees Simon raising his eyebrows at Fergus. Vanessa is obviously enchanted though. 'How thrilling. What does your wife do?' 'She spends my money,' answers Dirk. Tia, who has just joined the circle, shows no sign of having heard.

THE VALLEY OF THE QUEENS · 283

'That's nice.' Ruth realises that Tia is talking to her and looking at Muriel and Camille.

'Yes,' says Ruth. 'I'm hoping that will be me and my daughter one day.'

'How old is your daughter?'

'Fourteen.'

'I've got a son by my first husband,' says Tia. 'But it's complicated.'

'Nelson . . . er, Harry . . . has children from his previous marriage,' says Ruth. 'It's difficult sometimes.' She thinks of Laura looking after Flint, of Rebecca in Brighton, of George, who really wanted to come with them and ride on a camel.

'I haven't seen my son for years,' says Tia, 'and Dirk has never even met him.'

Ruth wants to ask more but she is distracted by Vanessa turning the force of her personality on Nelson.

'What do you do, Harry?'

'Police officer,' says Nelson. This causes a ripple of interest. Vanessa wants to know if he's had any 'gruesome cases' and Simon asks if he's concerned about recent scandals in the force. For her part, Ruth notices that Nelson doesn't describe himself as 'retired', although this is technically the case. Tia abandons Ruth to sit next to Dirk and listen intently to Nelson's laconic answers. Yes, it's a demanding job; no, he hasn't got a

284 · ELLY GRIFFITHS

degree; yes, he thinks bad apples need to be weeded out; no, he's never met a serial killer. This last, Ruth knows, is untrue.

'What about you, Ruth?' says Vanessa's husband, Miles.

Ruth prepares herself to give a brief, but hopefully interesting, account of life as a forensic archaeologist. But it turns out that Miles just wants to know if she'd like another drink. She asks for a gin and tonic. She has a feeling that it will be a long night.

The next day's itinerary involves a morning trip to the Temple of Karnak, after which the boat will set sail at last, heading for Esna. Ruth is looking forward to being on the move and watching the Nile drift past. She also hopes she might get a phone signal somewhere along the way. In the meantime, there is the immense temple complex near the ancient city of Thebes. Hammid tells them that it was constructed over a period of two thousand years and that more than thirty pharaohs contributed to the buildings, including Hatshepsut, who is Ruth's personal favourite, not only because she was a woman, but because she was known for making peace with surrounding territories. Sadly, she was succeeded by her nephew, Thutmose III, who tore down all her

THE VALLEY OF THE QUEENS · 285

monuments and embarked on an enthusiastic career of war and conquest.

It's hard to get a sense of the place, even with Hammid's descriptions of obelisks and ram-headed sphinxes. Ruth tries to link it to British archaeology. The pyramids were built at around the same time as Stonehenge. This is later, but not much. In fact, it was not long after work started on Karnak that the first timbers were erected on Ruth's beloved wooden henge in Norfolk. It doesn't help. This is so very foreign, the blue skies and the white pillars, it seems a million miles away from megaliths on windy plains.

They walk between corridors of columns, past vast stone images towering above the palm trees. Ruth thinks of Thebes and a T.S. Eliot quotation comes into her head. She thinks it's from 'The Wasteland', Shona's favourite poem. *I who have sat by Thebes below the wall And walked among the lowest of the dead.* There is something unsettling about walking through a land-scape created so many years ago, surrounded by images of the afterlife. 'The east of the Nile is life,' Hammid told them yesterday, 'the west is death.' They walk on, the relentless sun beating down.

Eventually they arrive at the sacred lake, looking rather sad and scrubby, partly fenced off by bollards.

286 · ELLY GRIFFITHS

Hammid points out a low pillar, topped by a squat stone beetle.

'If you walk seven times around the scarab,' he tells them, 'your wish will come true.'

Ruth suspects him of wanting a few minutes' peace. Tia has been demanding shade and cold drinks since they descended from the air-conditioned bus. Most of the group join the tourists already circling the column in an anticlockwise direction. Tia doesn't participate because she says it will make her feel dizzy. Maybe she *is* feeling unwell, thinks Ruth, because this time she has consented to wear Dirk's panama. Husband and wife walk away in the direction of the main temple. Raymond is also missing but he often wanders off on his own to have a vape.

Ruth wonders if she should ask for health and happiness for Kate, eternal life for Flint, or something selfish, like better sales for her new book, *Sacred Landscapes: the Archaeology of North Norfolk*. She opts for Kate and thinks about her daughter as she walks, counting the circuits on her fingers. She hopes Kate is enjoying skiing. She's with her best friends Isla and Megan, so should be having fun. She hopes the teacher in charge of their group, worryingly nicknamed Nutty Nellie, is taking good care of them. Kate had wanted to be with her favourite teacher, Miss Maughan, but was

THE VALLEY OF THE QUEENS · 287

assigned Miss Nelligan instead. The students aren't allowed mobile phones on the trip so at least Kate won't be worrying about Ruth not contacting her. All the same, she wishes she could get a signal. Three circuits done. What is Flint doing now? Laura is very good with him but she's out at work all day. She's a teacher too. Will Flint be bored and lonely? He's used to Ruth working from home at least one day of the week. Will he—

A scream drags Ruth from thoughts of her cat and breaks up the circle. Nelson is running towards Tia, who is crouched by the remains of a limestone boulder.

'It nearly killed me,' she sobs. 'It came from up there.' She points towards a high wall topped with pillars.

'Where's Hammid?' says Dirk. 'He should be here.'

It's hard to know what Hammid could do about falling masonry but it's odd that the guide, usually so assiduous, has vanished. Tia is now sobbing on Nelson's shoulder and there is quite a crowd around them.

'Maybe a cat knocked it over,' says Vanessa. 'There are stray cats everywhere. Poor little mites.'

'A cat couldn't dislodge that,' says her husband, Miles.

Simon offers Tia his water bottle. 'Have some water,' he says. 'Try to breathe.'

'I've got my own water,' says Tia, rather ungratefully, Ruth thinks.

288 · ELLY GRIFFITHS

'What's going on?' Hammid appears, accompanied by an official.

'I nearly died,' yells Tia. 'A huge stone fell from up there. It missed me by inches.'

Hammid and the official confer in Egyptian. Dirk puts his arm round his wife and Nelson makes good his escape.

'So much for my protective powers,' he says to Ruth, as they walk out of earshot.

'Do you think it was deliberate?' says Ruth.

'Put it this way,' says Nelson. 'Someone tells me Tia is in danger and today she's nearly killed. It's a coincidence and you know I don't like coincidences.'

'Are you going to tell her about the letter from Ashraf?' says Ruth.

'I think I have to,' says Nelson. 'Let's do it when we're back on the boat.'

'We?' says Ruth.

'I'm not talking to her on my own,' says Nelson. Adding, rather unfairly, 'After all, it's your fault we even know a mad druid.'

Back on the *Queen Nefertari*, Tia goes straight to see Ismael, the ship's doctor. Ruth and Nelson lurk outside his cabin. The rest of the group are up on the sun deck, enjoying the views of the Nile. Ruth thinks that Tia looks different when she emerges into the light, younger somehow and more unguarded. But maybe this is just because she has cried all her make-up away.

'Tia?' says Nelson. 'Can we have a word?'

They sit on the deck at the back of the boat ('the stern,' Ruth corrects herself). It's a quiet area, shaded by an awning. Nelson tells Tia about the circumstances of their holiday and shows her the letter from Ashraf Khalid.

'Daddy?' says Tia. She seems to be finding the news hard to take in. Ruth doesn't blame her.

'Your father seems to think you might be in danger,' says Nelson.

'I don't know why,' says Tia. 'I haven't an enemy in the world.'

People often make this assertion, thinks Ruth. Is it true of her? She's sure there are some disgruntled students out there blaming her for their 2:2 in archaeology. But would they try to kill her? It seems unlikely.

'The falling rock this morning,' says Nelson, 'could that have been deliberate?'

'Hammid said it wasn't,' says Tia. 'He says the stones get dislodged sometimes, due to erosion.'

This doesn't sound very plausible to Ruth. Stone, especially limestone, can erode over the years but for such a large piece to come loose Ruth suspects that force must have been applied.

Tia is looking at Nelson. 'You're a police officer, aren't you?'

'Semi-retired,' admits Nelson.

'Is that why Daddy asked you? Who's this Cathbad person he mentions in the letter?'

'It's a long story,' says Nelson. 'I've no idea why your father went to these lengths. I haven't been able to get hold of him. Can you give me a phone number for him?'

Tia searches in her designer handbag and comes up with an equally smart-looking pen. She scrawls a string of digits on a discarded cocktail menu. 'I think that's the right number but there's no signal on the boat.'

Nelson pockets the piece of card. 'What I don't understand,' he says, 'is why your father didn't tell the police—the actual police—if he thought you were in danger.'

'Daddy would never go to the police. He doesn't trust them. I suppose he trusts you because you have this friend in common.'

'Did you have any idea what your father was planning?'

'No,' says Tia. 'To tell the truth, I haven't seen him for a while. It means a lot that he still cares.' She rubs her eyes, once again looking vulnerable.

THE VALLEY OF THE QUEENS · 291

'What about our fellow passengers?' says Nelson. 'Could any of them have a grudge against you?'

'I never met any of them before yesterday,' says Tia. 'It seems unreal. Like something out of Agatha Christie.'

'It's funny that Tia and Ashraf both mentioned Agatha Christie,' Ruth says to Nelson, when they have left Tia and are back in their palatial cabin. 'I've been rereading *Death on the Nile* and guess what happens in that?'

'Someone's murdered,' says Nelson.

'Well, yes,' says Ruth. 'But, before that, someone is almost killed by a falling rock.'

The boat moors at Esna in the early afternoon. Hammid proposes a trip to the temple, which he says is a fine example of Ptolemaic—Greco-Roman—design. This description does not generate much enthusiasm and only Ruth, Fergus and the two French women accompany Hammid ashore.

'I'd better stay and keep an eye on Tia,' says Nelson.

'I know you hate to miss a temple,' says Ruth.

But, to be truthful, this temple is not as beautiful as Luxor or Karnak. It's below street level, which adds to the claustrophobic feel, and liberally streaked with grime and pigeon shit. The short walk from the boat

292 · ELLY GRIFFITHS

leads the small group through a bazaar, where stall-holders gather around them offering fridge magnets and plastic models of Tutankhamen.

'Just put your hand over your heart and say "*La shukran*", which means "no thank you",' Hammid told them yesterday. But Ruth hates feeling like a wealthy foreigner who can't even be bothered to make eye contact. All the same, she hurries past the vendors, keeping Hammid's shirt—bright green today—in sight.

Outside the temple, the small group gathers round Hammid as he tells them that Greco-Roman sculptures include sexualised details like nipples and navels. He gets out his torch and highlights the relevant body parts. Camille gets a fit of the giggles. Ruth finds herself next to Fergus as they walk around the dark interior of the building.

'What do you make of this morning?' asks Fergus. 'Tia's near-miss.'

'It must have been a horrible shock for her,' says Ruth.

'I wish it had hit Dirk,' says Fergus.

'Why?' says Ruth. She thinks of Dirk as essentially harmless, in the shadow of his extrovert wife.

'He's a tech billionaire,' says Fergus. 'Simon and I have heard a lot about him. None of it good. He treats

THE VALLEY OF THE QUEENS · 293

his staff really badly. And there are rumours that he beat up his first wife.'

'How awful,' says Ruth. She's reassessing the so-called venture capitalist. *What does your wife do? She spends my money.*

They both jump when Hammid materialises behind them, telling them to notice the marks where early Christians attempted to deface the Egyptian gods. She wonders how much he overheard.

Back on the *Queen Nefertari* they drink tea as the boat sets sail for Edfu. The river slides past them, cattle standing fetlock-deep in shallow water, children waving from the banks. Tia seems fully recovered, laughing at Hammid's stories of previous tours. 'You're lucky we're not a demanding group,' she tells him. Ruth sees Simon and Fergus exchange glances. Muriel and Camille are, once again, sitting slightly apart. Raymond is plugged into his headphones.

Supper is a rather formal affair, served by white-gloved waiters as the ship glides through the night. Afterwards, Ruth and Nelson go up onto the top deck to enjoy the cool air. At first Ruth thinks the area is deserted, the plunge pool spotlit and surrounded by shrouded sun-loungers, but then she sees that Tia is standing at the prow, talking on her phone. Ruth's

294 • ELLY GRIFFITHS

first thought is 'Hooray! She's got a signal,' but her own mobile is still incommunicado. Ruth edges nearer, hoping Tia has found a hot spot, and hears her talking in Egyptian. This is a surprise at first—she thinks of Tia as American—but, of course, Ashraf is her father. Tia's first language is probably Egyptian Arabic. Ruth catches the word 'habibi' which Hammid has already told them means 'friend' but also 'my love'. Tia turns, sees Ruth and Nelson, and hurries away without speaking to them.

'What's up with her?' Nelson has been busy with his own phone.

'I don't know,' says Ruth. 'But she was talking to someone. I don't think she wanted to be overheard.'

Ruth thinks that she should keep an ear out for any unusual happenings on the boat that night. But, back in their cabin, Nelson says 'Ruth' and all other concerns are forgotten.

The morning brings Edfu, breakfast on the deck and a glimmer of phone signal. Ruth checks her messages and sees that Laura has sent several pictures of Flint. She hasn't got enough power to upload the images but the fact that they have been sent must surely mean that all is well in Old Hunstanton. There's also a message from Kate's school saying that the ski trip is going well and that everyone is 'in good spirits'. Having checked on the family, Ruth tries a little light detection. She Googles Ashraf Khalid but, whilst there are several entries for him, all are in Arabic and incomprehensible to Ruth. Dirk Benedict's name produces a Wikipedia page but nothing uploads apart from the words 'dot com millionaire'. From Nelson's irritated mutterings, she assumes he hasn't had much luck either.

The temple of Horus at Edfu is a large, square building, almost industrial in feel. By the porticoed entrance are two stone falcons, the animal form of the god. Hammid organises them into a group photograph by the largest statue, an angry-looking creature wearing a crown shaped like a tall hat. Looking at it later, Ruth notices Raymond standing so far to one side that he has almost joined another party. Nelson is scowling, as is usual in photographs, and Ruth has been caught talking, her mouth half open. Dirk is looking at Tia, as is Simon, but Tia herself is smiling directly at the photographer.

After lunch, the boat sails to Kom Ombo and the temple dedicated to the crocodile god. In the evening there'll be a farewell dinner on the boat, followed by dancing. During the night, they will travel to Aswan, where the cruise will end. Ruth is worried about the dancing, which Hammid describes airily as 'just good fun'. There's also a chance to wear traditional Egyptian gallabiyahs but Ruth thinks this will make her feel even more like a thoughtless tourist, guilty of cultural appropriation and other similar crimes.

They reach Kom Ombo at night and the temple, floodlit against the navy-blue sky, is one of the most beautiful things Ruth has seen on the trip. Nelson makes eye contact with a vendor and ends up buying Ruth a pendant in the shape of a scarab beetle.

'Hammid told you not to talk to them,' Tia scolds.

'I'm sure the boy could do with the money,' says Nelson evenly.

Ruth says nothing; she is secretly delighted with her present.

While Hammid is showing them the well where the sacred crocodiles were kept, Nelson and Ruth wander off to look at the lights reflected in the dark waters of the Nile. They are followed by a grey cat with white paws. Ruth wishes she could take it home with her. She has already christened it Brother Dusty-Feet, after a favourite childhood book.

'Well, the holiday's nearly over,' says Nelson, 'and nothing terrible has happened.'

'Don't speak too soon,' says Ruth. 'There's still the dancing to come.'

'Nothing in the world will make me dance.'

THE VALLEY OF THE QUEENS · 297

'Not even Frank Sinatra on vocals?'

'They don't make them like ol' blue eyes any more.'

Ruth laughs. The *Queen Nefatari* is moored just below them and fairy lights are gleaming on the deck, presumably in honour of the gala night. As Ruth watches, she sees a man standing in the prow with binoculars held to his eyes. But what is odd is that he isn't watching the river but the temple, where the group are walking between the illuminated columns.

'Who's that?' says Ruth.

'Don't know,' says Nelson. 'One of the crew?'

'It could be Raymond,' says Ruth. 'He didn't come ashore.'

'I don't trust him,' says Nelson. 'He has the look of a man who carries concealed.'

'Carries what?' says Ruth.

'A gun,' says Nelson.

Ruth is shocked. She knows that Nelson has come across guns in the course of his work. He's never carried one himself, though he has been shot by one. She knows that armed forces are supposed to offer protection, but the thought of firearms always makes her feel the opposite of safe.

'Why would he be carrying a gun?'

'I don't know that he is. But he seems watchful. Like someone whose job that is.'

298 · ELLY GRIFFITHS

'Do you think? He's always listening to music.'

'He has headphones on. We don't know what he's listening to.'

Ruth realises that she has underestimated Nelson, not for the first time. Just because he isn't particularly interested in his fellow passengers, it doesn't mean that he isn't watching them with his keen policeman's eye.

They watch the figure on the boat for a few more minutes. At one point, Ruth sees him raise a hand, as if greeting someone on shore, but, when she turns round there's no one in sight.

The gala evening is as bad as Ruth fears. She dresses in her smartest outfit, a floral dress that she some-times wears for graduations, but is still outclassed by the other guests, who are all in gallabiyahs or formal Western attire. Tia is elegant in gold and white which contrasts well with Dirk's dinner suit. Simon and Fergus have dressed in traditional clothes too, which causes much hilarity. Camille wears a short, spar-kly dress and Muriel looks chic in green. Raymond is wearing black robes which makes him look a bit like a priest. Vanessa and Miles have gone to town. Miles is even wearing a fez, which seems more Turkish than Egyptian to Ruth.

'We like to make an effort,' says Vanessa, looking

pointedly at Nelson, tieless in a white shirt and jeans. 'It seems only polite.'

Vanessa insists on having her photograph taken with Hammid, who is wearing what he says are traditional Nubian robes, and with Jamal, 'my favourite waiter'. All the crew are wearing Egyptian dress and gamely join in with the dancing. The music lurches between traditional and disco. Dirk is roaring with laughter and attempting to belly dance. He's normally quite a reserved character but tonight he seems determined to let rip. Ruth sees Tia looking at him rather anxiously. Vanessa and Miles boogie to 'I Will Survive'. Ruth and Nelson soon escape to the deck.

'Do you think it was all in Ashraf's head?' says Ruth. 'Tia being in danger?'

'Who knows? He's probably a nutcase if he's a friend of Cathbad's.'

'Any word from Cathbad?'

'No. I tried to send him a text but it didn't get through. I'll try again when we get to Aswan.'

'There's a dam there, isn't there? Hammid says it's the reason why there are no Nile crocodiles any more.'

'I don't give a damn,' says Nelson. His Clark Gable impression is extremely bad but there's a gleam in his eye that reminds Ruth of last night and the curtains drawn in the presidential suite. When Nelson suggests that they go to bed, she agrees immediately. That is why she doesn't think of Tia, Ashraf, or even Kate and Flint, until she is woken at three a.m. by the sound of something heavy hitting the water.

'What's that?' says Ruth. But Nelson is already pulling on his clothes. Ruth does the same and follows him up onto the deck. There they find Tia sobbing in Simon's arms. 'It's Dirk,' she says. 'He was standing on the railing, trying to balance—he'd had too much to drink—and he fell in.' Hammid, still in his blue robes, is talking in Egyptian on his phone. Ruth assumes he's calling the authorities. The crew are throwing lifebuoys and ropes overboard.

'Can anyone see him?' says Camille, shivering in her sparkly dress. Why are all these people still up? wonders Ruth. It must have been a wilder party than she imagined.

Ruth looks down but she can't see anything but inky water. They must have reached Aswan because there are other boats moored nearby. She sees flashing lights and wonders if it's the police or a gala night on another ship.

'Did anyone see him fall?' asks Nelson. His policeman's voice, effortlessly commanding without being particularly loud, makes everyone turn towards him.

THE VALLEY OF THE QUEENS · 301

'I heard Dirk talking,' says Simon. 'He did sound drunk. Then I heard the splash.'

'You didn't see him standing on the parapet?'

'No. I was with Fergus, on the sun loungers.'

'I was talking to Hammid on the deck below,' says Camille. 'We heard the splash too.'

Interesting, thinks Ruth. She has noticed the tour guide being particularly attentive to the pretty French girl. They have now been joined by Muriel, wrapped in a scarlet silk kimono, and Miles, in a towelling robe. The ship's doctor has taken charge of Tia.

Ruth and Nelson stay on deck, watching as a police motorboat comes into view. Two officers come aboard the *Queen Nefertari,* crossing two other cruise ships in order to reach them. They confer with the ship's manager and with Hammid.

'Let's go to our cabin,' says Ruth. 'They'll call us if they need us.' She can see Nelson half-wanting to take charge of the investigation but he agrees and they descend the stairs. Two people are waiting outside the presidential suite. Ruth sees the gleam of silk and the sparkle of a party dress. Muriel and Camille.

'May we talk to you?' asks Muriel.

The four of them enter the cabin. It's equipped with mineral water, fruit juice and wine of every hue but, for the first time, Ruth regrets the absence of a kettle. If ever a situation called for a cup of tea, this is it.

Muriel and Camille sit side by side on the sofa. Ruth and Nelson take the armchairs opposite. Outside, Ruth hears shouts and the crackle of police radios. The *Queen Nefertari* rocks as heavy feet clatter overhead.

'I talk to you,' says Camille. 'Because you are a policeman.'

'I'm retired,' says Nelson. 'If you know anything about what happened tonight you should talk to the police up on deck.'

Camille looks at her mother and says, 'I'm not sure . . . but maybe . . .' She runs out of words, or maybe out of English. Muriel says, 'Camille thinks she might have seen something. Or someone.' Camille speaks in French and her mother translates.

'She was talking with Hammid and she thought she saw someone climbing to the upper deck. She thinks it was a man and he was wearing traditional clothes. Then, seconds later, she heard the sound of someone falling.'

Nelson persuades Camille to tell her story to the officers. As the two Frenchwomen leave the cabin, Ruth and Nelson look at each other.

'Do you really think someone pushed Dirk overboard?' asks Ruth. 'Could it have been the man Camille saw? Who was wearing traditional dress tonight?'

THE VALLEY OF THE QUEENS · 303

'The two boys from Brighton . . .'

'Simon and Fergus,' says Ruth. 'Neither of them liked Dirk much. They knew him through the tech world. But I can't see either of them killing him.'

'Never assume,' says Nelson. 'That's what I always tell my officers.'

Ruth moves on quickly before he can tell her that 'assume' makes an ass out of you and me. 'Vanessa's husband, Miles, was wearing a gallabiyah. So were all the crew.'

'Hammid's in the clear,' says Nelson. 'He was with Camille. Chatting, she says. Quite some chat if it lasted until three in the morning.'

'I did wonder if they liked each other,' says Ruth.

'I don't know how you find the time to notice stuff like that,' says Nelson. 'I barely know their names.'

That's not quite true, thinks Ruth. But, before she can say more, there's a knock on the door.

'Bloody hell,' says Nelson. 'What now?'

'Maybe it's someone offering tea,' says Ruth. She's ashamed of herself for becoming so used to being waited on but she really is desperate for a hot drink.

But it's not a friendly waiter. It's Raymond, still wearing his long black robes.

'DCI Nelson,' he says, 'may I have a word?'

Nelson looks surprised to be addressed by his correct

304 · ELLY GRIFFITHS

rank but says, rather grumpily, 'Be my guest.' Ruth notes that, once more, she is apparently invisible.

'Have they found Dirk?' she asks.

'No,' says Raymond. 'And one of the policemen told me that he doesn't think they will. It's the rapids, you see.'

Ruth remembers Hammid telling them about the treacherous currents around the Aswan Dam. 'This area is called the first cataract,' he had told them, 'the water flows especially quickly here. So, don't fall in,' he had added, with a grin.

'You seem friendly with the local police,' says Nelson.

Raymond sits on the sofa. 'As I think you've guessed, I'm a professional bodyguard.'

'Who were you hired to protect?' asks Nelson.

'Dirk Benedict,' says Raymond, with a humourless laugh. 'Ironic, isn't it?'

'Did Dirk think he'd be in danger on this trip?' says Nelson.

Raymond shrugs. 'No more than any rich man feels he's in danger abroad. He never mentioned anything specific. I was just hired to keep an eye on him. And I did. There was the falling stone at Karnak but I checked and it really did look like that was an accident. I thought we were nearly home safe. Job done. But . . .

tonight . . . I went back to my cabin after supper to have a vape and . . . I don't know why . . . I just fell asleep. I woke up an hour ago when someone hammered on my door yelling Dirk had fallen overboard. Pretty big failure, eh? I don't suppose his wife will pay me now.'

'How is Tia?' says Ruth.

'She's still with the doctor,' says Raymond. 'He's given her a sedative.'

'Why did you want to see me?' asks Nelson.

'I know you're a retired detective,' says Raymond. 'Quite a famous one too. I researched all the passengers before I came aboard. I just wondered what you thought about Dirk's death. Do you think it was just an accident?'

Nelson pauses before answering. 'I wasn't at the scene so I can't be certain. There are witnesses who say Dirk was drunk.'

'I heard that,' says Raymond. 'And I was surprised. He's not much of a boozer usually.'

That's a very British word, thinks Ruth. She hasn't really heard Raymond speak before. He has a flat Midlands accent that is curiously reassuring.

'Unless we hear otherwise,' says Nelson, 'it looks like misadventure.'

'That's what I think too,' says Raymond, stand-

306 · ELLY GRIFFITHS

ing up. 'Well, I can't say I'll be sorry to get off this ship. All those bloody temples and now a death. Makes Benidorm look positively attractive. Goodnight.'

'You didn't tell him about the man Camille saw,' says Ruth, after the door has shut behind Raymond. 'Or that you were hired by Ashraf.'

'No,' says Nelson. 'I'm still not sure if I trust our friend Raymond.' He stifles a yawn. 'I could kill for a cup of tea. Do you think someone would make us one?'

Ruth looks at her phone. 'We'll be on the plane home in a couple of hours.'

Old Hunstanton, Norfolk. December 2022

'**Ashraf is** an old soul,' says Cathbad.

'He's a very elusive soul at the moment,' says Nelson.

Nelson has been unable to contact Ashraf Khalid. The number Tia gave him doesn't seem to work. Google has revealed him to be a pharmaceuticals tycoon living in Cairo but emails to his office have gone unanswered. It turns out Cathbad met Ashraf when, as part of his world traveller phase, he briefly worked in one of his laboratories. Cathbad's first degree was in chemistry.

'Ashraf took an interest in his employees,' says

Cathbad, 'and we became friends. I haven't seen him for years, although we exchange letters sometimes.'

Only Cathbad still writes letters.

'Well, I wish you hadn't mentioned me in your crazy correspondence,' says Nelson.

'Of course I mentioned you,' says Cathbad. 'We have a psychic bond.'

'So you keep saying,' says Nelson. Judy, Cathbad and family have come for Sunday lunch. Cooking is a newly discovered skill of Nelson's. Apparently, Michelle 'never let him in the kitchen' but Ruth is more than happy to encourage him in that direction. Nelson particularly enjoys cooking roasts and doesn't even mind that Cathbad comes with his own nut version. Now the meal is over and the adults are chatting in the sitting room. The children are next door playing on the PlayStation that Nelson supposedly bought for them but, as far as Ruth can see, uses mainly to pretend that he's a football manager.

The high-ceilinged room, which faces the sea, is dominated by a giant Christmas tree. It's still three weeks before the big day but Kate wanted the tree early and her wish is Nelson's command. It's dropping its leaves already and Ruth predicts that it will be quite bald by the twenty-fifth but she has to admit that it looks lovely, especially in the twilight, all twinkling lights and home-made decorations. Flint is sitting under the lowest branches, looking martyred. Ruth once had to hang her tree upside-down because of marauding cats and children. The memory makes her feel both nostalgic for the past and grateful for the present.

'So, the Egyptian police thought the death was accidental?' says Judy, ever the detective.

'It appears so,' says Nelson. 'They accepted Tia's account that Dirk fell in when he was drunk.'

'"Accepted her account",' echoes Cathbad. 'Sounds as if you have some doubts.'

'I don't know,' says Nelson, draining the last of his wine. 'It seems a bit of a coincidence that Ashraf thought someone on the boat was in danger and then a man dies.'

'I know you don't like coincidences,' says Judy with a smile.

'Ashraf said Tia was in danger,' says Ruth, 'but was she in danger of killing or being killed?'

She's been thinking about this a lot, about Tia's face when she talked about her son, about Dirk's sudden raucousness on the last night, about Fergus saying that Dirk abused his first wife.

'Ashraf might well have wanted to prevent Tia from committing a crime,' says Cathbad. 'He wouldn't have wanted that stain on her soul.'

'Is that really what you think happened, Ruth?' asks Judy.

Ruth touches the scarab around her neck before answering. 'I think it's possible that Tia murdered Dirk and I think she had an accomplice on board. Her son.'

'You've never said any of this before,' says Nelson. 'Who was her son? Hammid? One of the tech boys? Raymond the bodyguard?'

'I think it was Ismael,' says Ruth. Nelson is looking blank, so she explains. 'He was the ship's doctor. Remember how Tia was always going to see the doctor? He was there on the gala evening and he was dressed in traditional robes. I think Camille saw Ismael going onto the top deck and then he or Tia pushed Dirk overboard.'

'Why?' says Nelson, frowning.

'Fergus told me that Dirk mistreated his first wife,' says Ruth. 'Maybe he was doing the same to Tia.'

'And he was a rich man,' says Nelson. 'I assume Tia inherited it all.'

'I don't think it was about the money,' says Ruth. 'After all, Tia's father is rich too. I think it was planned between Tia and her son from her first marriage. After Dirk fell, Ismael took Tia into his cabin and supposedly gave her a sedative. That meant that she couldn't be interviewed. And Ismael would have had the means to spike Dirk's drink. I don't think it was just chance that he got so drunk on the last night. And then there was Raymond, Dirk's bodyguard, who fell into a heavy sleep. I think he was drugged too.'

'But if Ismael was Tia's son, surely Dirk would have known him?' says Nelson.

'Tia told me that Dirk had never met her son,' says Ruth. 'That was the only time she mentioned him but, as soon as she heard that you were a police officer, she closed up again. She also told me that she hadn't seen her son for years. I don't think that was true. I think it was Ismael that Tia was talking to on the phone that night. The person she called "*habibi*".'

'What about Karnak and the falling rock?' says Nelson. 'Was that Ismael too?'

'Why not?' says Ruth. 'He could easily have followed us to the temple and got back to the boat before us. Ismael must have been aiming for Dirk but nearly killed Tia. Remember, Tia was wearing Dirk's hat that day? They must both have been very shaken when they found out. Tia looked really upset when she came out of Ismael's cabin. Of course, we thought she was there for medical treatment. If you want to make regular visits to a doctor, it's a good idea to pretend to be a hypochondriac.'

THE VALLEY OF THE QUEENS · 311

Nelson looks unconvinced and Judy clearly wants to ask more questions. Only Cathbad nods as if the story makes perfect sense to him. But, at that moment, the children rush into the room demanding pudding and the subject is dropped. Two weeks later, though, Ruth receives a photograph in the post. The envelope is postmarked Cairo and the picture shows Tia and Ismael on a balcony, toasting each other. There's no note but Ruth thinks she knows what it means.

It's funny, she reflects. No one on the trip bothered to learn that she was an archaeologist, but it was archaeology that gave her the clue. She remembers the story that Hammid told in the Valley of the Queens.

The Queen plotted with her son to kill the Pharoah Rameses the Third. She was found guilty and burned to death. Her son was buried in the sand and left to die. They found his mummy at Deir el-Bahari, not far from here. It's called the screaming mummy because of the expression of agony on his face.

And she remembers the name of the murderous queen.

Tiye. Pronounced Tia.

Ruth Galloway and the Ghost of Max Mephisto

'There's the theatre, Mum. Isn't it *immense*?'

Immense is Kate's new favourite word. Ruth knows that it doesn't always refer to size, which is just as well because the building in front of them is actually rather small. The Firebird is in the heart of London's theatreland but it's sandwiched between a Starbucks and a Pizza Express. You could easily walk past the entrance because it's set back from the road, a gleaming slice of gold and red with signs for '*Beowulf: The Musical*' and, in smaller letters, 'For one night only, Norfolk Youth Theatre. Scenes from Shakespeare'.

'My name in lights,' says Kate. 'That's immense.'

Her name is not on the poster and the lights aren't

THE GHOST OF MAX MEPHISTO · 313

on, but Ruth knows what she means. Kate has been rehearsing all summer but a village hall in Norfolk is not the same as a London stage. A *West End stage*, as Ruth's father said yesterday, to Kate's obvious delight.

Kate's grandfather and step-grandmother are both coming to the performance tonight. Ruth and Kate stayed with them last night, in the house in Eltham where Ruth grew up. Now they are at the theatre for the dress rehearsal. Nelson is on his way from King's Lynn and is going to join them afterwards.

Ruth and Kate are slightly late, thanks to Network Rail. Kate clearly blames Ruth for signalling failures at Charing Cross and looks anxiously at her photocopied directions. 'It says go in by the stage door. Which is the stage door?'

Ruth has no idea. They try the double doors at the front but they are firmly locked. Ruth knocks on the glass, much to Kate's embarrassment, but there's no answer. Ruth is just squinting into the lobby—signs for box office and refreshments, giant cut-out of Beowulf— when a voice says, 'Looking for the artistes' entrance?'

They both turn round and Kate says, 'Yes.'

A small man in a panama hat is smiling at them. He's wearing a cream-coloured suit that makes Ruth think of cricket matches, tea on the lawn, ladies in flowered hats.

314 · ELLY GRIFFITHS

'The stage door is always hidden in a side street,' he says. 'I'm Ernest French, the stage manager.'

'I'm so glad you appeared,' says Ruth, following Ernest French into an unprepossessing alleyway crowded with dustbins. 'We would never have found this on our own.'

'I have a knack of turning up just when I'm needed,' says Ernest. Ruth shoots him a curious look. This is the sort of thing her druid friend Cathbad would say. But Cathbad and his family are on holiday in Italy. He has already FaceTimed to wish Kate good luck.

Ernest stops at a blue door. There's nothing on it, not even a handle, but, as they approach, it opens slowly. Kate looks at Ruth and mouths '*immense*'.

The door has been opened by a man in a commissionaire's uniform, who directs them along a passageway and up some stairs. There's a door saying 'Quiet!' in passive-aggressive comic sans. Ruth pushes it open and, to her surprise, finds herself actually on the stage. Kate's teacher, Miss Bracebridge, is there too, surrounded by a scrum of teenagers. Kate makes a beeline for Tasha, her friend from primary school. The summer drama course has re-established their friendship.

Ruth feels self-conscious, standing on the very boards themselves. It feels high and exposed, brightly lit with a red lamp glowing at the edge of the stage.

THE GHOST OF MAX MEPHISTO · 315

Ruth can just make out the other adults sitting in the front row of the stalls.

'Hallo, Kate,' says Miss Bracebridge. 'I think that's everyone. Mums, you can collect in two hours. Now, let's have everyone who's in the first scene . . .'

It's a clear dismissal. Ruth finds the steps and descends into the auditorium, watching her feet carefully because, if there's one thing worse than being late, it's being late and falling flat on your face in front of the Drama School Mothers.

'Ruth!' Tasha's mother, Nicki, greets her affably. 'A group of us are going to Starbucks. Want to join?'

'That's very kind,' says Ruth, 'but I'm meeting someone.'

This is true but she knows it sounds like an excuse. Plus, she still doesn't know how to describe her relationship with Nelson. Kate's dad? My partner? The latter sounds like they're in business together, which Ruth supposes is sometimes true. Detective and archaeologist, crime-fighting duo.

Ruth pauses in the lobby waiting for the other mums to leave. They are almost all wearing summer dresses and trainers. Their dainty white feet pick their way through the alleyway like mountain goats. Ruth is wearing chinos and a cotton shirt. She knows that both are already fatally creased.

316 · ELLY GRIFFITHS

'How do you like our little theatre?' It's Ernest French again. He really does have the Cathbad-trick of materialising from nowhere.

'It's lovely,' says Ruth.

'The Firebird is one of the oldest theatres in London,' says Ernest. 'It's haunted. Well, all theatres are haunted. Did you see the red light at the front of the stage? The bulb in the wire cage?'

'Yes.'

'That's the ghost light. It's kept on all the time to keep the spirits company. Do you want me to tell you the story of the phantom of The Firebird?'

Try stopping you, thinks Ruth.

'This theatre was opened in 1662, after Charles II had been restored to the throne and people started going to shows again. It was called The King's Theatre in those days and it was famous for its musical entertainments. But the building was almost destroyed in the Great Fire of London. All the performers escaped the blaze except a young dancer who was trapped in one of the lower rooms. It's said that, when conditions are right, she can be heard crying for help.'

Ernest smiles at Ruth and she wonders if he is such a benign presence after all.

'This theatre was rebuilt from the ashes,' he says.

THE GHOST OF MAX MEPHISTO • 317

'That's why it's called The Firebird. After the phoenix, you know. The bird that's born again from the flames. Lots of variety stars have performed on this stage. The great magician Max Mephisto made his London debut here in 1928. People have seen his ghost too. An encouraging spectre, by all accounts. He appears to actors when they are suffering from stage fright.'

'He sounds harmless, at any rate,' says Ruth. 'Excuse me, I'd better be off now.'

Ruth waits for Nelson in a café called the Crooked Pipe.

'Typical of you,' says Nelson. 'There's a perfectly good Starbucks round the corner.'

'I prefer this,' says Ruth. 'It's got character.'

It's true that the tiny building doesn't seem to possess a single straight line. The timbered walls slope one way and the floor another. Nelson asks for tea and it's brought in a pot wearing a knitted cosy like a stripy jumper.

'Don't say it . . .' says Ruth.

'A proper pot of tea,' says Nelson, undeterred. 'Just like my mum makes.'

They drink their tea and discuss Kate's theatrical debut.

'I think she's quite nervous,' says Ruth.

'Well, it's a big deal, isn't it?' says Nelson. 'I think I was only ever in one play at school. *Julius Caesar.* I was one of the murderers.'

'Figures,' says Ruth.

'The one who has a "lean and hungry look". That got a big laugh on the night.'

'I hope Kate gets some laughs. Her scene is really funny. And she's so good.'

Kate's scene is from *A Midsummer Night's Dream.* She plays Helena, who is arguing bitterly with her friend Hermia because Hermia's boyfriend, Lysander, has been bewitched to fall in love with Helena, much to the anger of *her* boyfriend, Demetrius. Ruth is rather sorry that the row is over a man (especially because the boy playing Lysander is the weak link in the quartet) but she loves hearing the Shakespearean dialogue crackle between the girls. Kate's favourite lines are, 'O spite! O hell! I see you all are bent To set against me for your merriment.' Despite Miss Bracebridge's insistence that Helena is the meeker of the two, Kate puts real venom into the words.

Kate is also the tallest of the girls, which is central to the scene. Ruth loves Helena's description of Hermia, 'though she be but little, she is fierce'. It's all she can do to stop herself cheering for all the little people in the world.

THE GHOST OF MAX MEPHISTO · 319

Ruth and Nelson finish their tea and walk round to the stage door. As soon as they turn the corner, Ruth sees the blue lights. A police car is parked amongst the bins and two women are standing near a barred basement window. There is something about them, especially the younger of the two, that says they are on duty. Plus, both are dressed in the dark trousers and white shirts that police fondly believe are 'plain clothes'.

Nelson is there in a second, reaching for his warrant card.

'DCI Nelson.'

The younger woman raises her eyebrows. 'DI Harbinder Kaur,' she says. 'What can I do for you?'

'My daughter's in there.' Nelson points at the stage door. 'What's going on?'

'We heard reports of someone calling for help,' says the older woman, who has dyed red hair and a pleasant manner. 'Said to be coming from the basement.'

And Ruth hears Ernest's voice. *It's said that, when conditions are right, she can be heard crying for help.*

'Probably a cat,' says DI Kaur.

And so it proves. A few minutes later, a uniformed police officer emerges from the basement steps holding a scruffy ginger cat in his arms.

'Must have got trapped down there,' he says. 'Either of you two ladies fancy a new pet?'

'I'd love to,' says DI Kaur, rather to Ruth's surprise, 'but Mette and I are out at work all day. It wouldn't be fair.'

'I'll take it,' says the red-headed woman. 'It'll give Malcolm someone to talk to.'

She takes the animal and climbs into the car.

'Good to meet you both,' says DI Kaur, although no one has introduced Ruth. 'Enjoy London.'

Nelson is inclined to be irritated as the squad car pulls away, bumping gently over the cobbles, the redhead waving jauntily from the back seat.

'They should have taken that cat to the RSPCA. It might be someone's pet.'

'It looked like a stray to me,' says Ruth. 'I'm glad they were going to give it a home. It reminded me of Flint.'

'Flint is four times its size,' says Nelson. 'And twice as bad-tempered.' He has a rather strained relationship with Ruth's beloved cat. Nelson is silent for a moment before saying, with a slightly rueful grin, 'They're getting younger all the time, aren't they? Police officers, doctors, teachers.'

'Careful, Nelson,' says Ruth. 'That's the sort of thing old people say.'

'Harbinder Kaur.' Nelson shakes his head. 'She looks like a teenager. But I bet she's a pretty tough cop, all the same.'

THE GHOST OF MAX MEPHISTO · 321

There's no time to go back to Eltham before the performance so Ruth and Nelson take Kate for a pizza. She's uncharacteristically quiet and picks at her favourite American Hot.

'Nervous is only another word for excited,' says Ruth.

'I'm not nervous,' says Kate.

Nelson smiles at Ruth over Kate's dark head.

'What would Cathbad say? Something lunatic, no doubt.'

'Pray to Hecate,' says Kate.

'Light a bonfire,' says Ruth.

But talking about Cathbad makes them all feel happier. After the meal, they walk back to the theatre where Ruth's father, Arthur, is waiting with his wife, Gloria. Arthur looks a little frail in his old pinstriped suit but Gloria is smart in a red dress and sparkly scarf. She has brought Kate a black china cat for luck.

'Thank you.' Kate hugs her step-grandmother.

'Cats are always lucky.'

Ruth spares a thought for the ginger stray she saw earlier. He certainly looked as if he'd used up a few of his nine lives but maybe his luck has turned at last.

Ernest French, now in a black bow tie, greets them in the lobby. Ruth considers telling him about the cat

322 · ELLY GRIFFITHS

but decides against it. She thinks that Ernest would not want the legend of the imprisoned dancer debunked.

Kate goes backstage to join the rest of the cast. Ruth, Nelson, Arthur and Gloria take their seats. Arthur reads from the programme: 'Max Mephisto performed here once. Did I ever tell you, Ruth, that your mother and I saw him at the Theatre Royal, Drury Lane? It was a couple of years before you were born.'

'No,' says Ruth. She can't imagine her parents at the theatre and, surely, as devout Christians, they would have found the very name 'Mephisto' far too reminiscent of the Evil One. But, then again, didn't her mother once say that she'd wanted to be an actress when she was young? Yet another way in which Kate takes after her late grandmother.

'Had this act where he made a girl disappear,' says Arthur. 'She just vanished in front of our eyes. I said to Jean, "How the dickens did he do that?" She said, "There's only one answer, he must really be magic."'

Ruth, through her contacts with the police, has seen too many girls disappear over the years. But she likes the nostalgic note in her father's voice and the thought that her mother might once have believed in magic. Ruth is still trying to imagine the great magician when the curtain goes up. She is so nervous for Kate that her extremities are frozen—she has literal cold feet. But, when the

THE GHOST OF MAX MEPHISTO · 323

scene comes, it is perfect. Kate remembers all her words and 'O spite! O hell!' gets not just a laugh but a murmur of empathy. The actors get the loudest applause of the night.

Outside, Kate tells her fan club that she was never nervous at all. 'Well, just for a second, when I was waiting in the wings, about to go on. But I heard a voice—a bit like Uncle Cathbad's—saying, "Don't worry, you'll be great." And I was. It was immense.'

It's not the time to suggest modesty. Ruth silently thanks the ghost of Max Mephisto as she follows Kate, still a small figure between her grandparents, through the bright lights of London.

Though she be but little, she is fierce.

Note: The Firebird is a fictional theatre but ghost lights are real.

Acknowledgements

Some of these stories have appeared in print or on-line before so I'd like to thank the original commissioners including the *Sunday Express*, Jarrold of Norwich and Audible. I really enjoyed revisiting them and also writing new adventures for Justice, Harbinder, Max and Ruth. There are new characters and places in here too.

Thanks, as ever, to my editor, Jane Wood, and agent, Rebecca Carter. I'm the luckiest author ever to have these two brilliant women in my corner. Thanks to everyone at Quercus who works so hard on all my books. Special thanks to Katy Blott, Charlotte Gill, Florence Hare, David Murphy, Ella Patel, Emily Patience and Hannah Robinson. Thanks to Liz Hatherell for her meticulous copy-editing and knowledge of . . .

well, everything. Thanks to Chris Shamwana for the beautiful cover.

This book is dedicated to my friend Lynne Spahl with happy memories of collages, whale watching and burgers at In-N-Out. Love and thanks always to my husband, Andy, and our children, Alex and Juliet.

Elly Griffiths 2024

HARPER LARGE PRINT

We hope you enjoyed reading
our new, comfortable print size and found it
an experience you would like to repeat.

Well – you're in luck!

Harper Large Print offers the finest in
fiction and nonfiction books in this same larger
print size and paperback format. Light and easy to read,
Harper Large Print paperbacks are for the book lovers
who want to see what they are reading without strain.

For a full listing of titles and
new releases to come, please visit our website:
www.hc.com

HARPER LARGE PRINT

SEEING IS BELIEVING!